Remembering You

**Center Point
Large Print**

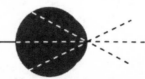

**This Large Print Book carries the
Seal of Approval of N.A.V.H.**

Remembering You

Tricia Goyer

CENTER POINT LARGE PRINT
THORNDIKE, MAINE

The text of this Large Print edition is unabridged.
In other aspects, this book may
vary from the original edition.
Printed in the United States of America.
Set in 16-point Times New Roman type.

ISBN: 978-1-61173-293-1

Library of Congress Cataloging-in-Publication Data

Goyer, Tricia.
Remembering you / Tricia Goyer. — Center Point large print ed.
p. cm.
ISBN 978-1-61173-293-1 (library binding : alk. paper)
1. Grandfathers—Fiction. 2. Soldiers—Fiction.
   3. Europe—Fiction. 4. Large type books. I. Title.
PS3607.O94R46 2012
813'.6—dc23

2011038002

Do two walk together unless
they have agreed to do so?

AMOS 3:3

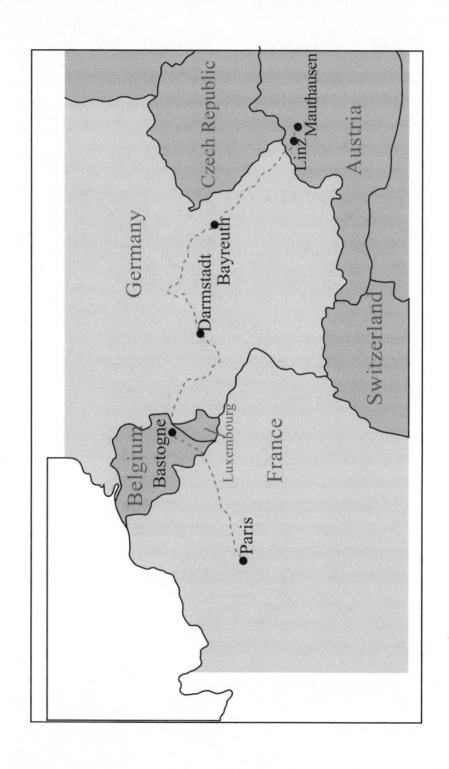

Chapter One

Ava Ellington pulled the lid off the red Sharpie with her teeth and drew a thick line from one corner of the clipboard page to the other.

As head producer of *Mornings with Laurie and Clark*, Seattle's top morning news show, she had booked best-selling author Dean Trust to talk about his dad, a fisherman who'd died in 1981 while rescuing a drowning teenager—a heroic father who was said to have inspired Trust's latest novel. Instead, as the cameras rolled, Trust had blabbered about the Seattle rain and an idea for a script that he was hoping to sell. *Rubbish!*

Ava bit her bottom lip as she strode down the television studio hall and pushed open the door to her office, resisting the urge to slam it behind her. She scanned her stacks of files and notes and wondered if she should pack her things now. Returning the lid to the pen, she tossed it on her desk. It rolled off and onto the floor. With a swift motion, she kicked the pen under the bookshelf filled with travel guides of places she hoped to visit someday. Places rimmed with stories she would never hear. Heart-tugging segments she'd never produce.

If Ava prided herself on anything, it was that she knew how to turn seemingly small ideas into breakfast-time entertainment that refreshed people's hearts. But all it took was one logjam to cause everything else to pile up—one babbling, unfocused guest—or at least that was her excuse today. But what about the last few weeks? Few months? It was hard to want to entertain and inspire people when her own heart was breaking.

Her cell phone buzzed in her pocket, and Ava hit IGNORE. Yet another task-reminder. She bent down to retrieve the pen, and her fingers brushed something else under the bookcase. A business card maybe? Pulling it out, her throat tightened. It was one of the photos of her and Jay that she used to have pinned on her bulletin board. She brushed the dust from his face with her thumb, and her heart clenched at his smile. She blinked the tears from her eyes and, before she could talk herself out of it, dropped the photo into the trash. It was the never-ending lists of tasks and calls that, perhaps, had cost her what she wanted most—a man who claimed to love her with all his heart.

Jay had seemed like the perfect guy. He was easy to talk to. He laughed at her jokes and e-mailed her funny YouTube videos. He encouraged her to find tales that would inspire people. He believed in her. Or at least she had thought he believed in her.

Ava refused to think about that now. Or about him. Right now she had to think about keeping her job. She'd moved to downtown Seattle to be close to Jay and had bought a condo she couldn't afford, believing it would be their home together. If she lost her job too, everything would be gone. Then where would she go? More than that—who would she be?

A soft knock sounded, and Ava glanced up to see her boss, Todd, standing in the doorway. He didn't say a word, but she noticed his tight-lipped grin and furrowed brow.

"I talked to Dean Trust last night," she tried to explain. "He told me he was happy to talk about his dad and the inspiration for this novel. . . . I—I don't know what happened."

Todd raised his hands. "Listen, I don't want to burst your bubble, Ava, but even if he had talked about his novel, the critics are giving it a C-minus just to be kind." He lifted his chin, which always seemed to have a five o'clock shadow. "You know what we need and what our viewers expect."

Ava slumped into her leather chair. The pressure weighed on her shoulders. "Obviously I don't. Everything I've put together lately has been a fumble." She glanced up at him under her eyelashes. "I have a worse record than the Seahawks this season."

Todd nodded and ran his hand through his dark hair. He opened his mouth and then closed it again. From the pity in his gaze she expected the worst.

"Listen, even though we never want our

personal life to affect our work, it always does. I tried to explain that to my boss—"

She stood, as if pushed from her seat by a spring. "I'm working on something. Something that'll knock your socks off. Something viewers will love."

Todd cocked an eyebrow. Then he crossed his arms over his chest. "You want to tell me about it?" Even if he knew she was fibbing, he didn't let on.

"Tomorrow." She brushed her long blond hair off her shoulder. "I have a few details I need to work out." Ten minutes before, she'd assumed this would be her last day, but now she planned to stick around if she could come up with something good.

She glanced at the photo in the trash. *You can't take my work from me too. You've already crushed my self-confidence, not to mention my heart. You can't have this too.*

Chapter Two

Ava pulled the container of leftover Chinese out of the fridge and sniffed it, trying to remember how many days it had been since she'd gone out to dinner with her best friend, Jill. Realizing it had been over a week, she tossed it in the trash and then poked her head back into the refrigerator. Her stomach churned, partly because she was hungry and partly because she had no idea what magical story could save her job. Like the takeout Chinese, every idea she'd generated so far had been far from fresh. Some ideas were just plain rotten.

She finally decided on a grilled cheese sandwich and apple slices for dessert. Setting a place at the table, she stood to flip on the light and then changed her mind. Her electric bill had been steeper than she wanted last month. Instead, she opened the kitchen cupboard closest to the dining room and held her breath as she stared at the fifty white candles she'd purchased for her wedding. In her mind's eye, she imagined the church altar twinkling with lights, but she quickly pushed those thoughts away. *I have the candles; I might as well use them.* With a quivering hand, she pulled two out and placed them in the candle-holders on the table. Then she retrieved her notebook from her purse.

She sat at the candlelit table, took a bite from her sandwich, and opened the notebook. She wrote *Ideas* at the top and then stared at the blank page.

Her cell phone buzzed again from her purse, but she ignored it. It was most likely Jill calling to tell her about Rick again. Jill called every evening, and the topic of late had been the show's cameraman Rick. Jill was a great associate producer, but she was a poor judge of character. Ava shook her head. *How many times do I have to tell her that Rick is only interested in getting better assignments?*

The buzzing of her cell phone stopped, but a few seconds later the ringing of her home phone split the air. Only a few people knew her home number. Only one person had called it regularly. Jay. They hadn't talked since the breakup. Still, she couldn't help but wonder. *What if it is him calling after all these months?*

She swallowed the last bite of apple slice, feeling it cut like razor blades down her throat, and her hands quivered. She'd asked herself what she'd do if he ever called. Her stomach tumbled just thinking of his voice.

Ava dropped her pen to the table and hurried to the phone. She didn't know whether to be relieved or disappointed when she recognized her mother's number on caller ID.

"Hey, Mom. Is everything okay? Are you okay? Or . . ." Her voice halted when a new worry filled her mind. Ava pictured her grandfather's thin frame. His white shock of hair. His easy smile. Well, the last time she had seen him, he hadn't been smiling, but she didn't want to think about that now.

"Ava, thank goodness you answered—"

"Is it Grandpa?" Her voice wobbled, and an ache as big as the Space Needle pressed on her chest. She knew she should have cleared the air with him. Life was so short—

"Grandpa's fine, but I wanted to tell you I had a little accident."

"Accident?" Ava pressed against the chair back.

"I was cleaning the winter debris out of the gutters, and the ladder wasn't as steady as I thought. The doctor said I was lucky that my leg was the only thing I broke."

"You broke your leg?" Ava pictured her mother—small, wiry, athletic, always on the go. She hadn't seen her mom with even a sprained finger before.

"Do you have a cast? What about work? Do you need me to come down to Bend this weekend to help you out?"

"Actually . . ." Her mom's voice trailed off.

Ava heard muffled voices in the background and the sounds of a doctor being paged over a loudspeaker.

"I need you to do something for me, sweetheart, but it's bigger than just making a few casseroles and taking my dogs for a walk. Grandpa has that reunion coming up in Europe. He said this morning he'd be fine traveling alone—that he'd meet up with a group when he got overseas—but that's not possible. He's been shaky on his feet, and last week he fell in the garden. The doc says there's nothing specifically wrong; he's just unsteady. He can't travel alone. I thought about asking your uncle, but—"

"Mom, hold up. The reunion's in Europe? I thought it was in Kalamazoo or Buffalo again."

For as long as Ava could remember, her

grandfather took a trip every August to the reunion of the Eleventh Armored Division, his unit during World War II. The reunion was organized by division members who'd trained together, fought together, and met together over the years to remind themselves that what they'd done had made a difference, even if the world didn't often know them or remember.

For three years her grandpa was one of fifteen thousand men who had soldiered on through Louisiana, Texas, California, and Europe. He'd seen frontline action in Belgium, Germany, and Austria, if she remembered correctly. Grandpa Jack had retold many of the same stories over the years, but Ava still had a hard time getting the dates and events straight.

"The division's doing their typical reunion in August, but the battlefield tour is next week. They'll meet up in Europe, travel to all the sites, and end with a large remembrance ceremony at Mauthausen concentration camp in Austria. According to your grandfather, it's their last overseas hurrah. Their bus tour starts in Paris and goes through Germany and—"

"Paris? Grandpa's going to Paris?" Ava cut in. The image of the Eiffel Tower at night, covered by a million twinkling lights, came to mind. Tana, her college roommate, had lived in Paris for the last few years, and she and Jay had talked about visiting.

"Yes, dear." Then her mom started reading the tour brochure as if she were trying to sell it on QVC.

Ava knew what her mom was going to ask: if she'd go. She rubbed her temple, feeling an ache coming on. She couldn't imagine traveling with a group of men in their eighties and nineties. Every tour would be done at half-speed. And if her grandpa was unsteady on his feet, she imagined the other guys would be too. She pictured one of them falling, followed by a visit to the emergency room in a foreign country. What if someone had a heart attack? Or got lost? How would they even communicate?

Then again, the stories could be interesting. There had to have been some close calls in battle. And then there were their experiences when they liberated the concentration camps. What did they think now, knowing their actions had saved the lives of thousands? Did they live each day knowing their actions continued to affect generations?

As her mother talked on, Ava sat up straighter, another image filling her mind. She saw herself in Paris, in Germany, at the concentration camp with her grandpa, recording his stories. She could be a younger, hipper, female Steven Spielberg, bringing World War II to life through the memories of those who'd been there. Goose bumps traveled up her arms and she rubbed them.

Her heart did a double beat, and she looked at the blank notebook, now knowing what to write under the word *Ideas*. Her pen moved across the page: Veterans. Battlefields. Sacrifice. Friends reunited—Grandpa's and mine. Europe. Paris. Concentration camp. Remembrance.

" 'The reunion concludes with a memorial service at Mauthausen concentration camp, where the veterans will be honored by the camp survivors,' " her mother continued to read. " 'Thousands return to Mauthausen every year to remember, to mourn, and to celebrate their freedom.' " Her mom cleared her throat. "So what do you think, Ava? Does it interest you? Have you ever thought you'd experience a piece of history like this?"

"It sounds like an honor. I want to go, Mom." She drew a heart around the word *Paris* as the words spilled from her lips. Anticipation bubbled up in her chest—the same feeling she'd had the night before Christmas or the morning of her birthday as a little girl.

"Okay, I understand. I could ask Uncle Mike. I figured with your schedule—"

Ava chuckled. "Mom, I said I *want* to go. I mean since you can't. I'm sorry you have to miss it." Ava rose and paced to the kitchen window with the view of the Seattle skyline, to her couch, and back to the dining room table again.

This could be *the* story. This could save her job

and restore her bosses' confidence in her once again. Not to mention it would be something to get her mind off of Jay and their derailed wedding.

"Well, I've already left a message on my brother's cell asking him if he wanted to go. I assumed you couldn't get off work. Or that you wouldn't want to. I mean, it's a group of old men."

"I think I can, if Grandpa doesn't mind. Especially after our last confrontation . . ."

"He forgives easier than you think, Ava. And knowing he'd have you there to travel with him would ease his mind. Grandpa's concerned about my leg, but I can tell he's even more worried about not getting to Europe. This is really important to him, and having anxiety at his age can't be a good thing."

Ava thought about how red her grandfather's face had gotten months ago when he finally confessed to her what was bothering him. She also thought about the unkind words that she'd shot back, and small rivets of pain drilled her heart. Before their last visit, they'd never had a harsh word between them. Maybe this trip would take things back to how they used to be. Maybe she'd once again feel like Grandpa Jack's girl.

Grandpa Jack. She pictured her sweet old grandpa and his plaid shirts in various earth-tone colors. Up every day by five o'clock, on schedule for his first nap at nine. He wasn't a real cowboy, but he always wore cowboy boots, grunting as he put them on. And sometimes, if he was in the right mood, Grandpa Jack talked about the war.

She remembered one fall evening when they had sat on the couch cracking walnuts. Ava had been ten or eleven and it had taken all her strength to crack the shell. Then she'd peeled it back and dug out the nut, popping each half into her mouth. Her grandpa had told her more went into her belly than the bowl. He would look at her and wink when Grandma complained there weren't as many nuts for her cookies as she'd expected.

It was on that night that he'd told her about crossing the Atlantic Ocean on a big ship. Most of the guys had been seasick, but not him. While other guys lost weight because they were unable to eat, he had gained because he ate their rations. He'd said the extra weight kept him warm during the cold winter's fight. At the time, sitting before the woodstove, cuddled next to her grandfather's side, it had been hard to picture him so far away, fighting in a different country, outside in the cold. It had been hard to imagine that the eyes she looked into were the same ones to witness all of this.

Ava pressed the phone to her ear and tried to act nonchalant. Tried to conceal that she was smiling like the Cheshire cat. "Don't say anything to Grandpa until I talk to my boss," she said. "I'd hate to disappoint him." She hoped Todd would say yes. She usually had a feeling when stories were going to hit it big. And the tingling at the base of her neck told her this one would.

Ava pictured herself and her grandfather in front of the Eiffel Tower—holding on to his arm to steady him—as they gazed up at the large structure. The twinge of sentimentality in Ava's gut surprised her. Her dad had disappeared long before she had a clear memory of him, and Grandpa had been the one man she'd always loved. She often wished she knew her grandfather better, but distance had made it hard. And strained silence over the last few months hadn't helped.

The buzzing of the cell phone in her pocket caught her by surprise. She silenced it and listened as her mom told her in greater detail about how her fall from the ladder had happened and how she'd spent ten minutes on the ground before her neighbor heard her.

Ava's cell phone buzzed again. She pulled the phone from her pocket and saw she had a text. Ava expected it to be from Jill, on course for their nightly chat. Jill always called to distract herself from the pain of riding her recumbent bike since she was too lazy to move the bike into the living room where the television was. But as Ava opened the message, the words were ones she hadn't expected to see. Not now. Not ever. Angry heat rose to her cheeks.

"Ava, can we talk? I've got a feeling I've made a horrible mistake. Love, Jay."

Chapter Three

"A reunion of veterans?" Todd stroked his dark-brown goatee and furrowed his brow. "I don't know. It sounds sort of *Saving Private Ryan* to me, except with old guys. Didn't Tom Hanks and Steven Spielberg already cover that?"

"There are so many stories. I'm not talking about making a movie here. I'm suggesting sitting down with veterans and hearing about the hard stuff. And the good stuff. Filming them talking, remembering. You know, making daily news features out of them." Ava adjusted the angle of her chair in an attempt to avoid being distracted by the stacks of books and papers on Todd's desk. His office was larger than hers, but you would never know.

As in her office, Todd's wall held a large bulletin board calendar with slots for the week's upcoming shows, but on his, the shows posted had aired six months ago.

"My grandpa has been friends with these guys for sixty-seven years. Their armored division liberated a concentration camp at the end of the war." Ava's mind scurried to remember some of the stories Grandpa and his best friend, Paul, had told as they sat near the lake, fishing poles in hand. "A small group of them were the first liberators and freed tens of thousands of Holocaust victims."

Todd straightened in his seat.

"Concentration camps always draw the viewers' attention." A smile tipped his lips. He lifted his chin and looked at the tiled ceiling. "Those segments last year on the Japanese interment camps got big ratings." After a moment of silence, he leaned forward and focused his eyes on hers. "But I think we need to connect with the younger generation too. I mean, why would they care? Think of the stay-at-home, Gen-X mommy who likes to spend her morning with us."

"I care. It's my grandfather. I bet there are many people like me who heard the stories of the war but didn't take the time to really listen. That could be the hook. My journey with my grandfather and his stories." Ava hadn't realized that was important to her until she said the words. Maybe this trip wasn't just about Paris. Or making up for their last tiff. Or saving her job. Maybe there could be something more . . . for them . . . for their relationship. Something she couldn't know until she journeyed with her grandfather to the places that had changed him.

Todd stared at Ava so intently that she felt like she must have something on her face. She shifted again. "It wouldn't just be his story. It would be mine too."

"I like that. Makes me think of my grandpa." He

leaned across his desk. "My grandpa was the one who was always there. He was never too busy for me." Todd's voice trailed off. "We made a birdhouse that I still have. I often think of his advice: 'Make yourself the most valued person in a company, even if you're just mopping floors.' "

Like a statue coming to life, her typically distant boss softened before her eyes.

"He sounds like a great man." Ava glanced at her watch and realized it was nearly time for their weekly production meeting to start.

Todd straightened and then nodded. "So sum it up for me. What's the story that's worth letting you head off to Europe during a very busy network season?"

She didn't answer right away but played with the black stapler on his desk, trying to wipe off the fingerprints with the sleeve of her sweater, as she tried to find her words. "When I think of World War II, I think of black-and-white photos from *Life* magazine, of soldiers in foxholes. Those images don't mesh with my sweet old grandpa who spends his days watching *Gilligan's Island* and *Bonanza*. Let's reconcile the two. He'll show me the places I've heard about my whole life. He did something that really mattered and . . . the world is different because of him." She tucked her hair behind her ear. "It wouldn't just be his story either. It would be mine too. Ours."

"I think that'll work." There was tenderness in

his tone. "You should do it. We could follow you . . . the show I mean." Papers fluttered to the ground, brushed off by his arm as he rose. "You can debrief in the evenings and send back video." Todd stood, walked around his desk, and then leaned back on it, crossing his arms. "Eat cheap. Don't buy too many souvenirs." He winked. "We can pawn off your duties during the meeting." He looked at his watch, which had likely cost more than Ava's car, glanced at her with those sexy, dark eyes, and rapped her chin with his knuckle. "You've never let me down, Ava. Don't mess this up."

Ava sank into the faded red velveteen chair in the small coffee shop a few blocks from the television studio and set her cell phone next to her laptop. She ran her fingers over the tiled table, brushing away the crumbs. Even though the Mean Bean was a block farther than the chain coffeehouse, it was worth the walk. She enjoyed the quaint atmosphere—the mismatched tables, comfy plush chairs, and old photos of Seattle squatter settlements of the thirties.

She usually went there in the afternoon to get a little caffeine pick-me-up and to work away from the office. Today, she had come to research where she'd be going and to research stories she'd most likely hear. On the walk over, she'd called her grandfather to get more details.

Grandpa Jack hadn't answered, and he didn't have an answering machine. He wasn't the least bit interested in a cell phone. In fact, he still used a gold rotary phone that had hung in his small kitchen for as long as she could remember. Her mom had told her to keep trying to reach him, but Ava wondered if not talking to him until she got there would be better. Maybe a face-to-face apology would be a good start to their trip.

She opened her laptop and connected to the free wireless, also making eye contact with the barista, Jed, behind the counter. The fresh-faced college student tipped his chin at her, which was their signal he'd get started on her order. She ordered the same thing every day—no need to stand in line.

Today the coffeehouse was especially busy—a mix of white-collar workers like her, moms with babies in designer strollers, and artsy people nestled in the corners with books and magazines. The chatter of voices swirled around her, mixing with the scents of coffee, vanilla, and cinnamon.

She opened the search engine and typed "Eleventh Armored Division reunion."

The first link took her to information about their Louisville reunion and news about the previous reunion in Chicago. Her grandfather had attended these gatherings since before she was born, and he always roomed with his friend Paul. While Paul was a wealthy business owner who traveled often, her grandfather had worked in a door factory his whole life. Paul was a city boy and Grandpa Jack, a country bumpkin. The two would have never met without the war. Yet, because of their time together in the trenches, they'd been best friends ever since.

After adding in a few more search words, she found a site with all the information about the European trip. The tour was traveling from Paris to Belgium, and then through Germany into Austria, where it would end with the annual commemoration ceremonies of KZ Mauthausen and Gusen.

Ava didn't understand what KZ meant, so she searched that term next. *Konzentrationslager*, or KZ, was the German term for concentration camp. Numerous websites popped up with information about Nazi concentration camps, including those in Upper Austria, where their tour was headed. She clicked on some of the pages, and her stomach turned at the photos of bodies stacked on horse carts, of underground weapon production plants, and of American tanks rolling through tall gates with skeletal men cheering healthy-looking GIs.

She clicked to enlarge one photo of the liberation of Mauthausen concentration camp. Her eyes scanned the men in striped prisoner uniforms, thin right arms lifted in cheers. Then she looked at the men on the tank and truck behind it. Her heart swelled as she viewed smiles that hinted of both joy and sorrow. And then her eyes focused on one man. She knew that face. Her stomach flipped as if being tossed like a pancake, and her heart swelled with pride.

"It's him."

Jed approached with a steaming latte, and she nearly knocked it from his hand as she reached for his arm. "Look, it's my grandfather."

Jed tossed his blond hair from his eyes and peered down.

"Cool." Jed nodded and then handed her the mug. "Sweet old photo," he called over his shoulder as he scurried back behind the counter to attend to the line.

Ava sank back into her seat. In the photo, her grandfather looked happy, relieved, overwhelmed. To actually see him entering the gates of the concentration camp made her grandpa's stories seem so much more real. Jay would have been excited too, but she couldn't call him. Wouldn't call him.

Instead, she opened her purse and pulled out a photocopied page that had been folded and tucked into a Christmas card. Two years ago her mom had tried to come up with a Christmas gift for her grandfather, who always claimed he didn't need anything. Her mother's idea started when she'd been reading some of the letters written by her father during World War II. Ava hadn't even known about her grandpa's letters until her mother sent one to family members with a special request. Since Grandpa had asked for cookies in his letter sixty-seven years ago, her mother had asked everyone to send him a tin of homemade cookies, along with their own personal Christmas letter—in honor of the one he had sent to his parents during the war. The cookies and letters had arrived throughout December, and Grandpa had loved it. Likewise, Ava had loved getting a glimpse into her grandfather's life during the war.

March 8, 1945
Mother dear,

I keep dreaming about your cookies and hope some will come in the mail. I haven't been getting any packages lately. I know it isn't your fault. It must be the mail service.

It's good to get out of Belgium—to make it out alive—but we have a lot of Germany stretching before us. The Germans held out against our bombing better than I thought. These towns have a lot of caves in the hills, which they run into. There's plenty of food. When we go into a town, the people are always huddled in the basement. They have their beds down there, their food, and most of their valuables. Of course we only bomb towns when they refuse to surrender.

The houses here in Germany have slogans

written on the walls to bolster the people's fighting spirit. One of the prominent ones is "Sieg oder Siberien," Victory or Siberia. I guess they worry that if they don't win, they'll end up as slaves up in Russia.

We traveled through some beautiful country coming here. It was wonderful, broad, fertile farming country. It reminded me of back home.

The farmhouses and barns are very neat and kept up well. The industrial cities and the houses are very modern. Everything here is much better than anything I have seen in France or England. The Hitler regime has made many improvements here.

I am enclosing a German army insignia which I took from a uniform I found in a basement today. There were a lot of German soldiers that got away from us. Some of them threw away their uniforms and put on civilian clothes. I wonder if we'll find them. I wonder if I want to. I wonder if they ever wrote letters home to their mothers to ask for cookies.

Love,
Jack

Ava paused. She folded up the letter and held it tight between her fingers. If she'd gotten her dates right, by this time her grandfather would have faced many battles, including the Battle of the

Bulge. Yet his letter skimmed over the bombings and fighting and focused more on the scenery.

Had he ever discussed the battles he fought in his letters? Or the friends he'd lost? Had he ever written about his fear? Ava wondered if her mother had access to the other letters. She scribbled a reminder in her notepad to ask about them.

Goose bumps traveled up her arms as she imagined driving down the same streets he'd gone down all those years ago. What had it been like to be fighting? Or to be on enemy soil? Or what had it been like to compare the improvements in Germany with the destruction found within the walls of the concentration camps?

"He had no idea of what was to come," Ava jotted in her notepad. Maybe her grandfather had a hard time writing about the battles, which was understandable, but he had no idea what awaited them. As Ava sipped her coffee, she mapped the trip. They would start in France, traveling by bus through Belgium, and then through Germany into Austria. Instead of stopping at obvious tourist spots, like Berlin, they'd spend their time at small villages where her grandfather's major battles took place.

The tour operator's specialty was World War II, and he had traveled with similar reunion groups from all over the world. Ava had recognized town names like Bastogne and Bayreuth from shows she'd watched on the History Channel, and even though she'd started reading through the history of her grandfather's division, it was still hard for her to keep track of all the battles, the dates, the places. Being there would help put the pieces together, she hoped.

Her cell phone buzzed, and she saw Jill had sent a text message. Reading the three simple words made it even more real: "Seriously, Paris? OMG!"

She smiled as she read the words, but the joy of the moment was disrupted by the text message right above it that she hadn't deleted—the one from Jay.

Does Jay really think he made a mistake? Maybe she should call him. Then again, how could he do this? How could he say he loved her after all he'd done?

Mostly, she hated herself for even considering responding. *Where's your backbone, Ava?* She'd always considered herself strong and independent, but that was before Jay.

I'm not sure I know who I am anymore. Or what I want. Somehow on the path to a rewarding job and marrying a man who also wanted to start a family, she'd lost herself.

She closed her laptop and stood. She didn't know how to respond, or if she should at all. She needed time to decide what she thought about Jay, and if she could risk her heart once more.

But even as she deleted Jill's text, she couldn't

make herself delete the one from Jay. She tucked the phone in her pocket, but his words replayed in her mind: *I have a feeling I made a horrible mistake.*

Was she the one making a mistake now by not giving him a second chance?

Chapter Four

After driving most of the day, Ava pulled into Cal-Ore trailer park just in time to see the sunset cast a pink glow on Mount Shasta. She could have flown down from Seattle to Northern California, but she told herself she needed the drive—to think, to plan, to process. She'd done a little of each, mostly the processing part, trying to come to terms with the fact life wasn't turning out as she'd always dreamed. She wasn't succeeding at her job. Didn't have someone to share life with. Most of her other friends were married; some had kids.

As the miles had clicked by on the odometer, Ava had tried to focus on the many ways this trip was a gift. Not only would she and Grandpa embark on this journey together, she'd also get to see Tana.

And this was a chance to fulfill at least one of her long-held dreams—to see Europe—since the dream of living happily ever after with Prince Charming wasn't going to happen any time soon.

Mentally, she kicked herself for hanging on to that dream. Before leaving the house, she had caved and sent a quick e-mail to Jay: "Got your message. Will be out of the country for a week. Would like to talk when I get back."

All those thoughts flittered away like dandelion seeds on the wind as soon as she pulled into the trailer park. Her grandparents had moved there before she was born, and Grandpa had chosen to stay in the doublewide after Grandma's death, even though his two kids lived four hours north in Bend, Oregon.

A smile curled Ava's lips as she scanned the trailers—the same ones she remembered from when she was five. She looked to the hill near the cow pasture and remembered rolling down it with Michelle from down the street. Ava chuckled, seeing that it wasn't much of a hill. Five feet high at the most. *It's amazing how everything changes, or rather how changing makes everything look different.*

She parked in front of the mobile home, and as soon as she turned off the engine, a strange peace washed over her. Tucking her cell phone into her purse, she got out and locked the car, immediately chiding herself for doing so. She wasn't in Seattle anymore.

Ava smiled as she hurried up the front steps and then paused at the cowbell hung by the door. Her grandpa had picked it up at a yard sale and used it as his doorbell. She rang it twice and waited. When no one answered, she opened the door.

"Grandpa?" The kitchen smelled of coffee, bacon, and his old woodstove. Emotion filled her chest when she noticed the pansy wallpaper that she'd helped her grandma hang. She moved through the kitchen to the living room and tears rimmed her eyes. Walking in this place was like turning seven again, and she had a sudden urge to make some popcorn and curl up next to her grandfather for some John Wayne movies.

"Grandpa?" she called again, moving down the small hall to the master bedroom. The bed was made and everything was picked up. The carpet even had lines from the vacuum cleaner, which meant he'd cleaned for her. Turning around to head back out of the bedroom, she noticed a suitcase by the bedroom door. Hard-bodied, with tarnished, bronze-colored clasps. He was packed and ready to go, even though they weren't heading out until morning. She imagined he was excited about seeing all his old friends, going back to the places that had transformed his life. The places he hadn't been in sixty-five years.

In the kitchen, the coffeepot was full, which meant Grandpa Jack had made a fresh pot for her. She poured a cup and opened the fridge for milk. On the top shelf she spotted hazelnut creamer. *He remembered.* She poured some and headed outside, knowing he couldn't be far.

Ava took a sip as she walked. Mrs. Sanchez had a new deck, and Mr. Harrison next door already had pink roses on the arbor next to his front patio.

Six trailers down, she spotted him. Grandpa Jack's back was to her. He was leaning against the fence talking to ol' Henry. Henry had to be at least twenty years younger than her grandfather, but he'd been in bad health since she'd known him. Grandpa did Henry's yard work for him, as well as the yard work for most of the others on his street. Her mom always said it kept him young.

Henry spotted her first and pointed. She was nearly at her grandfather's side when he turned. Uneasiness crept over her as she again remembered their last conversation. She wondered if he was still angry with her, or if he was disappointed that she was the one going on this trip with him.

Grandpa turned and his brow was furrowed slightly. Then, seeing her, the lines on his forehead softened.

"There she is. What took you so long?" With hedge clippers in one hand, Grandpa Jack had only one arm to offer for a hug, but she gladly accepted it. He smell like Old Spice and lawn clippings, just like he always did. But something was different too. He looked older. His shirt seemed to hang on him. His cheeks looked pale. His hair was thinner too.

Ava pressed her lips together. Suddenly the idea of his getting on an airplane and traveling to the other side of the world didn't seem like a good plan, but she pushed those thoughts down and held on for an extra second. "Oh, you know those coppers in Oregon. They were out in force. I decided to do the speed limit for once."

She turned to Henry and offered him a hug too. "How's it going?"

"It's going. It's going. Good to see you." He folded his arms over his barrel chest.

"Still got that candy jar on your coffee table?"

"Yeah, hold on." He turned.

"No, no. I don't need any." Ava laughed. "Just remembering."

Grandpa Jack handed the clippers to Henry. "You better keep these here. I'm going to be gone for a few weeks, and you might need them while I'm gone." He cleared his throat.

"Going on a vacation, Jack?" Henry wiped crumbs off the T-shirt stretched over his large belly.

"Yes, uh, just spending time with old friends."

The way he said the words made Ava look more closely at him. He offered her a quick smile and then averted his gaze. Why hadn't he mentioned the tour?

"Did you see all the snow still on the mountain?" He pointed to Mount Shasta and the white-capped peak filling the skyline. "Enough for skiing, I'd imagine. Wish the park was still open."

"You didn't come up to ski this year, Ava." Henry butted in. "You always come."

This time she was the one who averted her gaze. "I've been busy at work." She didn't want to mention that she'd spent most of ski season planning a wedding.

"Next year, then."

"Yes, I'll have to do that." She looped her hand around her grandfather's arm. "You have a good evening."

"Bring back lots of photos!" Henry called after them.

"Sure thing." She cast one last smile and wave over her shoulder. Her grandfather's hair was silver and fell into his eyes as he walked. She wondered if she should apologize now—just to be done with it. But, as they walked along together, everything felt like it always had.

"Ready to fly across the deep blue sea?" She took a sip from her now lukewarm coffee.

"I'm all packed. Your mom mailed me a list."

"What do you think about being back there again, Grandpa?" Ava couldn't help but ask. His comments would give her an idea of where to start her news features. His feelings about the trip could be a great launching point to pull viewers into the emotion of the experience. Ava made a note to contrast their former strength with their weakness now. *Even with shaky steps they still walk with pride.*

Her grandfather shrugged, but he didn't slow his steps. "Never thought it would happen. The day I stepped off foreign soil, I thought I'd never return. I almost decided not to go. Then I got to wondering. If I wanted to see the place again, now was the time. Some of the guys are old. They might croak soon." He winked. Yet even though he was trying to play it off as a joke, she could see the pain in his eyes.

"That's sad—to lose your friends."

"It's a part of life, Ava."

"Yes, I know it's part of life, but at least they died knowing their efforts changed the world."

He nodded but didn't answer, and the way he rolled his eyes told her it sounded like a lot of fluff to him.

"Your mom said you're making this a work trip." His curtness took her by surprise.

She slowed her steps and looked over at him. His eyes were fixed ahead. Even from the side his frown was evident.

"I don't think the guys will like having a camera in their face the whole time."

"But they have to know this is a special event."

"It was just part of life. We did what we had to do. You can find some other way to do your work without making a show of my friends."

She tightened her grip on the handle of the mug. She hadn't thought about Grandpa and the other guys not being excited about being filmed. She

37

just assumed they would be. She placed a hand over her stomach as the burger she'd eaten near the Oregon border grew into a boulder in her gut. She hadn't prayed for months, but now seemed like a good time to start.

"Grand-Paul loves telling his stories. Personally, I think he's going to be excited, don't you?" She forced a smile, as if doing so would keep her plans—her job—from crumbling around her.

"That's right. You called him Grand-Paul that summer," he said, not answering her question.

"Grand*pa Pa*ul is like a tongue twister. We just shortened it."

With the mention of that summer, a hundred memories filled Ava's mind, and her heart warmed. *My first love.* She thought about those days, the perfect summer, more often than she wanted to admit.

She didn't need to descend into those *I wishes* and *what-ifs* again. This was about her grandfather and her job. And getting her grandpa to let her do her job. Maybe if she knocked the videos out of the park, Todd would let her travel to other places, tackle other stories. It would be better than checking off tasks and living alone in a condo designed for two.

"Let me just take my coffee cup in the house, and then we'll go for a spin," she said.

"Just leave the cup on the porch. No one will bother it there." He waved a hand at her.

Ava took a sip of the coffee and then set down the cup. Her grandfather's roses—already in bloom on the bush near the porch—filled the air with their sweet scent.

Grandpa Jack waited by the car.

"Here, let me get that stuff out." Ava unlocked the car with the click of a button and then grabbed the video camera case and tripod, moving them to the trunk.

He stood by the passenger door without getting in, and he pointed to her camera. "Is that the only reason you came, Ava?" His white eyebrows folded down.

"Of course not."

Grandpa Jack opened the door. "Good, then you don't have to worry about the video. You can tell your work that you decided not to do it."

Ava paused at his statement. Her stomach tightened. Suddenly her neck ached and a headache pounded—a headache she was sure hadn't been there a minute before.

She put the equipment in the trunk and slammed it shut and then tried to calm her breathing as she walked to the driver's seat. Grandpa Jack was already buckled in. Ava started the car and pulled out, waving to various neighbors as she drove by at the posted five miles an hour. The sign also read CHILDREN AT PLAY, even though there hadn't been any children living in this park for quite some time.

"Did you watch the DVD I sent, you know, of our morning talk show? I thought you'd like seeing what I did. And seeing how important my work is. With these videos, the story of your division will be told all over the Northwest. Isn't that great?"

"I don't have a DVD player."

Ava's fists tightened around the steering wheel. She pushed out a slow breath. They'd have more time to talk about her work later. More time to get him to understand how important this was.

She tried to weave around the potholes, but there were too many. The car rocked as she drove through them. Her heart sank at the realization that making things right with him wouldn't be easy. She'd thought that even if he wasn't thrilled that she was the one coming, he'd at least be excited that his division was getting the honor they deserved at the liberation ceremony at Mauthausen concentration camp.

"Grandpa? Are you feeling okay? Do you—"

"I'm hungry, that's all." He stared out the window at the mountain. "I—I just want a piece of pie. Can't a man have pie when he wants? Why does everyone have to make a big deal outta nothin'?"

Chapter Five

Ava wrapped her arm around her grandfather's thin waist as they exited Charles de Gaulle Airport. Above her, the Parisian sky held no hint of clouds, and with her free hand she slid her sunglasses from where they rested on top of her head onto the bridge of her nose. She scanned the horizon, hoping to spot the top of the Eiffel Tower, but she couldn't see it from where she was. Behind her, the wheels of the luggage cart squeaked as an airport attendant followed them, pushing the cart with their suitcases and her camera equipment.

Grandpa Jack leaned close to her ear. "Paris, Ava gal." His eyes were bright despite the weariness on his face. Yet though his words chirped and lilted, like the birds flitting around the overhang near the exit door, her grandfather's body trudged forward with weariness.

"That's right, Grandpa." She squeezed his waist. "You'll be the perfect tour guide."

Ava took in a deep breath of muggy air and took in the blur of all the people, cars, and planes.

Paris.

The city had piqued Ava's interest from the time she was five and overheard conversations spoken in hushed tones at the kitchen table. Stories of

American tanks and GIs fighting against Nazi soldiers. For her grandpa, it had all started in France.

She'd imagined France being a horrible dark place until she got to Mrs. Garret's art class in ninth grade. The teacher said Paris brimmed with architecture, culture, and amazing food. Maybe the contrast of what Paris was, and what it had become during World War II—a city occupied by the enemy—intrigued her the most. Like a dragon taking over a fairy-tale castle, Hitler had conquered the wonderland.

Yes, she'd made it there, but not like she'd imagined. On this trip, there would be no romantic strolls through Parc Monceau or candlelight dinners at midnight. If the walk through the airport was any indication of what was to come, she'd be seeing Europe at half-speed.

She clung tightly as she supported her grandfather, who took slow, deliberate steps. She was still not used to how unsteady he was on his feet. She was used to his being the one who strode around the mobile home park, or pushed a mower, or climbed up onto his roof to clean the gutters. She hoped that his sluggishness was due to the plane ride and nothing more. She didn't like to see him like this. He stumbled slightly and his hand grabbed hers.

"Doing okay?" Ava asked as respectfully as she could.

"Darn airplane seats," Grandpa Jack mumbled. "Don't they know what legroom is?" He tipped his Eleventh Armored Division cap farther down over his eyes, squinting against the sun and forcing a smile. "My legs feel as if they've been shoved into my chest for the last eight hours."

Ava chuckled as she helped to steady him. "Watch your step, Grandpa. Let's get you out of the sun. In fact, why don't you wait in the shade while I get a taxi?" She helped him back and then motioned to the airport attendant to stay with him. She'd always wanted to ride the Paris metro, but that wouldn't happen today. Even though the taxi would be ten times more expensive, they were having a hard enough time making it down the sidewalk. She couldn't imagine trying to maneuver her grandfather around busy, bustling people—getting on and off the metro, shouting at her in a different language—and managing their luggage too. She moved to the curb. The taxi stand on the island seemed a hundred miles away.

The name of their hotel was written on a piece of paper in her sweater pocket. Ava patted it for reassurance. She didn't speak French, and she hoped the hotel's name would be enough to get them there.

Ava moved toward the line of taxis and then paused. Parked a mere ten feet away was a large black car. Next to the door stood a tall man sporting dark sunglasses. He held a sign with her grandfather's name written on it. She didn't remember the tour information saying anything about an airport shuttle, but who else would have her grandfather's name on a sign?

Ava pushed her sunglasses to the top of her head and hurried back to Grandpa. "It looks like we won't need our own taxi after all."

She nodded to the baggage handler, who followed their slow pace.

As they neared, the man with the sign flashed a bright grin, and Ava stopped. She *knew* that smile. She'd seen it a hundred times that summer. She'd fallen in love with the smile first, and then . . .

Her heart beat hollowly in her chest. She studied the way the man stood with his feet planted wide and one hand tucked in his left jeans pocket. His dark hair was shorter—so short that no one would be able to tell it was curly. And even though he wore sunglasses, she saw he was watching her. His brow furrowed as if he couldn't believe what he was seeing.

"Dennis?" she mouthed. Her grandfather released her arm. Then he placed a hand on the small of her back, pushing her forward. For the briefest moment she wasn't worried about her grandfather or the suitcases. She hurried toward Dennis, but when she got within a few steps of him, she hesitated.

"Ava?" He removed his sunglasses, setting them on his head, his eyes wide. He eyed her and turned to his grandfather, Grand-Paul, who was already sitting in the backseat of the car, overly interested in a map of the city. When Dennis turned back to her, the look on his face was clear. They'd been set up. Ava felt a slight trembling in her knees. It *was* him. He was really here. A hundred memories of their time together came flooding back.

"Dennis," she said again. She hurried to him and wrapped her arms around his neck in a hug. He gave her a hug and then placed his hands on her arms and took a step back.

"Ava." He put the sign on the roof of the car and then took her hand into his.

His eyes met hers, and then he studied her face. She wondered if he was remembering their summer. She was wondering if he was comparing how she looked then to how she looked now, and for some reason, she hoped he approved.

He looked at her mouth, her smile, and then looked back at her eyes. There was sadness in his gaze. Ava bit her lip. Yes, he was remembering. He no doubt thought back to the way that summer had ended. Another thing she hadn't made amends for.

"Last I heard, your mom was bringing your grandpa. In fact"—he cleared his throat as he looked to his grandfather in the backseat—"that's who I was told we were picking up today."

Ava forced a laugh and shrugged. "Change of plans. It happened last minute. My mom broke her leg last week. I took her place." She looked past Dennis to Grand-Paul, who quickly focused his gaze back on the map. "Maybe the news didn't make it to your grandfather." Even as she said the words, she knew they likely weren't true.

"I'm sorry for your mom. I hope you still like the trip." He forced a small smile, but it was still beautiful to her. More beautiful than the Paris skyline beyond.

"I don't know what to say. I can't believe you're here." She tilted her head up to meet his gaze.

Dennis's eyes were darker than she remembered. They were blue, but a dark blue like the color the ocean had been when they'd been flying over it just before dusk.

She removed her hand from his and let it fall to her side. "It's been so long."

"Yes, well, that's the way you wanted things." He glanced over his shoulder toward a bus rumbling by.

Ava opened her mouth. She didn't know what to say. He was acting as if their big fight had been last week, not all those years ago.

"Here, let me help you with that." Dennis stepped forward, moving to the cart with their suitcases. In one fluid motion, he tipped the attendant and then took the cart around to the back of the car. She should have been thankful for his help, but instead she was concerned. He seemed to be helping her so he could get her to the hotel and drop her off. His lifted chin and stiffened shoulders made that clear.

"Grandpa, let me help you." She turned back to him, telling herself he was what she was here for. Let Dennis give her the brush-off. She didn't need any more complications on this trip anyway. Taking care of her grandfather and getting videos to Todd would be consuming enough.

Still, deep down in a hidden part of her heart, she felt a small loss. Even if nothing was to come of it, she at least wanted Dennis to be excited to see her again. Even though their relationship hadn't ended well, there'd been a lot of happy memories. Was he forgetting all those?

Her grandfather reached the car door.

"Is that you, old man?" the voice from the backseat called.

Ava looked again to the hunched figure in the backseat. Grand-Paul waved and smiled.

"Grand-Paul!" Ava waved back.

"Who's calling who old?" Grandpa Jack chuckled. "Your birthday's before mine." His laughter lightened Ava's heart.

Grandpa Jack extended his hand, and Ava thought it was to shake Grand-Paul's hand. Instead Grand-Paul grasped it and used it to help pull himself out of the backseat. The two men stood there, gazing into each other's eyes, and what seemed like a hundred memories passed between them. Then, with a quivering chin, Grand-Paul opened his arms and pulled Grandpa Jack into an embrace, saying something that Ava couldn't make out over the noise of the airport.

With a firm hand, Grand-Paul patted Grandpa Jack's back and then sat down again, sliding across the seat to the other side. Ava approached and helped Grandpa Jack into the backseat next to his friend. She chuckled as they both began talking about their trip. She wondered which one was supposed to be listening.

Dennis slammed the trunk shut. His shoulders were wider than she remembered. His cotton shirt stretched across his muscular back as he lifted the suitcases and placed them in the trunk. He looked strong. Handsomely strong.

"Have you been here long? Or did you just arrive too?" She tried to make her tone friendly, hoping he realized they could still be friends despite what had happened.

"I had some meetings in Versailles, so I rented this car. Grand-Paul told me your grandpa and mom were coming in today, and we thought it would be a nice surprise to pick them up."

"Thank you. I was going to get a taxi, but this is better."

"You're darned right it's better," Grand-Paul called through the open door. "Do you know how much those guys charge?" She approached the elderly man through the open side door. She

48

leaned down and gave Paul a big hug. "It's been too long, old man. You look great, by the way."

He shrugged. "Not as sharp as the first time I was in these parts, but not so bad, considering the wear and tear."

"You look like a spring rooster," Grandpa Jack chimed in.

"A rooster with graying feathers."

Then Dennis—a very grown-up version of the boy she had once known—opened the passenger door for her. His eyes stayed on her as she got in, and she wondered again what he was thinking.

Ava tried to hide her own trembling as Dennis climbed into the driver's seat and started the car. He looked in the rearview mirror.

A smile brightened his handsome face. A true smile. Obviously Dennis was happy about seeing her grandfather. "Mr. Andrews, how's one of my favorite heroes? It's been far too long since I shook your hand."

"Dennis, my hand shakes on its own these days." Grandpa lifted his hand and over-emphasized its natural quiver.

More than anything, Ava wanted to ask about Dennis's life. For all she knew, he could be married with a few kids at home. She hadn't heard anything for the last five years at least—and then she'd only heard that he was in India somewhere working on homes for the poor. Handsome and a humanitarian. Someone would have snagged him up long ago. Then again, there was his attitude . . .

Ava glanced at his left hand on the steering wheel. He wasn't wearing a wedding band, but she knew that didn't mean he didn't have a wife, or kids, or a girlfriend somewhere.

Dennis spotted her looking at his hand. He lifted it. "Nope, not married. You?"

Heat rose to Ava's face. She laughed, trying to make light of her obvious curiosity.

"Nope, single as ever." Then she let out a sigh. "It's nice we got that out of the way."

Ava buckled her seatbelt and did her best to push the rest of her questions into the hidden recesses where she'd been carrying her memories of Dennis for nearly fifteen years.

It had been a summer romance, nothing more. They were young. They were stupid. And when she'd tried to be realistic, it had ruined everything.

Silence filled the vehicle, and it was only then that Ava realized the old guys in back had stopped talking.

Dennis realized it too. He pointed to the skyline ahead. "Quite a thing, isn't it?"

"I've always wanted to see it," she said, knowing full well that Dennis knew. If she'd told him once about her dreams of traveling in Europe, she'd told him a hundred times.

After awhile, they pulled onto a narrow street. Tall buildings lined both sides of the curvy, cobblestone road. Blocks and blocks of buildings that looked as they must have five hundred years ago. The ground level consisted of small shops. Apartments were layered above them with black wrought-iron balconies graced with flower boxes. On the narrow sidewalks, men and women strolled along at an easy gait, and on one bench a young couple shared an intimate kiss.

Heat rose to Ava's cheeks.

"Thanks again for the ride." Ava didn't know what else to say. Dennis's arm rested on the armrest between their seats, brushing her elbow. Needles danced up and down her arm, and she told her body to stop responding like that. The old guys in the back again launched into conversation about the trip, the flight, and the weather. Ava looked at Dennis's profile, wondering what she should say.

It's been so long.

You're as gorgeous as I remember.

What if . . .

She didn't have to worry about making small talk. Even as he drove, Dennis kept glancing into the rearview mirror, joining in with the conversation in the backseat, chuckling after each comment. Acting as if she wasn't even in the car.

Their car merged into traffic and then stopped at a light. Ava turned her head just slightly, noticing Dennis's eyes on her. "So, do you have big plans for tonight?"

"Just making sure my grandpa gets settled in,

and then I'm meeting my old roommate for dinner. I might have told you about Tana—way back when. We've been friends forever it seems."

Dennis nodded, and she wished she'd seen a hint of disappointment over the fact she had plans. More than that, she wished she wasn't suddenly so concerned about what Dennis thought.

O Lord, I need help here. I can't let my emotions get wrapped up in this. She hadn't prayed much lately, but the thought was there before she knew what to do with it.

His arm brushed against hers as he changed the flow of the vent, and she tried to ignore the quiver in her stomach. Ava instead focused on the strange world outside the car window. There were shiny cars everywhere, but different models than she saw in Seattle, mostly smaller. Big, white, historical-looking buildings lined the spotless streets, and ornate fixtures covered them like decorations on a wedding cake—not that she should be thinking of wedding cake either.

Ava stared at the people sauntering down the sidewalks. The women dressed far differently from those in the Northwest. Classier. One lady strolled along wearing a large hat, elegant coat, and high heels—with a saucy sway of her hips. The woman turned her face to their passing car. Her skin was wrinkled and hung under her chin. She had to be eighty, at least. Maybe she remembered these veterans rolling through town many years before? Ava almost wished she could have stopped and asked.

Another lady walked a poodle on a shimmery silver leash. Even the dogs here were high class.

Finally, Dennis parked in front of a swanky-looking hotel. Down the street she spotted the Plaza de Concorde, and in the distance, the Eiffel Tower.

She was here, just like she'd always imagined, and Dennis was here with her. Being with him reminded her of what she'd walked away from.

It also churned up painful memories that had nothing to do with Dennis—of being the one left behind.

She thought again of Jay's text. Maybe he was serious. Maybe he really did want to make things right. Seeing Dennis again reminded her that breakups not dealt with properly would just lead to more hurt. She was reassured that it would be better to at least smooth things over with Jay before fifteen years passed.

It's not like I'm going to get back together with him, Ava told herself. But Jay seemed to be open to the idea—unlike the handsome man who seemed intent on staring straight ahead. Not glancing at the hotel they'd just parked in front of, lest he glimpse her in his peripheral vision. Trying to ignore her and the fact they were together once again.

Chapter Six

Ava glanced up at the hotel, which was just one section of a block-long building. Rows of windows and small balconies looked down onto the sidewalk, the street, and the lush park on the other side. A blue and white canopy fluttered softly in the breeze, shading the doorway. Ava climbed from the car and was met by a squeal. Before she knew it, arms wrapped around her, and she recognized Tana's signature fragrance that smelled like a rose garden after a misty rain. Ava didn't remember the name, but it was a scent she'd never forget. It had been all over Tana's schoolbooks, her clothes, and in her car during the two years of college that they'd roomed together. It seemed Tana hadn't lightened up on the stuff.

Around them, well-dressed Parisians cast glances but continued their pace. Peering over Tana's shoulder, she took in the street. It was lined with small shops on the ground floor and apartments on top. A bell from a bicycle jingled. The smell of fresh-baked bread mixed with Tana's perfume, and Ava guessed there was a bakery nearby.

Ava squeezed Tana tighter, trying to convince herself it was really her—that she was really here. "I thought you weren't going to come by until tonight. Didn't you have to work today?"

Ava took a step back and eyed Tana, realizing that France had been good to her—a sophisticated elegance had replaced the grunge look from years prior.

Tana waved a hand. "I called in sick. I couldn't wait to see you. Oh, and Grandpa. Where is he?"

Ava turned and helped Grandpa Jack out of the car. "Grandpa, do you remember Tana?" She felt bad for leaving him there while she hugged her friend. She felt worse realizing how embarrassing it must be for him to receive help just to climb out of the backseat of a car. She had to remember to help Grandpa first. Dennis was on the other side of the car, helping his grandfather out too.

Grandpa Jack neared Tana, eyeing her. Then he tapped his chin. "Well, I recognize those eyes, but what happened to the purple and orange streaks in your hair?" He held tight to Ava's arm, trying to get his balance.

Tana shook her dark locks. "Actually, I think I was blond at that last Thanksgiving our senior year of college, remember? It was blond until I jumped into a hot tub at a New Year's Party and the highlights turned the most horrible shade of green. I cringe just thinking of it." She laughed, and again her laughter caused more of the locals to turn and look. Despite the number of people on the street, the atmosphere was quiet, subdued. They obviously didn't appreciate loud Americans.

"I'm sorry to interrupt, ladies, but this is a no parking zone." It was Dennis's voice. He touched Ava's arm, getting her attention. Grand-Paul was at her side and his face was pale.

"If you help me get your things from the car, Ava, I can lead the guys inside. There are a few steps they might need help with. Then I can park."

Her skin burned from his touch, and Ava mouthed "thank you" just as he turned away. She saw something in his eyes, something deeper, pained. Something that had nothing to do with their grandfathers. Could Dennis's heart really be broken after all these years? They'd had that perfect summer, but they'd been so young. When they parted, Ava had hoped for a while that he'd contact her and try to reconcile. When he didn't, she assumed he'd found someone else. But what if he hadn't? Could he still care for her? If he did, he had a funny way of showing it. *I'm just imagining things, aren't I?* She tried to catch his gaze again, but he ducked his head into the trunk as he reached to retrieve her bag. Ava turned away, focusing again on the Parisian street, reminding herself she was really here.

There was a bakery next to a flower stand. Taking a deeper breath, the air smelled of flowers and . . . *Frenchness,* which was the only description that came to mind. It was May, so she expected the air to be light and fresh, but it was more than that. It was as if scents from the sunshine, flower boxes, cafés along the boulevard, and the park across the street melded into something enchanting.

Ava grabbed her purse from the front seat, and then she moved around to the trunk where Dennis was unloading her things.

"Didn't you get the message from the tour handbook? One suitcase per person?" He placed their suitcases and all her recording equipment on the sidewalk.

"Excuse me?"

"This is a lot of stuff. I can tell you don't travel much." Dennis pulled her grandfather's suitcase out and placed it next to hers.

"No, I really haven't had the chance. I—" She tried to think of a good excuse. Nothing came to her. The truth was she'd been waiting until after she got married. She'd wanted someone to share this with, but how could Dennis understand that or anything else about her for that matter? He was a stranger to her now.

"I don't mean to be rude," he said, his gaze softening slightly. "But you're going to have a hard time getting around with all that stuff and help your grandpa too." He let out a heavy sigh. "If you want I can come back—"

"No!" Ava jutted out her chin and began gathering up her things. "I can get everything. I'm fine."

Without another word, he turned away and

guided Grand-Paul into the hotel lobby, a firm grasp on his grandfather's elbow. Paul seemed even more unsteady on his feet than Grandpa Jack. Thinner, weaker than she remembered. Her grandfather followed—more steady now than at the airport—and insisted on pulling his own rolling suitcase. Ava was glad to see that his legs were getting unkinked.

Ava and Tana gathered up her things, and Ava took a step, following the men. Tana's grasp on her wrist stopped her. "Who's *he?*" she whispered in Ava's ear.

"That's Dennis, Paul's grandson," Ava whispered back, trying to sound unimpressed. Tana's eyes widened in acknowledgment, and it was then Ava remembered there was one person she'd told about Dennis. That was one thing about being former roommates. There wasn't any need for explanation when it came to old flames.

Tana's eyes widened. "That's him? That's *the guy?*" She elbowed Ava. "If he's here, what do you need me for?"

Ava didn't want to admit it, but when she had first seen Dennis, she almost wished she were going out to dinner with him tonight, but now she was less impressed. He had rushed in like Prince Charming, saving her from the evil taxi fares, and then pointed out that she'd packed too many glass slippers.

Then again, maybe he wouldn't have wanted to

take her out even if he'd had the chance. She thought of the pain in his eyes. *Surely he's not still hurt by something that happened so long ago.*

She looked at her friend. Dinner with Tana would be more fun anyway. She'd have fun with Tana. It was Paris after all. Then, she'd have a whole week with Dennis to try to get to the bottom of his attitude. Maybe they could sit together on one of the bus rides and catch up. Or maybe he'd be civil but keep his distance. She hoped that wouldn't be the case. Just the thought of being near him and not talking and laughing like they used to caused her heart to ache.

Ava hadn't made it five feet into the lobby when she noticed that a cluster of gray-haired men had stopped Grandpa Jack and circled around. She approached, and Tana paused at her side, her arms full of equipment.

"Jack, there you are." The elderly men's voice quivered with excitement, and Ava noticed tears springing to her grandpa's light blue eyes beneath the Eleventh Armored Division cap he had pulled low over his bushy gray eyebrows.

"How was your trip?" another elderly man asked.

"Is this your granddaughter?" a third asked.

Grandpa Jack paused in the middle of the cluster of men and scanned their faces. He placed a hand over his heart. He opened his mouth to say something, but—overcome with emotion—he closed it again. He looked at the faces, his eyes resting on each one before moving on, and she wondered if he saw them as they used to look— young, strong, handsome, brave, a bit scared. From the look in his eyes, he did.

"I'm Ava." She stepped forward. "Yes, I'm Jack's granddaughter, and we're excited to be here."

"Jack, it's good to see you." The jumble of voices started up again.

"Jack, remember that time back in forty-two when you passed out when you saw it was a female nurse who would be giving you your physical?" The man's chuckle was deep and filled the ornate foyer.

"Or the time your boots got baked in the oven when you'd been trying to dry them?" another man chimed in.

Everyone seemed to be talking at once. Their faces were bright with excitement. Their eyes sparkled. Gray heads bobbed as they spoke. Hands patted her grandfather's shoulders and arms pulled him into hugs. Ava looked around for Dennis and Paul but didn't see them. Maybe Dennis had taken his grandfather upstairs to his room before parking the car?

The men continued, their voices ricocheting off the sparkling tile floor, the burgundy plaster walls, and around the crystal chandeliers, before drifting back down to them.

Ava turned to Tana, attempting to speak up over the many voices. "What do you think? Should I ask the front desk clerk if he has one of those portable defibrillators on hand?" She chuckled.

"This many excited seniors worries me," Tana said.

Ava laughed and gave her friend a one-armed squeeze and then went to the front desk to check in.

"The room is under Jackson Andrews." Ava leaned against the counter.

"Yes, I have the room here," the clerk said, impressing her with his English. "One hundred seventy euros a night."

Ava glanced at Tana. "How much is that in dollars?"

"Approximately 225 American dollars," the clerk answered for her. "Will that be on a credit card?"

"I don't understand. I thought the hotel rooms were already covered."

The clerk frowned and cocked one eyebrow.

"Maybe you should ask your grandfather," Tana suggested.

"That's a good idea." Ava tucked a long strand of blond hair behind her ear. She hurried over to her grandfather, still deep in conversation, sharing old war stories. Tana followed.

"Did anyone tell Jack yet?" a shorter man interrupted, glancing at his watch. He was stocky and round, and his face looked jolly, even with concern in his eyes.

"Tell me what?"

The room quieted, and it was only then Ava realized that their flushed faces had to do with something other than just meeting old friends.

"It's a big problem." A tall man strode forward. He didn't look as if he had lost an inch of his height over the years. The man's commanding presence showed he used to be in charge of many of these guys. Even after sixty-seven years, they looked at him with respect.

"Ava, this is Mitch Thompson, one of our former commanders," Grandpa Jack said.

"The tour guide's been hospitalized somewhere in North Africa. They were doing a tour with veterans there. There was a bus accident. All the guys are okay," he continued, but before he could finish, a few of the other veterans started in about friends they knew who'd fought in North Africa. Friends they hoped weren't on that tour.

"Excuse me." Ava moved closer to Commander Mitch. "Are they bringing in another tour guide?"

"There is no one else. Our tour guide had his own company. He ran the show himself."

"Is the tour canceled then? Did we come here for nothing? Are we going to have to head home?" Ava placed her fingers on her temples, pressing them hard. Trickles of sweat beaded on her brow and the men's voices faded in and out as if someone was turning the volume in the room up and down.

"There's more," the man added, running his hand through his graying hair. "We're also out of luck concerning the hotels on the battle route. The hotel manager said the guide usually paid as he went. We'll get our money back later, but that doesn't help us now."

An older woman approached, placing a hand on Ava's elbow. Her permed hair and the laugh lines around her eyes indicated she was much older than Ava, but not as old as the veterans. She was probably a daughter, Ava guessed.

"What he means, honey, is that the rooms have been reserved, but they haven't been paid for yet."

"My sister here called the chairman of the Mauthausen memorial committee," the man said, "letting her know that we might not be coming for the ceremony next week. The committee was horrified we'd been left in such a situation. They've booked hotel rooms for us in the village of Mauthausen. They—" Emotion filled his voice, and he lowered his head, focusing on the floor's marble tiles. "They are covering the cost of our rooms and food for the week. They also chartered a bus to drive everyone there. It should be here soon. We're packing up and leaving for Austria."

"We're heading to Austria tonight?" Ava pictured the map of the battle route. The tour was supposed to start in France and then travel through

Belgium and Germany, finally ending in Austria. Looking over the agenda for each day, she'd written a short outline of places where she'd shoot footage and things she'd talk to Grandpa Jack about along the way. By heading to the last stop now, the veterans would lose so much . . . and she wouldn't get the footage she needed. She suddenly felt sick, and her eyelids were weighed down with the weariness of every mile the airplane had just carried her.

The permed-haired woman continued talking about how nice everyone on the committee was and how generous their gift, but Ava wasn't listening. Instead, she glimpsed her grandfather's face out of the corner of her eye. His head was lowered, his shoulders slumped. This had meant so much to him. Back in California, his dining room table had been covered with maps of the trip, along with maps of Belgium and Germany from 1942. He'd studied them on their airplane, his quivering finger following the lines on the map. There was a seriousness in his gaze that told her the path itself was just as important to him as seeing his friends again—if not more important.

Grandpa Jack lifted his head and turned to her. He swallowed down emotion and his chin trembled. "We're not going to Belgium?"

His face became blurry. Tears filled her eyes as she saw his disappointment. He was the one who always took care of everyone else, and she'd never seen such desperation in his eyes.

"Ava, I need to go to Belgium." His voice was no more than a whisper. "I just have to."

"I don't know how that's going to work, Grandpa. But I'm sure Austria is nice." She took his hand in hers. She felt Tana's hand on her shoulder and appreciated the strength in her friend's touch.

Even though Ava tried to comfort her grandfather with her words, her heart pounded in her chest, and she knew this could be the end of it all—of her idea for battle site videos, of Todd's trust in her, and maybe even her job as head producer. She pictured another red marker crossing out the script she'd planned for this trip.

Her grandfather opened his mouth and then closed it again. He, too, was struggling with his words.

"I can't imagine coming all this way and missing out on so much. I just won't have peace until I see a few things—places I've been." His chin lowered and he fingered the handle of his suitcase, looking even wearier than he had when they first got off the plane. The spunkiness he'd had during the car ride was now gone.

"There's nothing really to see, just fields and trees." Tana offered Grandpa Jack a smile. "I've gone before and there are only a few places that have actual memorials, and you'll see the same types of little villages on the way to Austria.

There's really not much difference."

Ava knew Tana was trying to help, but Grandpa Jack's eyebrows furrowed even more. "It's not just the countryside. There are other things. There is . . ." His voice trailed off, and then he looked away.

"What, Grandpa?" Ava again thought about him on the plane, studying his maps. Moving from the hand-drawn battle-site map to the topography map. He studied every turn in the road and every hill, as if he was trying to find a path he couldn't quite place.

"What matters most is returning to the places that mattered to me." His voice rose in volume. "I didn't spend all this money just to see a hill someone else fought on." He leaned against a high-backed red velvet chair for support.

Tana looked to Ava. "I don't think I said the right thing."

"It's not like he'll have a chance to come back in a few years," Ava whispered, more for herself than Tana. She'd never gotten around to apologizing to her grandfather for their last confrontation, and even though they both tried to pretend it hadn't happened, the underlying tension was there. She couldn't imagine the tension—the sadness, the regret—if they didn't get to tour the battle sites.

Then again, could she do it alone? It would mean renting a car and driving in several countries. There were people who liked to prey on tourists. They could get lost or robbed. Her grandpa could get sick . . . and then where would she turn for help?

If they went to Austria, everything would be paid for. She wouldn't have to worry about food, hotels, the dangers of solo travel—or the limited budget on her credit card.

Then again, she also had her assignment to consider. Todd was expecting video footage from battle sites. He'd gone out on a limb to help her. There were *two* guys counting on her. Her boss and her grandfather. She didn't want to disappoint either one.

"Have you seen Paul? Or Dennis?" Grandpa Jack scanned the room, his eyes widened, desperate. "I'd like to talk to them. Maybe we can make different plans than the rest of the group."

Ava looked around too. A boulder grew in her stomach, and she wished she had made more of an effort to talk to Dennis on the ride over. Maybe she should have apologized for what had happened so long ago. Maybe now that he knew it would be her with Grandpa Jack, he was hightailing it—trying to put some space between them.

Ava rubbed her forehead, and she wondered when the guys had gotten the news. Surely if Dennis had known about the problems with the tour, he would have said something.

He didn't even say good-bye.

"You're right, Grandpa, we need to talk to Dennis and Grand-Paul."

"Ava, what are you going to do?" Tana no longer seemed put together or sophisticated as she chewed her thumbnail, eyes wide.

"I'm not sure," Ava muttered, pressing her fingers to her lips. She didn't need to worry about where Dennis was. Even her worry over her job took a backseat for the moment. The videos weren't the most important thing here. She needed to focus on her grandfather first. He needed this.

Ava turned to Grandpa Jack and saw the deep sadness in his eyes. Tana grabbed Ava's hand and patted it. Then she pulled Ava to the side. "Look at him, he's heartbroken. You have to go." Tana squeezed her hand tighter.

"I'm not sure I can do it. I've never travelled in a foreign country. This isn't like driving from Seattle to Northern California. I don't know the language, or rather the *languages*. I don't know how to drive on the roads."

"It's not that hard. If I can survive here, so can you."

"Can you come with me? It would make me feel a whole lot better."

"Sorry, I have to work. But I can help you with the arrangements."

As Ava watched her grandfather's age-spotted hand wipe tears—tears he was trying to hide—she knew what she had to do. She had to drive Grandpa Jack across Europe, taking him to the places that mattered most.

He had places he needed to go, and a past he needed to confront. And she was the only one who could take him.

Ava took a deep breath. "Okay, where do I start?"

Chapter Seven

Ava paused at the hotel room door before knocking. She heard voices inside and a tinge of anger punched at her lungs, making it hard to breathe. Grandpa Jack had asked the hotel clerk if Dennis and Paul had checked into a room. To Ava's amazement, they had. Either they were clueless about the problem with the tour, or maybe they had the same plan as she did. Maybe they were going to strike out on their own.

But Dennis could have at least let her know he was heading up to their room. He could have looked for her to try to talk about changes in their travel plans. Obviously, if they hadn't taken the time to find her in the lobby, they weren't interested in Ava and Jack's plans. Ava wasn't here to ask for company. She needed advice, though.

She knocked, and Dennis answered the door.

"Did you hear about the big problem?"

"The tour cancelation? Yeah, I heard about it, but it's not going to change our plans. I was on the phone with the rental car place asking if I could keep it for another week."

"So you're not going to get on the bus?"

"No. I know my grandpa wants to spend time with his friends, but he didn't come this far to miss out on the battlefields. I was going to talk to you to see if you'd be interested in going together—following the original route." He sounded all business.

"Yes." The word slipped out of her mouth and with it, some of her pent-up anxiety. "We'd already decided that too—that we weren't going to head to Austria with the others." She bit her lip. She looked into Dennis's dark blue eyes and heat rose up her neck. She looked at his jaw, his neck, remembering when she'd snuggled under his chin with his arms wrapped around her. Ava pushed her lower lip out, trying to hide her attraction. Even though he wasn't the same charming Dennis she remembered, she couldn't deny how handsome he was. She hoped that the uptight Dennis from earlier was gone. He seemed a little more at ease, and he had asked if she would—they would—join them. "I've never driven around Europe before. I was hoping I wouldn't have to do it alone." She tried to make her voice sound natural.

"Great." Dennis nodded. "We'll head out in the morning."

"You want to meet downstairs at breakfast?" Nervous energy seemed to radiate from her chest, and she wondered if he could feel it. They were really going to do this—head off across Europe alone. The small hairs on her arms rose at the thought of all those miles spent together. As she looked at him, it was the old Dennis who stood before her. There was no snobby attitude, just an easy presence that made her wish they could begin their adventure now.

"Sounds like a plan." He stepped back from the door.

Ava turned and started down the hall.

"Ava!" he called after her.

She turned. "Yeah?"

"I'm sorry you thought I abandoned you."

She knew he was talking about today, but deep down she wished the apology was for fifteen years ago. Even though she was the one who'd broken things off, she wished he had come after her. She wished the apology was for all the times between then and now that he could have reached out.

She brushed her hair over her shoulder and shrugged. "That's okay. No harm done." She thought about saying more—about adding that she was looking forward to the coming week. He stepped back inside the door before she could.

As she hurried to find Tana, she smiled at the adventure awaiting them.

The elevator doors opened, and another hotel

guest waved her inside. Ava crossed her arms over her chest as she stepped into the small elevator. A handsome Parisian with slicked black hair and wearing a business suit eyed her, but she focused instead on the lighted, numbered panel. Even then, she could feel his eyes on her. His closeness. She was consumed with his presence in the small space. Being in close proximity with Dennis in a car for a week would have the same effect. She wanted to be close to him but feared it just the same. Feared all the memories it would bring back. Feared attraction and yet another longing for something—someone—she couldn't have.

Chapter Eight

After Ava checked in, she made sure her grandfather got dinner. Then she and Tana hoofed it over to a mobile phone shop around the corner and picked up a cell phone for Ava, putting Tana's number on speed dial. While her grandfather got ready for bed, Tana called to check in with her boyfriend, Pierre, and Ava found their previous itinerary online and called the hotels. She also took a minute to check to see if she'd gotten a return e-mail from Jay, but there was nothing.

"You've come here at a good time." Tana linked her arm through Ava's as they walked down the hall toward the lobby. "Europeans go on holiday in August. It's a nightmare trying to find a rental car and hotel rooms then."

"Good thing World War II ended in May. Wouldn't want to mess with everyone's holiday." Ava chuckled, trying to ignore the unsettled feeling she had over using her expense credit card for the room. Todd knew that her expenses would be on the card, he just didn't realize how much they would be. She'd thought about calling him and explaining, but he hated dealing with the financial side of things. It would be better for her just to take care of everything when she got home—save him from all the forms that needed to be submitted, the hassle. She also tried to ignore the unsettled feeling she had over Jay's not e-mailing her back.

She pushed both thoughts out of her mind and squared her shoulders. A lot had happened to disrupt their plans, but tonight was her one and only night with Tana. She needed to be present for that.

She scanned the front lobby of the hotel. The clock was already inching toward ten o'clock. Her stomach grumbled, but she doubted there would be a restaurant open this late. Ava had eaten her last granola bar hours ago when her grandfather was enjoying dinner with friends.

The foyer that had previously been packed with old men, suitcases, and anxious family members was now empty, and Ava assumed everyone was on their way to Austria. Well, everyone except Grand-Paul and Dennis. She hoped they were upstairs resting peacefully.

Grandpa Jack had told her he planned on hitting the sack after dinner, and even though it meant waiting longer, Ava made sure he had everything he needed before she headed out.

Ava yawned and rubbed her eyes, wondering if she would be able to keep going despite losing half a day and sleeping poorly on the plane ride. But instead of being tired, she was excited and anxious. The idea of heading off across Europe with a map, Dennis, and their grandpas was as good as two venti lattes, at least.

Tana knew a great restaurant within walking distance, and Ava wondered what type of place would be open this time of night.

Just go with it, Ava. It's Paris. Let your hair down, she thought as she played with the red beads on her bracelet and cautiously scanned the near-empty streets for any sign of danger.

A few cars passed, but no one seemed threatening. She walked by Tana's side through what appeared to be a shopping and business district and passed a plain-looking bank with an ATM machine on the side of the building, just like at home. She was disappointed to see that so many things—like the ATM—were similar to Seattle. She found herself wishing that every street was filled with ornate architecture and quaint shops.

As they walked, Ava's heels echoed off the pavement, and Tana rattled on about Pierre's parents.

"Fabian and Magalie have an estate thirty minutes south of the city. Magalie is his third wife, and much younger. They built a house for Pierre's sister when she married, and Magalie's hinted about us looking at house plans. Not that I'm ready to marry anytime soon. That's what I like about the French, though. Family matters. They dislike the idea of living too far apart, unlike Americans who scatter around the country like tiddlywinks. Oh," she continued hurriedly, "you should see their swimming pool. . . ." Tana rattled on. Ava's mind was on her grandfather, the trip, Jay, and Dennis, but she feigned interest.

As she glanced at her friend, Ava remembered that they used to have deep, insightful conversations, but she couldn't remember what they used to talk about. Their lives had gone down two different paths, in opposite directions. Tana lived in the Paris art scene and lived a creative lifestyle with no regular schedule. Ava organized her day down to the minute. She needed to pull off a show every day, five days a week.

A soft breeze blew, ruffling Ava's hair, and she brushed it out of her face, worried the same thing would happen with Dennis. After all these years, was it foolish to believe they'd still enjoy each other's company? She pulled her arms tighter to her, considering what a long ride it would be with someone whom she no longer connected with. Maybe teaming up with Dennis hadn't been the best idea. This had the potential for being the longest week of her life.

Just when Ava seriously doubted Tana knew where she was going, they turned onto a street with a few lighted restaurant windows. Tana led Ava into one, and she sucked in a breath as she entered. Stepping through the front door was like moving from a black-and-white movie into a 3-D, Technicolor adventure. Every table in the place was full, and there were people ahead of them waiting to be seated. Blue smoke trailed through the air, and Ava attempted to stifle her cough. Glancing around, it was evident she was far, far from Seattle.

As Tana jabbered with the host in French, Ava felt her senses being assaulted. Everyone spoke rapidly in words she couldn't understand. Music played in the background. The scents of warm bread and garlic made her stomach growl again. Even the air felt thick, heavy, warm, strong.

Tana returned to Ava's side just as Tana's cell phone rang. She picked it up immediately. From the brightness in her friend's eyes, Ava assumed it was Pierre yet again. Ava watched her and shook her head in amazement as her friend rattled on in French.

Ava glanced around and attempted to focus on different conversations, trying to pick out a few words. It was hopeless. She'd taken Spanish in high school and college, and that did little to help her here.

Finally, a waiter approached, and Tana continued to chat on the phone. The waiter spoke quickly, and Ava shook her head. "I'm sorry. I don't understand."

His eyes widened, and he smiled. "American, yes. Come with me." He grabbed two menus and placed his hand on the small of her back, leading Ava to a tiny table. Very tiny. The table was nestled between two others of equal size, with only a foot or so between them.

One side of the table was a booth and the other had a solo chair. Since Tana followed, it was only polite for Ava to slide to the booth side. It was awkward, mostly because her rear felt like it was going to bump the food off the table next to her. Even though she was an average, healthy American size, compared to these French women, she felt like a bull in a china shop.

They sat and studied the menus. To the right of them, an older couple ate quietly. They were as neat and proper as the queen of England. On the other side, two young women shared a table. Ava couldn't say they were dining together because one was puffing a cigarette while she talked on her phone and the other ate her salad in silence.

Thankfully, Tana had gotten off the phone as soon as they sat.

Ava glanced at the menu and then looked to Tana for help.

Ava's eyes darted to the older woman next to her, who had a plate full of what looked like raw meat. "I'll try anything, except what she's having."

"That's steak tartare." Tana pursed her lips.

"You've eaten that?" Ava wrinkled her nose.

"Yes, I've eaten a lot of things."

"It's raw meat."

Tana glanced up. "It's just food."

"I know, but seriously," Ava whispered, leaning close, "there are so many other things on the menu. It makes my stomach churn just looking at it."

Tana placed her menu on the table, shaking her head in disbelief. Then she glanced down at her manicured nails as if she was indicating to those around her that she too was bothered by the American.

With Tana's help, Ava decided on mushroom ravioli for an appetizer, and a walnut salad and grilled fish for dinner. Crème brulée would finish the meal.

"So, how are you doing? I mean really doing?" Tana studied Ava's face as they started in on their appetizer.

"As long as I don't get my hopes up about

someday finding love, getting married, and having kids, I'm fine. At least I still have my job." Ava sighed. "I'm hoping this trip will help turn around the career slump I've had lately."

Tana twirled a lock of hair around her finger and glanced at her watch. She looked at Ava briefly before turning her attention to the couple next to them, who were laughing and talking in French. Ava didn't want to make their time together a total bomb and decided to change the subject.

"But I don't want to talk about that. Have you noticed something strange about my grandpa?"

"What do you mean?"

"There's something in his eyes."

"Glaucoma?" Tana winked.

Ava almost choked on her ravioli. "No." She swallowed, laughing. "I'm serious. It's like he's searching for something. Every chance he gets, he looks at the old maps. He did it at home and then on the plane."

Tana put down her fork. Then she leaned forward and clasped her hands together. "What if he's not searching for some*thing,* but some*one?*"

Ava cocked an eyebrow. "After all these years?"

"Maybe it's your grandpa's true love."

Ava pointed her fork. "We're talking about my grandfather here."

"He was young once. I bet he met some girl during the war. Maybe a milk maiden on a farm. It was love at first sight and they spent every moment together before he moved on. He's never forgotten her, but he can't say anything. After all, he doesn't want to make you think he didn't love your grandmother." She took a small bite of her salad, eyes wide.

"All those romance novels have gone to your head."

"Well, just because I'm romantic doesn't mean it's *not* true." Tana jutted out her chin. "Find ways to work questions into your conversation, or when he's in the shower, check out his suitcase. Maybe he has a photo of her tucked behind his socks."

Ava smiled and again shook her head. The waiter came and took their plates and then laid out clean silverware.

Some*one*. It wasn't possible—was it?

Their entrees came, and Ava switched the conversation again, focusing it on Tana. They talked about Tana's job as an English-speaking tour guide around the city. She joked about the American tourists, their cameras, and their need to record every moment of their trip on video. Ava thought about her own video journal that would start the next day.

"Everyone loves the Louvre, but they miss so much when it's the only place they visit. There's also the Musée d'Orsay, which is in an old train station. And the Musée Jacquemart-André has amazing displays of art from the Italian Renaissance. Édouard André was a banker, and he and his wife were art collectors. Can you imagine one couple's collection being enough for a museum?" Tana took a sip from her water. "Of course, the way Pierre's parents are buying up art, that could be them soon."

Ava rubbed her forehead, feeling a headache coming on. She pulled her European cell phone out of her pocket to check the time and tried to think of a good excuse to head back.

"It's getting late." Ava leaned back from the table. "And I haven't gotten much sleep."

"In Paris, the night is still young. But I understand."

The walk back to the hotel was quiet, and in the hotel lobby they said their good-byes.

"Remember, if you have any problems I'm only a phone call away," Tana offered.

"Thank you. I'll let you know how it goes, but I think we're going to be okay." Ava tried to sound upbeat, as if convincing herself of the words. They gave each other a hug. It was quick, without tears. It was the same polite good-bye Ava had given to the nice older lady she met on the plane.

"It went by too fast," she said, hoping her words sounded sincere. "Let me know if you ever make it back to the States."

"Of course."

"E-mail works too."

"Okay, bye then. See you on e-mail." Tana waved as she strode away, a *foreign* version of

Ava's old friend, in every sense of the word.

Ava breathed a sigh of relief as her friend walked out the door. Then a lump swelled in her throat as she realized she missed how things used to be. Again she questioned if it would be a good thing that she'd be spending so much time with Dennis. Maybe she'd just be disappointed to see how he had changed too.

Ava's grandfather was sound asleep as she entered, his snores shaking his side of the room. Before she turned in for the night, Ava checked her camera, battery, and mic to make sure everything was working properly and charged. Then she made a list of some raw footage she hoped to get over the next few days—battlefields, gravestones, distant and close-up shots of her grandfather. She also made a list of basic interview questions: What is one incident you'll never forget? Who were your friends? Did you lose any of them? What was it like fighting in one of the most famous battles in history?

Ava also labeled her video cards with a fine-tipped permanent marker—Europe 1, Europe 2, Europe 3—which would help when she needed to grab one fast. It was always easier to grab the next number than to sift through all the video cards to see which ones she'd used and which ones she hadn't.

Finally, she turned her notebook to the back page where she'd kept her log. One of her media teachers had told her to log each shot to make things easier to find.

Ava realized she was smiling as she prepped everything, and she was reminded of why she'd gotten into this business in the first place. She liked systems. She liked creating order. She liked taking a jumble of words and photos and preparing a package that told a story.

She also liked the idea of her stories being appreciated by others. Sometimes when she watched Clark and Laurie on set, she thought about the young mom watching as she fed her baby rice cereal, or the worried woman in the hospital as she waited for her husband to get out of surgery, or the retired man eating his sandwich on a TV tray and chuckling at Clark's jokes and spouting his opinion back to the television set.

Maybe sharing her grandfather's story would make a difference to these people. It would remind viewers to spend time with their elders. To listen to their stories and learn from them.

Ava took a deep breath and then released it slowly, knowing that whatever came would make a good tale. Even if they got lost and ended up down a dirt road in the middle of nowhere with a cow and a kid on a bicycle who didn't speak English, she would experience it with her grandfather and get a glimpse through his eyes of what he'd been carrying in his heart for all these years.

Chapter Nine

The following morning, Ava looked up expectantly as the elevator bell in the lobby dinged and the doors opened, but the man who stepped out wasn't Dennis. She tried to hide her disappointment as she chatted with Grandpa Jack, who was finishing his breakfast in the lobby—croissants and jam.

Concern about how unsteady Grand-Paul had been the night before and anxiety about spending the day with Dennis weighed heavily. Her breathing felt labored—like she was trying to breathe through a straw. She fretted. Would it be a good day? Would she and Dennis have things to talk about? Would they still enjoy each other's company?

It was strange, she realized, how you could be so close to someone—feel so strongly about them—and then have them disappear from your life completely. Looking back, she could see how young and independent she'd been. If she could transport her thirty-three-year-old self back to talk to who she'd been then, she'd tell herself a thing or two. Mostly that being on your own and facing the world with shoulders squared and chin cocked wasn't all it was cracked up to be.

Ava gazed out the window, taking in the Paris

view. Across the street from the hotel was what looked to be a park. If she had more time, she would have headed to the park to find a good bench to do some people watching. She could imagine old ladies feeding pigeons and mothers pushing their babies in prams.

On the street next to the hotel, there was a shopkeeper setting up an outdoor display of trinkets—miniature Eiffel towers, colorful scarves, postcards. She remembered what Todd had said about not buying too many souvenirs but decided she should buy something to take home. She would pay for it herself.

"Grandpa, I'm going to run outside real quick to get a souvenir. Do you want anything?"

"No, there's enough stuff around my place that your mom's going to have to sort through one of these days. Better not."

Ava wanted to argue, but she decided to just pick out something nice and give it to him later.

"Okay, I'll be back in five minutes." She checked her purse to find her wallet and then hurried outside.

She'd just finished paying for a few postcards and a watercolor print of the Seine that would look nice in her grandfather's dining room when someone approached from behind and grabbed her elbow. Ava froze and sucked in a breath. She clutched her purse tighter and took two quick steps away, turning to eye her perpetrator. Her heartbeat stilled and then began pounding again when she saw that it was Dennis.

"What are you doing? Are you crazy?" Ava spouted. "Are you trying to give me a heart attack? I should have figured it was you—*Dennis the Menace*."

"Sorry, *Ava-tude*. I didn't mean to scare you. I just wanted to let you know we were back."

"Back?"

"Yeah, Grand-Paul wasn't happy with breakfast. He said he needed protein, so we headed to an American café a few blocks away and had ham and eggs."

Ava nodded, trying not to be upset that they had not been invited. She now understood that just because they were going to travel together didn't mean they'd be doing everything together.

"I don't know about you, but I'm ready to load up. How about I run and get the car and you get the guys to the sidewalk."

"Sure."

Twenty minutes later, Ava sat in the front next to Dennis. He'd scowled when he saw her luggage, so she'd pushed him aside to load it herself. She didn't understand why Dennis was making a big deal about it. It was as if he was trying to stir up trouble.

Their grandfathers sat in the backseat, with Grand-Paul behind Ava. Before he started the engine, Dennis bowed his head.

"Dear God, You guided the Israelites across the desert. If You could get us to Bastogne today, it would be greatly appreciated. So glad You know the path and the journey, Lord. Amen." Dennis finished praying, and then he glanced over at Ava. "My mom always prayed the Israelite prayer whenever we headed out on a long trip. It never fit as well as it did today. Strange people in a new land."

"And, Lord, in fewer than forty years would be great," Grandpa Jack quipped.

"Amen," Grand-Paul chimed in.

Dennis smiled, giving Ava hope for the trip ahead. She liked it better when he smiled.

Dennis started the engine, glancing into the rearview mirror at Grandpa Jack. "Is my navigator ready?"

Her grandfather unfolded a roadmap on his lap. She'd heard long ago that her grandfather had been put into the recon unit because of his sense of direction. Maybe it was Paul who'd said it. She only hoped Paul wasn't being sarcastic.

"Go out of the parking garage and make a right and then your first left," Grandpa Jack ordered. She glanced into the backseat, noticing her grandfather's eyes were bright.

Dennis left the parking garage and did as he was told. As they merged into traffic, Ava let out a sigh, relinquishing all the things she'd hoped to see in Paris: Notre Dame Cathedral, the

Catacombs, the Louvre, especially the top of the Eiffel Tower. There were still plenty of years for her to return. Grandpa Jack and Grand-Paul, she knew, didn't have that luxury.

From the corner of her eye, she saw Grandpa Jack marking out the route with his finger. "If we follow this road, it will take us by the Arc de Triomphe, and then we can get a better view of the Eiffel Tower on our way out of town."

"That sounds like a good plan. Are you sure you don't want to go to the top?" Ava asked.

"No." Grandpa Jack sighed. "Just like last time, we have a greater calling. We need to head to Belgium."

"Amen!" Grand-Paul called out again. Laughter filled the car.

Dennis drove around a roundabout. When they paused for a traffic light, Ava spotted the Eiffel Tower in the distance, and she wished the old guys would change their minds just this once about sticking to the planned route. How fun it would be to go to the top, to see the view, to experience it together. She told herself to focus on the reason they were here.

"So what was your division doing in Belgium?" she asked, looking back and making eye contact with her grandfather. Even though she had studied the Battle of the Bulge on the flight over, she wanted to hear the story from his point of view.

But before her grandfather had a chance to

answer, Grand-Paul cut in. "Our unit drove the enemy troops out of a small Belgium village near Bastogne." Even though he sounded excited, his voice wobbled with weariness as he continued. "Boy, were we anxious. It was our baptism by fire—the first combat action of our division. Then in Chenogne . . ." Grand-Paul started and then paused.

She looked over her shoulder. "What about Chenogne?" she prodded.

"Do you see the Eiffel Tower up there?" Grandpa Jack cut in, pointing.

Ava noticed her grandpa's face was flushed.

"Is it too hot back there? Do you need me to turn on the air?" She flipped the knob for more air.

"I'm fine. Are you, Jack?" Grand-Paul gazed at his friend with a penetrating look. A message passed between them.

"Grand-Paul, I'd really love to hear about Chenogne," Ava said, returning to the subject. Her hand gripped the armrest, and she knew she was on to something. Dennis glanced in the rearview mirror and then back to the road.

"I—I decided I don't want to talk about it." Grand-Paul cleared his throat.

"Are you sure? I know it must be hard . . ." She let her voice trail off.

Instead of answering, Grand-Paul pointed ahead to a gleaming white arch in the distance. "Look!"

"Maybe we can talk about it later." Ava smiled.

"Paul doesn't want to talk about it later," Grandpa Jack snapped. "There are some things that just have to be that way."

Ava sucked in a breath and swallowed hard. Her shoulders tightened. Her grandfather had never talked to her like that. Tears sprang to her eyes and she blinked them away, taking in a deep breath.

Jack pointed out the window. "Look, the Arc de Triomphe! Can you believe it, Ava?" His voice was too chipper.

She nodded, swallowing down her emotion.

Hundreds of cars filled the roadway, and trees lined the road that led toward the majestic monument. It was taller than she had expected, growing before her as they neared. A large white square with a perfect arch cut from the center. Ava couldn't look at it without recalling the black-and-white images she had seen while researching. A photo of Nazi guards marching in straight lines through the arch sent a shiver up her spine. The Nazis' foreboding presence seemed to still be there, dominating the bricks they'd strode over with precision and power.

The road curved around the arch, and Dennis slowed so Grandpa Jack could snap a photo from the car window. The car behind them honked.

"Hey, buddy, these guys waited sixty years for this moment, they aren't about to miss it," Dennis mumbled.

"Yeah, if you'd waited sixty years, you'd want a

photo too," Ava chimed in, pushing her grandpa's harsh tone out of her mind.

As they continued, the traffic grew more congested. Dennis's hand gripped the steering wheel as he maneuvered through the lanes.

"Okay, right up here, you're going to make the next left," Grandpa Jack told Dennis.

After they passed the arch, Grandpa Jack guided them past the Eiffel Tower.

Ava leaned forward in her seat to eye it and then gave a small wave. "I'll be back someday. Just give me some time to let my life calm down," she called to the tower.

"Don't let it get too calm. Life's full of adventure, especially if you have someone to share it with," Grand-Paul said.

In the driver's seat, Dennis cleared his throat.

"Maybe someday. We'll see." She shrugged, keeping her eyes straight ahead. Years ago, when Grand-Paul and Dennis had spent the summer in Northern California with her grandpa and grandma, the hints had been more subtle, but they'd been there just the same. Ava had been only too happy to oblige then, but now . . . she was a different person. Dennis was too. They were strangers beginning a journey together, and they had a long way to travel toward trust.

"*We'll see?* What kind of attitude is that? Too passive, if you ask me." Grand-Paul scoffed. "We wouldn't have accomplished anything in our lives with that type of attitude, would we, Jack?"

"Don't let life just come to you, Ava," Grandpa Jack added. "Look for the one thing that won't leave your thoughts and pursue it, even if it costs you everything." His voice trailed off. She could tell he was thinking of something specific. Someone?

Ava looked back and eyed him more closely, unsure what to think. It seemed strange to be getting advice like this, especially from a man who hadn't traveled two hundred miles outside his home in sixty years. Maybe that was it. Maybe he regretted waiting until he was eighty-four years old to follow his own advice.

As they drove out of Paris, somberness settled over her soul. It was as if she'd been living her life in a dim room and someone had come in and opened the drapes, giving her a peek of how the world really was.

She was awed by Paris. Overwhelmed by its beauty. More than the beauty, she understood better the impact of what had happened here during World War II. A foreign invader had come and had taken complete control of the French people. This wasn't just a little village. Hitler had shown great power when he occupied Paris. She understood that feeling of helplessness, of other people's decisions changing everything you believed to be true. She thought of Jay's text and her e-mailed response. She wondered now if she'd made a mistake in responding to him. Jay had promised her the world and then walked away. Fear and doubt had invaded her heart. She wished she could be completely free to love again but didn't know how that would ever be possible.

Chapter Ten

As they drove, Grandpa Jack talked about his first experiences of the war, and it wasn't the eighty-four-year-old man riding with them any longer but the nineteen-year-old soldier. As he talked, his voice lost its quiver. He spoke in shorter, more clipped sentences—so different from his usual slow, lazy drawl.

"When we first got to France, we expected to fight the Germans still hanging on from D-Day. Then our orders changed." Grandpa Jack didn't appear to notice the ride or the countryside flashing by. In fact, she was sure that though his body was riding with them, his mind was back there again. Back in '44. She jotted down a few of her thoughts. Then her pen stilled.

She tried to focus on her grandfather's stories, but the view out the car window drew her attention. Rolling hills, covered with vineyards, stretched both directions. Rectangles of green and brown striped a nearby hillside—various crops at different stages of cultivation. The scenery looked as delicately beautiful as the elegant clothes the French women wore.

"We headed north to the combat zone on December seventeenth. It was a four-hundred-fifty-mile, breakneck march. We weren't actually marching, of course, but those jeeps, half-tracks, and tanks seemed to crawl."

"You must have taken this road. Do you remember it?" Dennis asked.

"All I remember is white." He sighed. "Snow poured from the sky. I'll never forget the unique crunch of a tank moving slowly across new-fallen snow."

"I bet it was cold," Ava said.

"You ain't a-kiddin'," Grand-Paul added. "The only thing that kept us all from freezing was our own fear and adrenaline."

"Every now and then, we heard a high screech," Grandpa Jack continued. "It was the tracks locking up on the ice." His voice quivered. "We were convinced the enemy was around every turn."

Ava leaned her head against the headrest, picturing what he was saying. She'd jotted down a few more notes, but the motion of the car and the warmth of the sun coming through the window were getting to her. A nap sounded nice.

"We neared Neufchâteau, Belgium, on December twenty-ninth. The first day of battle, the Germans came over the hill, and that's when we started to sustain casualties."

Ava tried to imagine the now-serene landscape covered with snow, ice, and the bodies of men who died their first day of battle.

Grandpa Jack was quiet for a while, and Ava could tell he was thinking, remembering. Grand-Paul was quiet, waiting for his friend to speak again.

She wanted to make sure Grandpa Jack didn't get all his storytelling out before she could record it, and she was glad when he grew silent. The sunshine warmed her. Ava's eyelids fluttered closed.

Ava didn't know how much time had passed, but when she opened her eyes again, she knew France was long behind them. *Belgium.*

Ava rubbed her eyes just as Dennis was pulling into a rest stop. Even though the sign called it a rest stop, it was more like a luxury travel center with a nice hotel and store. She chuckled when she thought about the mini-mart gas stations back home in Seattle. The ones with bars on the windows and paddles hooked to keys that opened locks to smelly bathrooms.

After using the fancy bathroom, she headed into the store. Grandpa was checking out the cheese and baguettes, and she moved to the soda case.

Dennis approached, and Ava realized that even though they'd been together for hours, they still hadn't said much to each other.

He glanced over at her, his eyes studying her

face for a moment, but he quickly looked away, pulling an orange Fanta from the cold case. "This is nice—getting the chance to hear your grandfather's stories."

Ava agreed, and when they got back in the car, the stories continued. Both Grand-Paul and Grandpa Jack started in about the pranks they used to play on each other. After a while, the stories became fewer and farther between. The laughter faded, and the backseat grew quiet. Before long, both men were snoring. Ava sat quietly too, wondering what to say. Dennis turned on the turn signal, preparing to take the next exit. As they got closer, Ava saw that the sign read BASTOGNE.

She settled deeper in her seat. Warm rays of sunlight filtered in the front window, and a sweet peace filled her. Even though she was in a foreign country with someone she hadn't seen in years, she felt more comfortable and at ease than she had in a long time.

"Do you know what's up with Chenogne? My grandpa didn't seem happy that it was brought up."

He shrugged. "Mostly my grandpa and I just talk about the end of the war when they liberated Mauthausen."

"I can see how something that big can overshadow everything else, but something must have happened in Chenogne. It must have been something horrible for him to change the subject and then to act that way when we brought it up again."

"You should ask him about it when it's just the two of you. Maybe he'll open up more," Dennis suggested. From the pinched look on his face, she suspected he knew more but just wasn't letting on. She thought about prodding him, but once again the view out the window captured her attention.

The car wound down a narrower road, leading them past houses, fields, and farms—many of which she assumed looked the same as they had sixty years ago. Or one hundred years ago, for that matter.

She twirled a strand of long hair around her finger and studied a small herd of cattle moving with quickened steps through a lush green field. "I'm afraid to see him cry or get angry. I'm afraid I won't know what to do or how to respond."

"I've never known you to be afraid of anything."

"Well, I was afraid before I found out we'd be going on this trip together. When I first considered heading out alone, I was scared of getting lost, getting robbed. Of being out of my comfort zone."

"That just doesn't seem possible. Where is the adventurous girl I once knew?"

"You're making it sound like it's a bad thing I'm no longer adventurous."

Outside the window, the hillsides were covered

with forests. She tried to picture the United States Army moving through these parts. She imagined young guys, fearful of what was around the next bend.

"I didn't mean for it to sound like that. It's just that for so long I used you for inspiration. Every time I'd come to a challenge, I'd think, *Ava would do it, so why can't I?* Then I'd go for it. That strategy worked, because I've traveled more places and accomplished more than I thought possible."

Ava's fists clenched on her lap, not appreciating the way it made her sound like she'd accomplished nothing. "I'm still a take-charge person—just not in this situation. I'm the lead producer at a morning television show. I call the shots." She thought of Todd. "Well, I mostly call the shots."

"Okay, if you say so. I just see something in your eyes. It's not fear. Not concern. There's something else. I can tell—" He started and then stopped.

"What?"

"Nothing."

"You have to finish now." She waited, tapping her toe against the floorboard.

Dennis took in a deep breath. "Well, at first when I saw you I was mad. Mad at Grand-Paul because he knew you were coming and didn't tell me. It would have helped if I could have prepared." He paused and pressed his lips tight.

Ava eyed him, trying to get a hint of what he meant.

"Even though I don't know what's happened in the last fifteen years, I could tell you've been hurt. You just seem so lost, so uncertain."

Ava balled her fists and placed them on her lap. "Don't you think that's a bit presumptuous?" She twisted her hair around her finger again. Faster, harder.

"That's also something I forgot. How fiery you can get. I was just trying to open up."

Ava opened her mouth, ready to shoot back that maybe he should say nothing at all, when guilt wrapped around her chest like a rope. What bothered her most, perhaps, was he was right. She *was* hurt, and it angered her that he could see that. Instead of answering, she pointed to a road that looked as if it led into the center of town. "I think you're supposed to turn right here. Isn't that the way to Bastogne?"

"I'm going to head down the road a little bit. This is the route the guys took back in forty-four. I'd like to stop near the hill where they first saw battle." His smile had slipped a notch, but he still had a pleasant tone to his voice. She didn't know why. She wouldn't try to be nice to herself if she were in his shoes.

"Good. That will be great for my videos," she said, glad to get off the subject about her life and how pitiful it was.

Dennis's brow furrowed. "Videos? Like family movies?"

A cold trickle moved down her arms. Would he be excited about her assignment? For some reason she doubted it. She pressed her lips up, forcing a smile.

"Didn't I tell you?" She attempted to keep her voice light. "It's for my job. I'm shooting news features, and they're going to show them on the morning program where I work. We have three million viewers who're going to follow us through Europe. Isn't that great?"

"Did you talk to the guys about it?" Dennis's voice was curt.

"What do you mean?" She opened her fists, sliding her hands down her jeans.

"I mean this is the first I've heard about it. If you're planning to use my grandpa's stories, he ought to give you his permission."

"Of course I'm going to get their permission. I may have changed, but I'm not totally incompetent."

Dennis's face wore a scowl. "I don't like the idea of using their pain for your advantage. And what about the viewers? If they're not entertained, they just flip to the next channel. These stories are special."

"The viewers will be touched. Maybe some of them will be inspired to talk to their own grandpas or uncles about the war."

He nodded but didn't answer.

"It's not about ratings. It's a chance for me to spend time with my grandpa. The job comes second." She nodded, as if trying to convince herself.

Dennis glanced at her. "So if they said no, you'd just drop the whole thing, right?"

"Yes, of course." Ava said the words, but they didn't sound convincing, even to her. She hoped it didn't come to that.

Chapter Eleven

The Ardennes area of Belgium was more beautiful than Ava had imagined. Thick groves of trees lined the roadway. As they drove, the groves opened up into wide meadow plateaus. It was hard to believe such a horrific battle, the Battle of the Bulge, had happened in such an idyllic place.

"How far are we from Bastogne?" Grand-Paul asked in a groggy voice.

Ava had first heard the name Bastogne before she even understood what *war* meant. It was the epicenter of the Americans' fight against the Germans. Thousands of men had died fighting for this position.

Dennis glanced at the clock. "We passed Bastogne a few minutes back. I thought I'd stop at the hill where you first saw battle. Should be there in two minutes."

They passed another small village. It reminded her of something she'd see in a Disney movie. Farms and small houses with gardens. A gas station selling petrol seemed like the only modern structure. There was no Walmart. Not even a 7-Eleven. Outside the village they passed a sign that read CHENOGNE, 4 KM. She didn't dare ask if they were going to visit Chenogne—not after her grandfather's reaction. She'd ask Dennis about it later.

"That's it, up ahead." Grand-Paul pointed to a distant hill. "See over there, off the road a ways."

"No. I don't think that's it. We weren't that close to a village," Grandpa Jack countered. Ava heard the rustling of paper behind her and guessed he was opening one of his maps to look.

"See," Grandpa Jack said to Paul. Then he called from the backseat, "It's a little bit farther up the way."

They drove a mile more, and then Grandpa Jack patted Dennis's shoulder as if signaling him to slow. Both older men sat forward in their seats, studying the terrain. Ava shook her head. She couldn't remember a shopping list of more than four items. How could they remember one hillside after sixty-five years?

"That's it." Grand-Paul pointed to a tree-lined field with a rising hill.

"Yes," Grandpa Jack agreed. "Do you think it'll

be okay to walk over there? It might be someone's property."

"Of course it's okay," Grand-Paul spouted. "We liberated that hill. Who's going to stop us?"

Dennis pulled to the side of the road. He and Ava helped their grandfathers out of the car. Grandpa Jack removed his Eleventh Armored Division cap and held it to his chest. Grand-Paul took two steps forward and then paused as he stared at the hill to the left of the roadway. To everyone else passing along this road, it was just another hill, but not to the men who had traveled thousands of miles to see it.

Ava approached the two older men. "Before we head over there, there's something I need to talk to you about."

"Is it about the videos?" Grandpa Jack scowled. Dennis stood next to him, frowning too.

"Yes." She turned to Grand-Paul, hoping for an ally. "They're for my job. My boss wants me to do short news features about our journey across Europe. They're going to show them on-air. I thought it would be a nice way for you and my grandpa to share your stories. For the younger generations to hear your experiences firsthand."

Grand-Paul turned to Grandpa Jack, scratching his head. "Let me guess, you're giving your sweet granddaughter a hard time about this."

"I don't like the idea of a camera in my face . . ." He trailed off, but she could see there was more to it. Something he wasn't saying.

"You should be honored." Grand-Paul elbowed Grandpa Jack. "It's not like you're Clint Eastwood. You should be thrilled someone wants to look at your ugly mug."

Grandpa Jack turned away, looking back to the hill. Then he shrugged. "Paul can be your star, Ava. I'll watch."

Ava didn't want to argue. "Can you pop the trunk?" she asked Dennis, disappointed. "I need to get my video stuff out."

He nodded but didn't comment. She hurried past Dennis, afraid to look into his face to see if he still agreed with Grandpa Jack. She hoped that once they got going, Dennis would warm up to the idea. Maybe, if she prayed hard enough, Grandpa Jack would too.

A minute later, she had her video camera case, mic, and tripod in her hands, and she looked at the horizon, hoping it would stay light long enough for her to finish.

Since her hands were full, Dennis walked between the two older men, a steadying hand on each arm.

The grass was dry and high, but when she pushed it down with each step, she saw new green blades sprouting from the moist soil.

As they walked toward the hill, she remembered that officially Grand-Paul should sign a release before she taped them, but she decided not to bring it up. Not yet. It wasn't like she was taping strangers. She'd get to that minor detail later. She was just happy that Grand-Paul had knocked some of the fight out of the other two.

"We're really going to be on television?" Grand-Paul slowed his pace, as if the idea was just sinking in. Then he looked at Grandpa Jack as if saying, "How come you didn't tell me about this?"

"Three million viewers!" Ava exclaimed. Why couldn't Grandpa Jack and Dennis appreciate how exciting this was?

"Maybe there will be some pretty white-hairs watching." Grand-Paul chuckled. "I better start practicing my autograph and jitterbug. Both are getting a little shaky these days."

"Well, if we get fan mail I'll be sure to pass it your way." She loved seeing that Grand-Paul was enjoying this. Loved to see she was proving Dennis wrong.

"I can set the equipment up over here, where you won't be able to see it." Ava moved the tripod far enough away for them not to feel as if she was in their faces, but close enough to get a good shot.

Grandpa Jack eyed her and then turned his back to her, studying the hill.

Paul steadied himself with his cane and then ran his fingers through his hair. He turned and faced Ava with the hill behind him. "Do I look okay?"

"Perfectly handsome." Ava set up the camera.

"This is set to autofocus, so let me figure out the view for the shot."

Grand-Paul leaned forward on his cane, looking directly into the camera as if he was the president preparing to give an address. Despite his enthusiasm, his whole body sagged, as if he had a hard time carrying his own weight. She set the shot so it showed him midchest up, with the hill in the background. As she stepped back, he looked up at her and winked.

Ava laughed. It was Grand-Paul's eyes that she loved the most. Lively and light blue. That was the first thing she noticed that summer evening when he and Dennis had shown up at Grandma and Grandpa's place. Her grandparents had received Christmas cards from Paul and his wife for years, but Paul decided to visit after his wife passed away. At first Ava had been upset she had to share her summer with her grandfather's old war buddy, but as they sat on the porch sipping lemonade, Paul had asked Ava about her life, her hobbies, her dreams for the future. She felt like an adult. She also felt special because Dennis was constantly averting his gaze when she glanced his way.

Standing in front of that hill, Grand-Paul's eyes seemed bluer than she remembered. Maybe his beard—neatly trimmed and gray—had something to do with that. His beard had been dark before, but his smile was just as wide.

Yet now, in front of this camera, Ava got a glimpse of the serious businessperson he was. She could almost see the script of what he wanted to say running through his head.

"Watch out, Robert Redford." He winked.

Ava put down her notebook and picked up the remote for the video camera. "Okay, Grand-Paul." She focused on his face. "Can you start by telling me why you ended up here?"

He nodded and cleared his throat. "The Germans weren't ready to give up, and they attacked the Americans, who were set up near Bastogne. We came in to help and to win back Belgium for the Allied forces."

From the corner of her eye, Ava notice Grandpa Jack pause and turn. He tilted his head and then tentatively stepped closer to listen.

"We'd never faced the actual enemy before that," Grand-Paul said. "All at once everything started. Shouts came from the sergeants. Tanks and the first wave of men crested the hill. Then they disappeared on the other side."

Grand-Paul continued, describing how the fifteen tanks in their unit were knocked out, and how he and the other infantrymen ran over the hill to find a wall of German weapons focused on them. "It was a miracle any of us made it out alive."

Ava glanced at Dennis for a brief moment and couldn't help but notice his pride. And sadness.

She crossed her arms over her chest, pulling them in, as if that would hold her emotions in too.

"It must have been hard, losing those men." As soon as the words were out of her mouth, Ava felt foolish. Of course it was hard.

"Yes, but what we did made a difference. That first battle was hard—nearly a failure—but we kept at it. We slowly pushed them back. Inch by inch, we took the countryside and the towns. Why, I'd never seen such a celebration as when we kicked the last German soldier out of Bastogne."

Her grandfather didn't say anything but took more steps toward Paul. Ava widened the angle to get him in the shot. He looked so small. He glanced at her with a look of uncertainty, as if he was wondering if she still approved of him even if he refused to tell his stories.

"We were just kids. We had no idea what we'd see. No idea," Paul said, looking into the camera.

Ava took the remote from her pocket and turned the camera off. She wanted to go to her grandfather, to tell him it was okay if he didn't share, but inside she knew that wasn't the truth. She wanted him to share his stories—needed him to. She just hoped he'd change his mind now that he saw how simple it was.

"See, the camera doesn't bite," she called to Paul, trying to act as if everything was normal.

"Are we finished?" Dennis approached.

"Almost. I need to get a few more shots." She

glanced around, noting the sun fading into the horizon, and realized that she was running out of time.

Dennis guided the grandpas gingerly across the field, back to the car. Emotion again overcame her. It was hard to see their health fail. It was harder to know they still held so much pain inside.

She stood there for a moment longer. She didn't want to leave, not yet. She wanted to remember this place. Remember the hill where her grandfather had fought—even if he wasn't willing to share his memories.

Dennis got the old men settled into the backseat and then returned.

As she packed up, Ava jotted down the information she needed on her video log sheet, including the order of her shots, the description of the shots, the take number, and the location of the counter.

"I was thinking we should get dinner tonight and then do some touring around Bastogne tomorrow," Dennis said. "There's some cool museums and stuff."

She paused and placed a hand on his arm. "What about Chenogne? We're so close. Should we at least drive in and look around?" She thought again about her grandfather's reaction and couldn't help but wonder what it was about.

"No." Dennis picked up her camera bag. "I asked my grandfather about that. He said no."

"But don't you think—"

"Listen, Ava, this is their trip. It's not about you or your videos. It's about them."

"Yes, it's about them, but my grandpa was so excited about Belgium. His first question when he heard the tour was cancelled was, 'What about Belgium?' " She placed a hand on her hip, the frustration of the moment mounting. "So we're here, and now he's not going to do anything?"

Dennis took a step back, holding up his palms as if to protect himself from the onslaught of her words. "Listen, we are going to see things." He motioned toward the field. "But this is their trip and their memories. I'm letting them call the shots whether you like it or not. There are other places your grandpa wants to see, but not Chenogne."

"Do you know something about Chenogne you're not telling me?" She narrowed her gaze at him.

Dennis's eyes met hers for the briefest second, and then he looked away and crossed his arms over his chest. "I'm not at liberty to tell."

A harsh laugh broke through her lips. "Are you kidding me?"

He looked down at her camera bag. "I might have considered it before you told me about your *work*." He spread his arms wide. "But this isn't just a lead, Ava. This is their lives. Their memories. If your grandpa wants to tell you, he will. You've got to take time to understand him. You've got to trust him." Dennis took the tripod from her, easing her load. Then he looked at her, his eyes gentle. "And you've got to earn his trust," he said in no more than a whisper.

Ava wanted to argue, but she knew she was standing on shaky ground. Lash out at Dennis, and she could lose Paul's goodwill.

"Besides," he said, "we don't need to go there for the story. Your grandpa carries it with him. He always has."

They walked quietly side by side as they approached the car where the men were looking around. They looked so frail, tired. Ava lowered her head. Guilt ricocheted through her. This was hard enough for them—physically, emotionally—and here she was placing more demands on them. Still, she had no choice.

"Can I get one more thing before we leave?" Ava pushed the thought of Chenogne out of her mind. "Grand-Paul, can you state your name and unit into the camera?" Ava knew Dennis was right. Pushing her grandfather too hard wouldn't help anything. So she tried to push softly. "Grandpa, can you do just this one thing for me too? It'll be painless, I promise."

Her grandfather didn't respond, and if she didn't know better, she would have thought he had not heard her.

She got out the camera again and focused on

Paul. She turned it to the low-light setting and hoped that the high-tech camera would make up for the dimming sunlight. "Okay, go ahead."

Grand-Paul straightened and stuck out his chest. "Paul Prichard, Company B, Twenty-first Armored Infantry Battalion of the Eleventh."

"Great."

Then she turned to her grandpa. He narrowed his gaze, obviously still uncomfortable.

"I'm not going to ask you to tell any stories, but can you just state your name and unit for me?" she asked again.

He looked weary, and then he straightened. She turned the camera on him.

"Jackson Andrews, Company B, Twenty-first Armored Infantry Battalion, Eleventh Armored Division." Then he narrowed his gaze. "That's all you're going to get."

A lump formed in Ava's throat. She cleared it. "Okay, if that's how you want it." She quickly put away her camera, wondering why she'd ever pushed for this. *Everything in my life has to be so hard these days.*

It was quiet as the car pulled out and they headed into town. The guys' eyes were intent on the views around them, and Ava wondered what they were thinking, what they weren't saying.

Then, as they neared Bastogne, Grand-Paul started in singing "Auld Lang Syne." After the first verse, Grandpa Jack joined in. Ava tried not to let her frustration ruin the trip, and as softly as possible she hummed along. She was pleasantly surprised to discover that Dennis knew the words as he joined in with the guys.

As they approached the outskirts of Bastogne, Ava spotted large gun turrets on either side of the road. She sat straighter in her seat.

"Would you look at that," Dennis said. "Those are ours."

"They sure are," Paul said.

"I never would have thought . . . ," Grandpa Jack mumbled.

"That's amazing—that the town still remembers and honors the liberators," Ava said, trying to show the guys she could still be pleasant even if she didn't get her way.

Ava pulled her digital camera out of her bag, but instead of taking a photo of the turrets, she turned and took a photo of the men.

Turning back around, she clicked the button to view the photo. The men's faces were solemn, but their eyes held a special sparkle. The expression on their faces spoke what they didn't say.

We're back.

They still care.

They remember . . .

Chapter Twelve

Blue curtains with bright pink flowers fluttered in the open windows as Ava, Dennis, and their grandfathers sat in the hotel dining room enjoying dinner that night. The white floor was spotless, the chairs had comfortable blue cushions, and a painting of a medieval village hung near their table. Other tourists sat around the room, enjoying quiet conversation.

Grandpa Jack leaned forward, arms on the table, telling them how—after weeks of fighting—the people from Bastogne had been so thankful that the Americans had finally pushed the Germans out.

"The women brought us flowers. The men had tears in their eyes. We passed out chocolate to the children."

Grandpa Jack spoke a little too loudly compared to the others at neighboring tables. Other customers looked over, and Ava shrank down a little bit in her seat. She didn't want to interrupt to tell him that he was talking too loudly or that he had bread crumbs making indentions in his lower arm where his sleeve was rolled up. She couldn't remember the last time he had told a story with such enthusiasm. Part of her was happy. The other part was frustrated. *Why can't he share his stories with this much enthusiasm in front of a camera?*

"Could you imagine the lives of those kids? All they knew was war," Dennis said.

"Worse yet were the ones who didn't make it. The bodies . . ." Grand-Paul lowered his head.

"Let's not talk about that, Paul." Grandpa Jack's voice quavered. His face looked pained, as if a clear memory had surfaced.

Ava looked at him and noticed tears. Her own eyes misted. She looked at Dennis and saw him looking at her—watching her as she watched Grandpa Jack. Heat rose to her cheeks, which made her even more frustrated. He'd been rude to her on much of this trip, so why did she still blush under his gaze? Part of her wanted to ignore his attention. After all, he knew about Chenogne and refused to tell her what had happened. Yet another part of her wondered if they could ever have the type of friendship they had after high school. Could they pick up where they had left off? Was that possible? The idea both excited and frightened her.

Cigarette smoke filled the room, giving it a dim and hazy feeling. She leaned closer to the open window, appreciating the no-smoking policy in restaurants back home.

They finished their simple meal of goulash, frites, and vegetables, and Grandpa Jack seemed more solemn than he had at the beginning of the meal. Grand-Paul pushed back his chair. Without a moment's pause, Dennis rose and helped him.

"So are you going to have a long night working on that video?" Grand-Paul asked.

"I hope not. I need to work on it, but I'm really tired." She stood and stretched. "The jet lag's finally hitting me."

"Maybe you should get some rest. This is just the beginning of the trip. You don't want to make yourself sick." Her grandfather talked to her with the same tone as when she was five and wanted to eat a whole package of Oreos by herself. But this time he wasn't just being grandfatherly. *He just wants me to rest because he hates that I'm doing the videos.* She squared her shoulders and tried not to let his comment pull her down.

"I wish I could rest, but I have no choice. Todd made it clear the video needs to be there three hours before the show so they can review it." She wrinkled her nose, imagining the team assembled in Todd's office, viewing her work. She knew she could make something decent, but could she, in this amount of time, meet their high standards?

"You seem a little nervous about it." Grand-Paul cocked an eyebrow.

"A little is an understatement. I just want to get it right, you know? My boss is counting on this." She didn't mention that her boss was also counting on her to understand her grandfather in new ways. Understanding was far from what she'd achieved so far. Rather, each new

116

destination had only brought more questions— ones her grandfather had no desire to answer.

"Let me tell you something I used to tell the people working in my company," Paul said, stepping closer to her. "Inside, all of us feel as if we're still in junior high. We feel awkward and think everyone around us is more handsome, smarter, or better. The best thing you can do is to take long strides ahead and tell yourself you're at the top of the class. Have confidence in yourself, in your abilities, Ava."

Ava looked at Dennis, remembering what he told her: *"I used to tell myself, Ava would do it, so why can't I?"* Thinking of that, she wondered when things had changed. For too long she'd focused on what she could do well, instead of trying new things. This trip was a huge step for her—she hadn't realized how big until now.

"I'll be fine. A little nervous, yes, but nothing hard work and a few prayers and tears can't solve. Besides, I can't think of a better story to lose a little sleep over. I have to get this right because I have one amazing subject."

Her grandpa rose from his chair and tried to get his balance.

"Off to bed, all of you." She waved her hands to shoo him away, trying to pretend she wasn't bothered by his decision not to participate in the videos. "Get some sleep."

She pointed at Dennis. "Especially you. You'll

need a good night's sleep, because I have a feeling you'll be dragging me around tomorrow in my half-asleep state."

"I can do that." Dennis grabbed her hand and playfully tugged her arm. "Just as long as your feet move to follow." His hand felt warm and the heat from it moved up her arm, spreading through the rest of her body. She took a step toward him, the tenderness in his eyes drawing her, and she rubbed her thumb over the back of his hand.

"I can do that," he repeated.

Ava previewed the video while Grandpa Jack got ready for bed. She smiled into the camera, noticing that the shots were nice. The audio was clear. The scenery came across beautifully—a nice contrast to the stories Grand-Paul was sharing. Her grandpa seemed to give no mind to the video playing on the computer screen as he got into bed. It was almost as though he believed the whole project would go away if he just ignored it. He snuggled under the down comforter and was asleep nearly as soon as his head hit the pillow.

While the video was uploading onto her computer, Ava set to work on the script for the extra video she wanted to shoot. After she got everything written out as she wanted it, she changed her clothes, put on fresh makeup, restyled her hair, and then she headed downstairs.

The dining room was empty except for a

young waitress who was sweeping.

"Excuse me." Ava approached the young woman, whose hair was dyed burgundy—a color popular in Europe. "I was wondering if I could videotape." Ava pointed to a table in the corner.

"No, *nein mur* food today." The waitress's accent was strong.

"Oh, no food. My camera." Ava lifted her video camera and pointed to the table. "Vid-e-o." She nodded.

The waitress shook her head, still not under-standing.

Ava was too tired to explain. Instead, she pointed again, moved to the corner, and began setting up her tripod. The waitress watched her.

"Hollywood movie star!" She nodded, hurried to the bar, poured a beer from the tap, and then sat down to watch.

Ava set up the video camera, thankful the cameras used for fieldwork these days were smaller and less complicated than the one she'd used in school.

Ava knew how to set the manual shots, but full automatic would work just fine. Fine sounded good to her. This wasn't about being artsy. It was about doing her best as quickly as she could so she could get some shut-eye, although the excited nervousness of putting the video together had banished her fatigue. Even though she was disappointed that her grandfather hadn't been part of the first taping, she was excited about this project. It was an excitement she hadn't found in her work in a long time.

She put the camera into auto focus and sat down at the table. The streets outside the hotel were silent, and inside, the hotel was quiet. In fact, the only noise other than her own breathing was the sound of the waitress sipping her beer as she watched.

Ava adjusted her shirt collar, and then she pulled out her script. It had taken her over an hour to write and rewrite it. She'd used the Internet to search out facts about the Eleventh Armored Division and Belgium during the war. She glanced at the words again, knowing she didn't have time to memorize it. She'd do her best and read what she couldn't remember. Surely viewers would understand.

After taking a deep breath, she started the recording with the remote control under the table.

"Hallo, Bonjour. This is Ava Ellington coming to you from Belgium." She glanced at the words on her notepad and then back to the camera again. "I'm here in Europe with my grandpa Jack. We were supposed to be on a tour with his division—the Eleventh Armored Division—but after some challenges, we headed out with another veteran and his grandson. Just two grandkids with the veterans they love. We've been traveling all day, heading into Belgium. We went to the hill where our grandfathers first confronted—I mean faced—the enemy, and the date was, uh . . ." She blew out a breath. "Cut." She stood, pointed the remote control, and turned off the camera.

"This is not going to work," she said to the waitress who was nodding and smiling.

Ava brushed her hair out of her face. *Okay, Ava, think through this. It's going to look dumb for you to sit and read these dates and facts.* She thought of her audience. Of the young mom. Of the lady in the dentist's chair. The guy watching as he grilled his cheese sandwich. They didn't care about dates and facts.

Deep down, Ava knew what she needed. She needed to engage the viewer first. There was footage of beautiful scenery, of the hillsides, of talk of battles, but that didn't matter as much as two old friends walking through a field where they'd once fought. The real story started with a couple of kids who'd gone off to war.

She looked at the waitress who still sat there with her beer, and then she reset the video.

"What is the first thing that comes to mind when you think about your grandparents?" she said into the camera. "I always thought about my grandma's homemade lemon meringue pie and the summer days when my grandfather took me fishing. I never thought of Grandpa Jack as young. Not until this week. The last few days have changed who I thought my grandpa was.

"Even though his hair is gray and his steps are slow and deliberate, I can see something else when I look into his eyes. I can see who he was in 1944—a nineteen-year-old kid from Kansas who found himself in the middle of a big war."

Ava bit her lip and glanced up at the tin-tiled ceiling. Then she looked back at the camera. "I can imagine him fresh from boot camp heading into experiences he didn't see coming. Experiences both good and terrible. Ones he's carried with him his whole life.

"Things have changed. War is fought differently now, but stepping along this journey with my grandpa and his best friend of sixty-seven years takes me back to how things used to be. I've always loved my grandfather; he's an amazing man. But . . . today I got to know a part of him I've never known before." Ava felt her voice choking up. "Join me every day as I share the story of a couple of guys who headed to Europe in 1944. It's a story of a war . . . and a journey of discovery."

Ava lifted the remote control from under the table and stood. She spread wide her arms and looked at the waitress.

"What do you think?" Ava wrinkled her nose.

"Oscar! Oscar!" The woman laughed and then rattled off something Ava couldn't understand.

"Thank you. I appreciate it." Ava packed up her camera. "See you in the morning."

"Pardon?" the waitress asked.

"I'll see you at breakfast?" Ava patted the table.

"No mur food." The woman smiled.

"Yes, I know. Tomorrow." Ava gathered her equipment and moved to the foyer, forcing herself up the tiled stairs. She liked what she had said for an introduction, but she wondered if it would embarrass her grandfather. Or anger him. In her own way, she was inserting him into the videos he wanted no part of.

As she neared their room, Ava dug out her key from her pocket—the real, metal kind, not the electronic card-keys that she was used to at hotels. Inside, she turned on her computer and connected the video camera and started the last transfer. It was 10:00 p.m. here, which meant it was 1:00 p.m. in Seattle. She tried to imagine what everyone was doing right now.

The day's show would be done, and if she were in Seattle, her whole team would be in her office, staring at her large whiteboard, going over the rundown of the next day's show. She smiled as she thought about how she liked organizing each day's segment information—the guests, props, and B-roll that were needed, but even those moments couldn't compare to this day. Even though she felt stretched—like Silly Putty getting pulled out of shape—Ava felt a sense of purpose she hadn't felt in a while. She could be brave, not get the material she needed, and still figure out a way to make it work. She could live a story, and not just capture someone else's. She could survive by sharing from her heart, and not just from a script.

Ava set everything up and connected to the Internet. Her in-box was filled with messages, and she quickly scanned them. It was mostly junk mail, but one stopped her from looking further. It was from Jay. With a trembling hand she opened it, and then sat back as if the words would jump off the page. She held her breath as she read.

Ava wow. Can't believe you e-mailed. I was worried you wouldn't. I'd like to talk. Know you're in Europe but wondering if you could call. Call collect if you have to. Jay

She read the e-mail twice. It was exactly something he'd write. He hadn't given away what he wanted to talk about. She assumed it was their relationship. The text he'd sent previously said he'd made a mistake and missed her, but he said nothing of that here.

Ava pressed her hand against her forehead. Most of her friends had fallen in love and had gotten married without the drama and the heartbreak she had to go through. She hoped that Jay was sorry and wanted to make things right, but she also doubted she could trust him. Why would she?

Dennis's face came to mind, and she shook her head, trying to clear it. The man she thought she had loved—whom she'd imagined marrying—wanted to talk. The guy she could very easily fall in love with—whom she now traveled with—disapproved of nearly every goal she had for this trip. She closed the e-mail and shut off the light. She'd e-mail Jay, but not now. In her weariness—her heart heavy—she longed to reach out for the line he was tossing to her, but her heart had betrayed her before. She had reasons to believe love would bring only pain.

The room was dim, and Ava watched as the bar indicated that the video was nearly done transferring. Behind her, Grandpa Jack snored.

Her new laptop seemed out of place on the antique desk. The desk was made of solid wood, with layers of peeling paint on the surface. She wondered how many people had sat here over the years. Maybe some wrote with quill pens and ink and others with pencils and pens. Now, here she was creating a video that would be sent halfway around the world and be shown to millions of viewers in less than twenty-four hours.

Thankfully, the small hotel had high-speed Internet. That's one thing she'd checked when confirming the reservations. *Hot showers, optional. High-speed Internet, a must.*

Pulling her spiral-bound notebook from her suitcase, she noticed something on the ground. A manila envelope that looked as if it had fallen out of her grandfather's suitcase. Her mother had written "Don't forget to pack" on the envelope.

Ava turned it over in her hand, wondering what was inside. On the back side of the envelope, her grandfather had written Ava's cell number. Was this something he'd meant to give to her? She looked at her grandfather, who was still snoring, and slumped into the chair.

A smile curved her lips. The envelope made her think about the notes her mom used to pack in her things when she went to summer camp. One note for every day she was gone. Most of the time she didn't open the notes until the bus ride home. Still, she'd open them and read every one, just so her mom wouldn't feel bad.

Ava unclasped the small hook and tipped the envelope upside down. It wasn't notes that first slipped out of the envelope. Photographs.

"Oh." She breathed out. Tears sprang to Ava's eyes. She picked up the photo from the top of the stack. It was a black-and-white photo of her grandfather in his military uniform. He was sitting in a rowboat. Behind him were water and a distant shore. The wind ruffled his hair, and his smile was wide. No, it was more than a smile. It was laughter. He was laughing at someone—most likely the photographer. She recognized the crinkle of his eyes.

In the next photo, he posed with another soldier. She recognized the second man, even though the man's eyes were closed in the shot. *Paul.* They were both smiling, and sun was on their faces. She turned the photo over. It read: "Attersee, AT after V-E day during occupation of AT."

AT . . . Austria.

Ava shuffled through more photos and then paused. Behind the photos was a stack of letters, bound together by a red ribbon that was now faded and tattered at the edges, tied into a small bow. She smiled, realizing her mother had gotten the message to her grandfather to bring his letters from World War II. Ava wondered why her grandfather hadn't given them to her sooner.

She turned them over in her hand, immediately recognizing her grandfather's handwriting. The first one had a postmark from Camp Cooke, California, where he had gone for basic training. Ava started to open it and then glanced at the time on her cell phone. She had only two hours to edit the video and send it on. Back in her college days, she could create a video in less than half that time, but to say she was rusty was an understatement.

Maybe she had enough time to read one letter.

March 13, 1944
Friday
Dear Mom and Dad,

The Army is doing a good job training me. I've been washing dishes all week and may have a shot at getting a job at a restaurant when I get home! That's just a joke, you know.

I keep thinking about back home, wondering if the spring flowers are coming up. Nothing but dust storms here. Every crack is filled with sand. It even gets into my teeth when I sleep.

No time for much sleep, though. When I'm not washing pots, there are the drills, calisthenics, hand-to-hand combat, and obstacle courses. We went on a compass course over rough terrain and a bunch of the guys found a patch of thistles. Thankfully, I steered clear of that. The sand is bad enough.

Lots of the guys from B Company head to Los Angeles on the weekends. I did last weekend, but I'm running out of dough so I thought I'd stick around. To answer Mom's question, I didn't go to church last week, but I plan to tomorrow.

I do enjoy cutting a rug at the Paladium or guzzling a Coke at Dave's Jukebox Joint. Last week I went to Pismo Beach. The water was cold, but we jumped in anyway. At first I forgot it was saltwater and that took me by surprise. I never thought I'd do a back float on the ocean. I can check that off my list. More later.

Monday
Dear Mom and Dad,

We had a gun drill. Guys are learning how to set up and fire the big guns on level ground. We can unload, set up, and fire in less than 30 seconds. It's amazing how things work when everyone knows how to do their part. I've been selected to be part of the 21st Armored Infantry Battalion. The infantry part means we'll be trained to fight on the ground. The armored part means that the tanks and big guns will destroy everything in our way to make it easier for us.

We're still having crew drills, and I got to fire the gun. I'm happy with this outfit and I know I'll be content overseas with them.

Around Christmas I sent a letter to Patty Long, but I haven't heard back. I'm guessing she hitched up with Roland Simpson as soon as I left town. What a thug.

Friday

Dear Mom and Dad,

We went out on the village fighting course to practice in street fighting and the taking of houses. I was in the cleanup squad and had to set off booby traps or neutralize them. They don't use full charges. Yesterday, we had a full inspection with the squads lined up in front of the half tracks. I can't write more as there is a bull session going on around me.

Oh yes, tell Mom I went to church. That should make her happy.

Give everyone back home all my love,

Jack

Ava smiled as she folded the letter, trying to picture her grandpa as that young man. She glanced over at him and realized he wasn't snoring as loudly as he usually did. She wondered if he was lost in a sweet dream. She also wondered if he'd snored back in the war. She guessed not. That would have alerted the Germans, for sure.

There were at least two dozen more envelopes, but she wouldn't read them all tonight. Her eyes burned and her mind was starting to dull from lack of sleep, and she still had a video to edit.

She placed the envelope beside her computer, telling herself to thank her grandfather for bringing them in the morning.

Ava started the edits for the segment, jotting down notes for her voice-over, while she waited for the various changes to load. She replayed her favorite quotes that she got from Grand-Paul and wrote them out on note cards. It was a trick that one of her old teachers had taught her. The note cards made it easier to move the quotes around to make the most powerful story.

She especially liked the quote, "We were just kids. We had no idea what we'd see. No idea." She wrote that down.

After she got the audio lined up, she worked on the cover shots and cut-ins. Her tired mind worked hard to figure out how to include her intro with the stories in a segment that was less than two minutes. As she worked, she remembered how much she liked the challenge of it. It was like putting together the pieces of a puzzle, with two other puzzles mixed in and no box for a reference. The tired, fuzzy-headed feeling she'd had after dinner was gone.

She rose and stretched and felt something under her foot. She thought it was a note card until she bent over and picked it up. It was a small slip of paper that she guessed had fallen out of her grandfather's envelope. On it was written only three words.

Find Angeline. Bastogne?

Chapter Thirteen

Ava rested the strap of her computer bag over her shoulder and attempted to rub the sleep out of her eyes. She'd been up late finishing the video. She'd been up even later wondering who Angeline was and why her grandfather wanted to find her.

When she'd awoken at eight o'clock, Grandpa was already gone, no doubt eating breakfast downstairs. They were in Bastogne, and she knew they wanted to get started on the day, but she didn't want to look frumpy.

She'd showered, quickly applied her makeup, and then blow-dried her hair into long, soft waves. Finally, she'd put on some lip gloss as she gathered her laptop.

She checked for her room key and hurried out the door. Downstairs, she found the three guys sitting at the same table where she had videotaped the night before.

Dennis lifted his eyes as she entered, and she couldn't help but notice his face brighten. His eyes rested on her hair. He'd always liked it when it was down. She smiled, glad he noticed.

The grandpas turned. A smile filled Grand-Paul's face.

"Look at you, sunshine," Grand-Paul said.

"Bright enough to light a cloudy day."

Ava paused in front of him and set a hand on her hip. "You know I'm going to have to take you all home with me, right? I never get such a welcome."

Her eyes moved to her grandfather, but he was not smiling. Even as she looked into his face, he seemed to be looking past her. His lower lip was turned down. *Is he still angry about the videos? Or is it something else?*

"It's a shame you aren't welcomed like this every morning." Dennis took a sip from his coffee. "Need to find a way to change that."

Ava felt heat rising to her cheeks, and she noticed the grandpas exchanging glances. She broke the silence as she pulled her notebook from her computer case. "I have something to show you."

"Is it the video?" Grand-Paul asked.

"I stayed up to the wee hours. Your encouragement really . . . encouraged me. I felt top of my class as I worked on it. Ready to watch?"

"Of course." Grand-Paul leaned closer, but both Grandpa Jack and Dennis had reserved expressions on their faces. *So much for the warm welcome.*

Ava started the program and then clicked PLAY.

Music started, followed by images of Ava and Grandpa Jack. There was one of him teaching her to walk, holding her hands. And one of them fishing. And one of her and Grandpa with Grand-Paul and Dennis hiking around Castle Lake.

"These were on my computer . . . ," she said and then quieted.

"What is the first thing that comes to mind when you think about your grandparents? I always thought about my grandma's homemade lemon meringue pie and the summer days my grandfather took me fishing. I never thought of Grandpa Jack as young. Not until this week. The last few days changed all that."

The picture switched from her to Grandpa Jack as he stood by the hill. Underneath, the caption read, "Jack Andrews, near Chenogne, Belgium." From the corner of her eye she saw her grandfather bristle over being taped unaware.

"We received desert training at boot camp. That's where I met Jack." Grand-Paul glanced at the camera and then he looked away, focusing on

Grandpa Jack. "We knew what we'd been told to do, but we'd never tried it. And we were far, far from the desert—going up against an experienced enemy."

"We'd never faced the actual enemy before that," Paul said in the video. As she watched, Ava realized again how pale Paul looked. How sickly. *Must be from the lighting.* She'd have to watch that. "I knew things were kicking off when I heard a sharp crack from a thirty-seven-millimeter tank cannon."

There was an image of the hills and trees, but Ava had filtered it to look black and white, as if it was a movie from back then. She couldn't help but smile when she saw the effect. The grandpas smiled, looked at each other, nodded.

"We were just kids. We had no idea what we'd see. No idea," Grand-Paul said in the video.

More music played, more scenery, and then close-ups of the men. "Paul Prichard, Company B, Twenty-first Armored Infantry Battalion of the Eleventh."

"Jackson Andrews, Company B, Twenty-first Armored Infantry Battalion, Eleventh Armored Division."

Then there came the shot of them walking across the field. Finally, it moved back to her.

"Even though his hair is gray and his steps are slow and deliberate, I can see something else when I look into my grandfather's eyes," Ava said in the video. "I can see who he was in 1944—a nineteen-year-old kid from Kansas who found himself in the middle of a big war."

Finally, the video switched to a still of Grandpa Jack and Grand-Paul staring at the hill where they had first fought, and in the voice-over Ava added, "Join me every day as I share the story of a war . . . and a journey of discovery."

The video stopped and Ava closed her screen. She scanned the faces. "Well?"

"I'm impressed." Grand-Paul cocked his chin. "I like how it turned out, but I sure do look old." Grand-Paul gave a half smile that also hinted of sadness.

"That's because you *are* old." Grandpa Jack nudged his friend with his elbow, but he didn't comment on the video. At least he didn't get mad at her for including him in it.

Ava swallowed as she looked at Dennis, waiting for his reaction. He was looking at her, and she couldn't read his expression.

He finally nodded. "Well, I think you won my grandpa over. Did you already e-mail it off?"

"I e-mailed it before I went to bed." Ava bit her lip. "I haven't heard back yet. I hope it's what they were looking for."

"I bet it is, and I'm sure a lot of people will tune in and watch. It's amazing how you put it together like that. It's all you ever wanted." Dennis leaned forward.

She cocked her head. She still couldn't tell whether Dennis was pleased. It seemed that he did like it, but there was something in his gaze that she didn't understand, couldn't read. The joy that had been there a moment before fizzled out, like a soda going flat.

"I bet you're hungry." Grandpa Jack looked around, seeking out the waitress.

"I'll probably just grab one of the granola bars that I packed. If you can give me five minutes to take my computer upstairs and grab my camera, I'll be ready to go."

Ava hurried up to pack, and as she got all of her things loaded, she remembered the envelope of letters. She looked in her computer bag, in her suitcase—even in her camera bag—but they were nowhere to be found.

A knock sounded at the door. Ava assumed it was housekeeping. "I'm almost done," she called and then wondered if the person could even understand her.

"One minute," she said, looking under the bed to make sure the envelope hadn't slid underneath it.

"Ava, it's me." It was Grandpa Jack's voice. "I was just checking to see if you needed help."

She smiled, thinking of how sad it was that he really couldn't help her, but sweet that he would ask. She rose and hurried to the door, opening it.

He stood, hat in hand. "Need me to carry something?"

"Sure." She handed him her purse, the smallest of her items. "Thank you so much. I also had a question for you." She scratched her forehead. "Did you happen to see that envelope with the letters? I found it last night but didn't see it this morning."

He placed his ball cap back on his head and his eyes narrowed with the same disappointed look as when she had been a sophomore and skipped school. "I saw it on your desk and I took it. I was hoping you didn't look inside."

"I thought you left it out for me. I'd asked my mom to tell you to bring your letters—"

"Those are my private things." His hand trembled beyond its natural quiver.

"There was a note that you wanted to find Angeline. I assumed you wanted my help."

Her purse slipped from his fingers and fell to the floor, and Grandpa Jack bent over to retrieve it. "That note wasn't for you." He turned away and walked down the hall to the elevator, moving with slow steps.

A part of Ava told her to let him go. Not to bring it up again. Not to bother him. But another part of her wouldn't let it drop so easily. The note had also mentioned Bastogne, and they were here. If she didn't ask today, it could be too late.

"Was she a girlfriend? Or someone you rescued from the camp?" Her voice followed him down the hall.

Her grandfather kept walking. "No, no, she was not."

"So you're not going to tell me?" she called.

Her grandfather paused and turned. He still looked angry, but from the droop of his eyes and the curve of his lower lip, he mostly just looked tired.

Ava stood in the doorway and waited. She didn't argue. She didn't beg. Instead, she did what she often did when she was working with a guest whose story was hard to tell. She waited. Waited for his words to work past the emotions welling up inside.

"No. I don't think I will."

"But the note said you want to find her."

He shook his head. "I've changed my mind."

"Why?"

He looked away, gazing at the carpet in front of him. His eyes were wide, as if he could see a ghost from the past lying there.

Ava hurried through the lobby, balancing her camera bag, tripod, and sweater in her arms. Seeing her, Dennis took her camera equipment from her hands and carried it to the trunk and placed it inside.

"Thanks."

"No problem." He took her sweater and helped her find the armholes. He seemed more concerned about getting on the road than wanting to help her, but it was still a nice gesture.

She wanted to know if he knew anything about Angeline. He seemed to know a lot about their grandfathers' war experiences. If her grandpa wasn't going to tell her anything, maybe Dennis would.

She glanced at her watch. It was nine o'clock. People strolled up and down the sidewalks around them. Young women pushed strollers and older women walked side by side talking, laughing. A few tourists wandered the streets, their cameras in hand. A businessman walked by with a briefcase. It was something she saw often at home, but here—in this village—it seemed out of place.

The clock in the nearby clock tower chimed, and Ava lifted her head to listen. As it continued to play she realized it wasn't a typical chime at all, but rather the first six notes of the United States national anthem. She turned to her grandpa, who was right behind her.

"Did you hear that?" The clock continued chiming the half-hour, echoing from the nearest bell tower. "It's the 'Star-Spangled Banner.' "

Tears rimmed his eyes. He nodded, but he didn't speak. She didn't know if it was her questions or the song that were making him tear up. She assumed it was a little of both.

Ava wondered whether she could capture the chimes on video. Maybe she'd try before they headed out.

"I'll get in the back this time." Ava got into the backseat next to Grandpa Jack, offering him an apologetic smile, hoping they'd have a chance later to talk things through. She still hadn't apologized for the confrontation they'd had months ago, and now she was adding yet another thing to the list of things she needed to apologize for. His eyebrows lifted, and then he quickly looked away.

After they were settled, Dennis drove toward their first destination. The town was plain, simple. Nearly every building was a dingy tan color, which made it appear even drearier against the gray, cloudy sky.

The thing that surprised Ava the most were the US flags and other American symbols everywhere. "Are all the flags because of the war? Because of you guys?"

"Belgium wouldn't be free without them," Dennis said.

Ava wanted to ask Dennis to stop so she could get a better look around, but she could tell he was on a mission. She'd head out later, on her own, with her video camera. Capturing the streets, the American flags, and the countryside would be a great addition to her video.

"It's not just us," Grand-Paul commented from the front seat. "Our part was small. There were many who deserve the credit more, like the guys from Easy Company."

"Too bad everyone who fought couldn't be here to see how things turned out." Grandpa Jack shook his head. "It's good to see the place rebuilt."

"So it looks a lot different now?"

"Very different." Grandpa Jack's eyes widened as he looked around. "There wasn't much of a town when we arrived. Every home had been hit. Some had bullet holes, most much more. Many of the buildings down the main street were just rubble. The trees were blackened sticks"—he paused and closed his eyes—"like thin arms reaching into the sky."

Ava imagined tanks in the streets. The German snipers waiting for American troops. The guns. The citizens running, hiding, and crying. Goose bumps rose on her arms.

A few minutes later, they parked in a large parking lot, and in the distance, Ava saw a tall concrete monument that looked like a wagon wheel on its side with tall pillars joined at the top by an open ceiling. It seemed strange to see something like this in the middle of the countryside. It looked like something she'd expect to see in Washington, DC, not here. The people looked small standing next to it, and the blue-gray sky made a striking backdrop. Dennis got out of the car and opened Ava's door for her without making eye contact.

He pointed to two large buildings beyond the

monument. "That's Bastogne's official war museum. There's a screening room and a thirty-minute documentary recounting the defense of Bastogne."

"Hope they got it right," Grand-Paul piped up. "I've watched some of those documentaries and they don't always get everything right."

"Well, you have to think of it this way." Dennis walked around the car and extended a hand, helping his grandfather to stand. "There was a lot going on in the fighting and much confusion. I'm sure if you interviewed one hundred vets, you'd get one hundred different stories—everyone sees things through his own eyes, his own prejudices, his own fears."

"Humph." Grand-Paul grunted.

Grandpa Jack climbed from the car, reaching out to Ava for help.

"Could you imagine if things had gone differently?" Ava looked beyond the monument to the countryside. "If the right decisions hadn't been made at the right time, the people here could be speaking German. And the monuments could have been erected in honor of their great leader, Hitler."

"Ah, nuts!" Grand-Paul said, pointing his finger into the air. Laughter burst from Grandpa Jack's lips. Another group of people walking through the parking lot laughed too, but Ava didn't understand.

Dennis leaned close to her ear. His breath was warm. "It's a reference from the war. During the Battle of the Bulge, the Germans demanded surrender and that was General McAuliffe's response."

" 'To the German Commander: Nuts! The American Commander.' " Grandpa Jack slapped his knee as he said it.

"The Germans responded with bombs. They held on, though, until we—Patton's troops—arrived from the south," Grand-Paul said. "They said a prayer for help. A change in the weather allowed air reinforcements the following day. But if it had taken any longer to get reinforcements . . ."

"A prayer?" She looked at her grandfather.

"They prayed to God for the rain to stop, and it did the trick. The Allies were able to drop supplies," Grandpa Jack said.

"Wow, that really is amazing."

"Yes, it was amazing, but it shouldn't come as a surprise." Grandpa Jack jutted out his chin. "It's a good reminder, but it's no different today. I talk to God now, just like I did back then, and He answers. Maybe not so dramatically, but He answers just the same."

"You talk to God, and that's good." Grand-Paul swayed slightly as he leaned against his cane. "But how do you know that what happens wasn't going to happen anyway?"

"Because I can see Him at work. Things change. People change."

Grand-Paul didn't argue, but Ava could tell from the look on his face that he didn't completely agree. The conversation seemed to pique Dennis's interest, brightening his eyes as he waited to see how this was going to play out.

They continued their slow walk to the memorial. "Don't get me wrong, I believe there's a God. I'm just not a fan of prayer," Grand-Paul stated.

"What do you mean?" Dennis asked, scratching his head.

"I thank God for things. I just don't think I should ask God for stuff."

"But sometimes, Grandpa, God puts something on our hearts so we will ask. Then, when we get it, we know it's from Him, and He becomes more real to us. Why don't you try praying for something specific. Something that really matters." Dennis placed a hand on Grand-Paul's shoulders. "It wouldn't hurt to try, would it?"

"I guess not." Grand-Paul looked from Dennis to Ava and back again.

As they continued to walk, Ava waited for more. She expected Dennis to quote a Scripture verse or to list ways God had answered his prayers, but instead his eyes fixed on the tall, open-air building ahead.

They neared the memorial. It was a large pentagram with names of the forty-eight US states engraved around the top. Inside were paintings of battles. Ava took her camera out and snapped photos—of the men, of the place. Other people milled around. A group of old men—most likely another veteran's group—a young couple, a small group of children on a school trip. She looked at the inscription on the wall nearest to her and furrowed her brow.

"You wish for me read?" a voice interrupted. Ava turned toward a woman who'd approached to her left. She had short black hair—streaked with gray—and wore glasses at the tip of her nose. Her name tag said her name was Camille. The woman pointed to the Latin words on the wall.

"I would love for you to read it to me. Thank you."

" '*Liberatoribus Americanis Populus Belgicus Memor,*' " the woman said. "This translates: 'The Belgian people remember their American liberators —July fourth, nineteen forty-six.' "

"Can you repeat that?"

The woman repeated it, and Ava wrote it down in her notebook.

"Thank you for your help."

The woman turned, but Ava reached for her hand, touching her arm. "Excuse me. I have another question." Ava looked around her and saw Dennis taking photos of the two grandfathers with the American flag in the background. Ava thought about what her grandfather had said—about not wanting her to find Angeline—but she also couldn't get past the idea that they were here, and before her was someone who might be able to help. When would they get that chance again?

Ava took a step closer to the woman. "Do you happen to have records around here? Of citizens maybe? I'm looking for someone who might have lived in Bastogne during the war. A woman named Angeline."

Chapter Fourteen

The woman led Ava to the Bastogne Historical Center, next door to the memorial. With quick steps, they moved past the photos, maps, presentations, life-size battle re-creations, and even a wartime Harley-Davidson motorcycle. Ava knew she'd come back and look at the displays, but not now. First she had to see if Camille knew anything about Angeline. She'd told Dennis she was going to scout some areas for footage, and his look of distaste told her she wasn't in danger of his following.

The older woman led her into the back room of the center. Additional artifacts were stacked on metal shelves. Books about Bastogne filled a bookcase. Photos of old veterans in uniform and note cards were tacked onto a corkboard. It seemed that many men had returned here, to the place that had never left their thoughts.

"We have files of citizens who lived in town. I have them on computer here. It tells me if I have any information in our filing cabinets. Angeline is a common name."

The woman looked up some things on the computer. Then, finding what she was looking for, she approached a long row of filing cabinets and pulled out a file from the fourth cabinet down. "This has information on female survivors," the woman said.

"Do you mind if I look at that file?"

"I do not mind."

Camille cleared a spot on the desk. Ava sat on a wooden chair that creaked, and she opened the file. She pulled a small notebook from her purse. There were six Angelines. Four had been older at the time—at least forty. Much too old for her grandfather. One—a young woman, age twenty— had died before the end of the war. A little girl, age four or five, had disappeared, never to be found again.

If her grandfather thought he'd be able to find Angeline, the older women would be out of the question. That would make them far over one hundred years old. The child wasn't worth following up on. Children, she knew, were often killed as soon as they arrived at the concentration camps. They couldn't provide slave labor, so wasting resources on them didn't make sense to the Nazis. More than that, Ava knew it would be a dead end trying to find more information about the youngster since the note said she had disappeared. Had someone smuggled her to safety? Ava hoped so.

From the moment she'd read Angeline's name, Ava had assumed she was an old flame. Another possibility was someone he liberated from one of the camps. This most likely meant the woman he was looking for was indeed the twenty-year-old Angeline—and she was dead. Maybe Grandpa Jack knew this deep down. Maybe he didn't want it confirmed that he was right.

After going through the file, rechecking to make sure she hadn't missed anything, Ava approached the woman, who was busy typing data into a computer. "Excuse me. Do you have any information about this woman—Angeline de Vos? It says here she was twenty in nineteen forty-five."

"I do." The woman's face brightened. "I am familiar with that name. Her family owned restaurant in town during the war. They cared for much Americans . . . cooked for them."

The woman hurried to the far side of the room and searched through another filing cabinet.

"Yes! Good, good!" she exclaimed and then returned with a file, pulling out a photo. It was of a beautiful young woman with light hair and eyes. She wasn't smiling as she looked into the camera—at least with her mouth. Her eyes were bright and smiling, though, and she looked full of life. Ava turned it over and looked at the back. There was only one word. *Angeline.*

"She's beautiful." Even as she said the words, Ava had a feeling this was the woman her grandfather was looking for. She wondered how they had met. Her grandfather had fought the Germans in her town. Maybe he'd protected her family from danger. Maybe her family helped him. Perhaps they brought him in on a cold night and fed him. Maybe that's when the two fell in love, gazing at each other over the table. When he left with his unit, he promised to return but never did. After the war it was impossible to get back. She imagined her grandfather always wondering about her, and also wondering if she still thought about him. Ava let out a heavy sigh. And then she remembered. Angeline was dead.

"So when did she die? It wasn't during the battle, was it?" Ava asked Camille.

The woman looked in the file. "No, it says here Angeline became ill in April—few months after the Americans passed through. It doesn't say cause. Just illness."

Ava nodded, wondering if she should tell her grandfather. Would he get mad that she hadn't dropped it?

She brushed her hair back from her face and wondered why he wasn't back here asking these questions. Maybe he was too embarrassed—an old man dreaming of lost love. Maybe it was because of what he knew deep inside—that what he'd find wouldn't be good news.

"Is there any way I can get a copy of this?" Ava held up the photo.

"Do you know Angeline?" The woman's face brightened.

"I didn't. But I know someone who I think did." She didn't want to tell the woman about Grandpa Jack. The woman would no doubt make a big deal out of it, embarrassing him for sure.

Camille walked to the photocopy machine and made a copy. "We usually charge for copies, but not this time. It is good to know it goes to someone who will appreciate it."

"Thank you so much. My grandpa will be, uh, surprised."

"It was your grandpa, then, who knew Angeline? He was here in the war?"

"Yes."

The woman approached and took Ava's hand in hers. "Tell him thank you . . . tell him we will continue to remember."

Ava nodded and considered telling Camille that her grandfather was here and she could thank him herself, but she didn't want to risk the chance of the woman mentioning Angeline.

"Thanks again." Ava tucked the photo in her satchel. Leaving the back room, she walked around until she found the guys looking at the displays.

"It looks like you've been busy." Dennis pointed at the notebook in her hand.

Ava closed it, remembering the only thing she jotted down was the words on the monument's dedication. "Yes, it's been a good day." Excitement over solving the mystery mixed with regret that there would be no reunion . . . no happy ending.

Next, they decided to go to one more museum before lunch, and Dennis drove them to *Au Pays d'Ardenne l'Original*, which the guidebook said was the Original Museum of Ardenne.

When they parked, the guys seemed eager to get inside. The guidebook said it was the largest collection of American military items left from the battle. Even Grand-Paul climbed out of the car without assistance. Ava moved more slowly. Maybe it was because of the long night and lack of sleep. Maybe it was the fact she'd skipped breakfast. Maybe it was because Dennis was polite but distant. Or maybe that her mind was full—full of the romance between her grandfather and the Belgian woman. Her mind was also full of questions about how she should break the news about Angeline.

"You coming?" Dennis looked over his shoulder.

"I'll be there in a few minutes. A little down the

road, there was a great view of the countryside. I'd like to get some footage."

"Do you want me to drive you back there? Or go with you and carry your stuff?"

"No, it's fine. Go inside and enjoy yourself . . . and keep an eye on those guys. I'd hate to see what would happen to the curator if our grandfathers disagreed with any of his displays."

Dennis nodded, looking away.

Ava walked down the road to where the town ended and the countryside began. There, she set up her tripod and video camera. There were rolling hills, similar to those in Northern California. In the distance, she spotted another small village. Lilacs were in bloom. A content cow and a red-feathered chicken shared a grassy field.

She videotaped for a while and then sat on the grass, leaning against a stone wall. She tried to close her eyes but was afraid she'd fall asleep, not make it back, and cause the guys to worry. Or even worse have her equipment stolen while she snoozed.

As she rested, her mind wandered to her grandpa's little talk about prayer, and her own questions about what she believed about that. A year ago she would have agreed with Grandpa Jack, but lately she'd been acting more like Paul. She was afraid to pray—afraid she'd ask for the wrong thing. Afraid she'd be disappointed.

It's not that things had always been that way. For most of her life—after meeting Dennis and being inspired by his faith—she'd taken time to read her Bible and pray every day. Her dedication had slumped when she started working at *Mornings with Laurie and Clark.* Since the show went live at 10:00 a.m., she had to be in the office by six. Not being a morning person, she struggled just to make it to work on time. But she supposed it was her relationship with Jay that changed everything. As she found herself getting closer to Jay, God became less and less of a priority. And when their relationship ended, she seemed to lose her comfortable trust in God too.

She thought again of the e-mail he'd sent last night. Her mind had been so busy trying to figure out the mystery about Angeline, she hadn't dwelt on it too much. But each time she remembered, it was like a pinprick to her heart.

Why, God? A familiar ache was resurrected as she thought about her former fiancé, and as she considered their plans and the future she would have been living if he hadn't ended things.

She'd uprooted her life and moved from Portland to Seattle so he could keep his job. She'd found a new job, excelled at it for over a year. They'd bought a condo with the plan that once they'd saved a little, she would quit her job and they'd start a family. It's not like they'd drawn out a graph: work, condo, marriage, have a baby, but in her mind it was like they had. And then for him to end things and for her to be left without a husband and with a condo she couldn't afford. Ava covered her mouth with her hand and refused to let the tears come. Why had she even e-mailed him back?

A bird chirped from the top of the fence, and she glanced up, remembering where she was. She was in Europe with the first guy she ever loved. Actually the first two guys she ever loved, her grandfather and Dennis. God had a wicked sense of humor.

Fear gripped her chest, and she released a slow breath, wishing she could breathe it away. She couldn't fall in love again. She couldn't. The pain of loss was too great. Thankfully Dennis wasn't giving her the chance.

Ava rose, repacked her things, and headed back into town. An American flag flapped in the breeze, and she looked at the buildings, searching for bullet holes.

Walking by a small café, she saw them. At first, the holes appeared to be chipped paint, but as she looked closer she saw the pattern of machine-gun fire. Her heart felt riddled in just this way. She kicked at a rock on the cracked sidewalk.

Of course what she faced seemed trivial compared with what had happened in Bastogne. And here she was feeling sorry for herself.

Dennis was waiting outside the museum when

she approached. He glanced at his watch. "I was giving you five more minutes, and then I was going to look for you." He offered a sad grin. "Maybe all those photos of injured women and kids are getting to me. I was starting to get worried."

"I'm fine. I was just shooting video and wrapping my mind around . . . well, everything." She moved toward their car and he opened the trunk, taking the things from her and putting them inside.

"It's overwhelming, isn't it?" Dennis closed the trunk. "Seems like something out of a novel. Doesn't seem like a war that horrific could have happened." He nodded his head toward the building. "I read in there that eighty-one thousand Americans lost their lives or were injured in the Battle of the Bulge."

"Eighty-one *thousand?* That can't be right. They must mean the Americans *and* the Germans?"

"No, there were even more Germans killed or injured."

Ava looked around. This place seemed so peaceful now. She looked up at the American flag flapping in the breeze. *The people here choose to remember. They don't hide the pain, but they also remember to celebrate the victory.*

Dennis looked over his shoulder, back toward the museum door. "I better go check on our grandpas. Just a few minutes ago, Jack was outraged at the price of souvenirs." He moved to the door.

"Wait," she called after him, hurrying to catch up. "Can I ask you something first? Something important."

He turned back to her, concern filling his gaze. "Yes, of course."

"I know you've been a much better grandson than I've been as a granddaughter. I haven't always listened. . . ." She glanced up at him, remembering again how handsome Dennis's gaze was when he focused on her. "I was wondering if my grandpa . . . or if your grandpa ever mentioned someone named Angeline? Maybe someone they met during the war."

"Angeline?" Dennis looked up into the sky as if replaying old conversations. "I don't think so."

Ava folded her arms over her chest. "That's not what I needed to hear."

Dennis leaned back against the brick wall and cocked an eyebrow. "Why do you ask?"

"Well, I wasn't trying to pry, but I found a slip of paper in my grandfather's things. It said, 'Find Angeline.' And then it said 'Bastogne.' I asked him about it, and he got upset."

Dennis shook his head. "You're two for two."

"Yes, I know." Ava didn't tell him she actually was three for three.

"At the museum, I asked one of the curators about women who had lived here back then, and there were some Angelines. There was one woman who I thought might have been someone he met, maybe even someone Grandpa Jack cared about." She opened her satchel. "I have a photo—"

"I don't think it was a romance."

She glanced back up at him. "Excuse me?"

Dennis ran his fingers through his hair. "I, uh, I can't believe no one's told you."

Ava's stomach clenched. The wind blew again, but this time it caused goose bumps to rise on her arms. "What are you talking about?"

"Years ago, I overheard a conversation between our grandpas."

"Was it about Angeline?"

"No. Well, maybe. I can't be sure. They were talking about a girl."

"A girl?"

"Your grandpa was crying, and he said he thought of her every day and wondered how she was. My grandpa was demanding they travel here—back to Bastogne—to find her. He offered to pay, but your grandfather refused. Grandpa Jack said he had to focus on his family and not chase ghosts of the past."

Ava's knees softened. *A girl. He was looking for a girl. Could it have been the one who disappeared or—*She reached for the wall, needing something strong to hold on to. Dennis grabbed her arm, steadying her.

"Are you okay?"

She didn't answer. Instead, she looked at the window. Her wide-eyed expression reflected back. Then she dared to ask the question she hadn't wanted to consider. "Do you think my grandpa has a child over here? Maybe the baby's name is Angeline." She looked at Dennis, her gaze most likely pleading with him to come up with a better answer.

"That's what I assumed, but it was years ago. Maybe I'm not remembering correctly."

"What if you are? What if my grandpa met someone and this woman had a baby? It happened a lot during the war. I just never figured it would happen to my grandpa. No wonder he doesn't want to talk about it. He basically abandoned his child. And her mother."

"It was a different world back then. It's not like he could have just hopped a plane and returned at the end of the war. And he couldn't just Google her name in nineteen forty-six."

"What should we do about it?" Ava looked around, taking in the town. The flat-topped, narrow buildings of various heights reminded her of scenes from *Mary Poppins*. The large square in the center of the town was lined with trees and filled in with parking lots. She tried to imagine a relative growing up in a place like this.

"What do you mean what should we do?" Dennis's gaze narrowed.

"How amazing would that be to find her—to find Angeline."

"That's not for you to decide. He wanted to come to Bastogne. Now we're here. If your grandpa wants to find her, it's up to him."

"You think I should drop it? Just like that?"

"Yes, Ava. As much as you're trying to make it your trip, it's about him."

Movement caught her eye, and Ava turned to see her grandpa and Grand-Paul exiting the museum —supporting each other—and she swallowed hard.

"Shouldn't I at least ask? She could be here," she whispered.

"It's not your choice, Ava."

Both men looked sober as they approached. Ava looked at Dennis, as if wondering what to say, what to do.

"It's been a long, hard morning. Lots to take in." Dennis took his grandfather's arm. "Why don't we get some lunch?"

"Yes, that's a good idea." Her mind couldn't comprehend that perhaps her grandfather could have another child. Ava glanced at a couple coming toward them down the street. The woman's hair was blond like hers. Could she really have cousins here?

Chapter Fifteen

For the second night in a row, Ava found herself at the table in the corner with her video camera set up and the waitress as her audience. This time, all three guys joined her. In addition to her script about the Battle of the Bulge and the coldest winter in fifty years, she had something else she needed to ask. Something that could put her back on shaky ground with her grandfather. She should be thankful he was willing to be video-taped at all, but she also needed to add another element to these videos, because what she had now wasn't going to be strong enough.

"Grandpa, can I talk to you alone for a minute?" She pointed to the patio outside.

"Sure." He rose with slow movements. His hand trembled more than it had any other time on this trip, and she told herself he was tired from their travels.

They walked out into the cool air, and her eyes focused on his cowboy boots. "I know you didn't intend for me to find those letters, and I'm sorry. I should have asked. I—I just haven't been handling things as I should on this trip."

She was afraid to look at him. Afraid to see the disappointment in his eyes. "But the truth is, I'm going to need more for this video." She paused, thinking of how to say it. How to tell him there was nothing heart-tugging about what they shared today. "Could we do more taping? Maybe if you could share a few personal stories?" Her finger followed the grain on the wood of the patio deck. "Or, if you thought there was a letter that was meaningful . . ." She let her voice trail off and waited for her grandfather to respond, but the only sound was Paul and Dennis's laughter coming from the dining room. Their laughter didn't help the tension building within Ava. She recalled Dennis's words. *Would you walk away if he asked you to?* Her heart ached, knowing he had asked— not directly, but by his rebuff—and now she was wanting even more from him.

Finally, she dared to lift her head, looking into his face. The single light on the patio did little to penetrate the darkness. Yet, even though the night was dim, the rays from the moon lit her grand-father's worried gaze.

He shrugged. "The letters aren't any good. I was no Ernie Pyle or Ernest Hemingway."

"I know you don't think they're very good. But they'll give viewers an inside look at your experiences—a glimpse into your heart." She noticed he didn't offer to share any stories. Maybe sharing the letters seemed the less threatening of the options.

"If you think people are interested, I can pick out a few. There are others . . . well . . . I'll pick the ones you can look at."

Pain shot through Ava's heart. What could be so horrible that he would keep it from her? She was his granddaughter, and before last year's incident, they'd had a close relationship. She attempted to look into his eyes—to get a glimpse of what was going on in his mind, but he quickly looked away. It made her want to read the other letters even more.

"I understand there are some you don't want me to read." She swallowed her emotion. "And I'm okay with that. If there are some I could look at, well . . . I'm sure I can find something interesting. I think our viewers will enjoy the fact they're from World War II."

He nodded and turned back to the doorway leading inside. His shoulders slumped. It was as if he had gotten tired of fighting and was choosing the path of least resistance.

"I was thinking maybe you could read the letters for the camera." The words spilled out, and she hoped she wasn't pushing too far.

He tilted his head, unsure.

"Don't worry about the camera. I'm just using the voice track." She stepped forward and hurried to his side. "I won't even set the focus on your handsome mug if it makes you feel better." She offered a soft laugh, hoping he couldn't sense how hurt she was that he didn't trust her with the truth of what was in the rest of those letters.

Her grandfather nodded. "Do I have a choice?"

"Of course, Grandpa." She placed a hand on his arm. "I'm not going to force you to do anything you don't want to do."

He thought about it for a moment. "Fine. I do know how to read," he said, and then instead of returning to the dining room where Paul and Dennis sat, he went through the other door into the lobby. Ava assumed he was going to the room to get some letters, and she hoped there would be something she could use for the video. Ten minutes later, he returned with a half-dozen letters.

It took a few minutes for Ava to go through the letters, picking her favorite parts. There was nothing spectacular, but she could work with them. She got the camera set up and without putting up a fuss, her grandfather sat down— much to the amazement of Grand-Paul and Dennis.

"Okay, good. We're all set." She glanced up at him and then pushed the button on her remote. "Go ahead and start."

Grandpa Jack glanced over the sections she'd put sticky notes on.

"So these are the interesting parts?" Grandpa Jack shook his head.

"I think so."

"Here goes nothing." Grandpa Jack readjusted his glasses on his nose. He didn't seem excited, but at least he wasn't fighting her. Her grandpa cleared his throat and began.

" 'December 19, 1944. Dear Mom and Dad, I got my baptism of rain and mud, sleeping outside for the last few nights. As I laid in my pup tent, I heard your voice, Mom: "Jackson, you're going to catch your death of cold." I haven't got even a sniffle yet. We bivouacked in a quagmire of mud and water. Four of us pitch our tents together, Paul, Henry, David, and I.

" 'I haven't washed in a week. Another week might pass before I can. I've always wanted to try growing a beard. Now's my chance. Love, Jack.' "

Grandpa Jack set the letter on the table, and then he looked at the next one. He cleared his throat and then started.

" 'December 24, 1944. Dear Mom and Dad, There's going to be a Christmas service tonight here. Not that I know where "here" is. We've been on the move quite a bit. It's hard to believe in Christmas over here. It's sometimes hard to believe in the Christ child too. Even my memories of home seem like a made-up story.

" 'The other day we rolled through the city of Reims, in France. It was amusing to see people walking through the streets with long, thin loaves of bread. I thought they were baseball bats at first. The women of France are lookers. They really know how to use makeup and fix their hair. The buildings all around them may be crumbled down, but the ladies are fixed up. My buddy Paul says he likes it that way. He says ladies are more interesting to look at than buildings anyways.' "

Grand-Paul gave a low chuckle, and Ava glanced his direction. Dennis appeared equally amused.

" 'More than anything, I wished we could have gone to Paris so I could climb the steps to the top of the Eiffel Tower,' " Grandpa Jack continued. " ' General Patton said it was impossible to make a tourist stop. We were needed in Belgium.

" 'That's where we are—somewhere in Belgium. Over the last few days we went through a lot of towns, and the destruction of war was clear. In some villages there wasn't a house intact. There are many German vehicles wrecked on the sides of the roads, and some of ours.

" 'I know you worry, Mother, but don't worry too much yet. I'm a little cold and a little hungry, but otherwise in great shape. Keep praying and maybe God will listen to you. It will be a good thing if He does. Love, Jack.' "

"It doesn't work." Grand-Paul lifted his chin. "Jackson's voice sounds too old. The letters were written by a young man."

"I know, but the viewers will understand. They know that he's . . ." Then Ava paused as a new idea filled her head. She turned to Dennis. "You." She pointed.

He leaned forward, resting his arms on the tabletop. "What are you talking about?"

"I think you should be the one to read the letters." She rose and removed her sweater and placed it on the back of the chair. Excitement caused the hairs on the back of her neck to rise. For the first time that day a smile bubbled out from inside.

"Yes, that'll work!" Grand-Paul gripped Dennis's shoulder.

"What is this, video by committee?" Dennis shook his head, and he didn't seem amused.

"No, really. We should try." Grand-Paul scooted the letters across the table to Dennis.

"Grandpa, are you okay with it?" Ava searched his face for any sign of disappointment.

His smile brightened. "Fine by me. Maybe Dennis will breathe some life into those old words."

Ava turned the camera and focused in on Dennis. He glanced up at her and then let out a sigh.

"Ready?"

"Well, ma'am, don't really think I have a choice, do I?" He winked and then held them up to read. It surprised her, first his going along and then his playful attitude. What had changed?

He looked over the letters at her, and her stomach grew warm, as if she'd just downed a hot cup of coffee. She studied his face and was reminded again how handsome he was. She also wondered why she'd been so adamant about following her own plans so long ago. How could she have turned her back on him?

In the corner of her eye she noticed Grand-Paul's eyes on her. He had no doubt noticed her looking at Dennis, for a wide grin filled his face. Ava quickly looked away and focused instead on the camera, pretending to make sure all the settings were right.

Dennis started with the first two letters that her grandfather had already read. They sounded fine, but she still wasn't sure if it was that much of an improvement.

"Okay, now try these new letters, and really think about being here." She pointed to the window. "Or rather out there in the Belgium countryside, cold, scared, alone."

"Alone." Dennis cocked one eyebrow and pursed his lips. "I can understand that feeling." He cleared his throat. "Ready?"

Ava nodded and twirled her finger in the air to show that she was already rolling.

" 'December 26, 1944. Dear Mom and Dad,' " Dennis read. His voice was soft, hesitant.

" 'I know it is not polite to ask for Christmas presents, but is there any way you could send me a wool hat to wear under my helmet? There are some that protect your head and neck and have small holes for your eyes and mouth. Also, don't be concerned if my letters become less frequent. Know that I'm thinking of you all back home. We all think of those far away. Sometimes I write letters to you in my mind, saying all the things I don't have time to write or can't write because of censorship.

" 'There's so much I want to tell you. I've never felt so alone in my life. My friends are with me, but there's something wrong deep inside. I can't explain it. Maybe that's what war is. As much of a battle within as outside in this frozen place. Love, Jack.' "

"Wow," Ava whispered. "Read this last one just like that. It was great." She looked at her grandfather, and for a moment she saw that scared kid peeking out from his gaze.

Dennis nodded.

" 'January 2, 1945, Belgium. Dear Dad, I'm not sure why I'm here. I wish I could be anyplace but here. Something awful has happened in a place called Chenogne. I can't tell you—' "

"Not that one." Her grandfather's voice interrupted Dennis's words. "I didn't mean to put that one in there." Her grandfather reached for the letter. His face took on an ashen hue.

Before Ava understood what was happening, her grandfather ripped the letter from Dennis's hand and pushed back from the table, stood, and then turned. He moved more quickly than Ava had seen him move in years.

"Grandpa, wait!" The cord was stretched between the camera and the wall, and before Ava could get to them, her grandfather's leg and the cord connected.

She saw him going down, and she sucked in a breath, not believing what she was seeing. She stood and reached but couldn't get to him in time. He tumbled to the ground. His arm hit first, then his shoulder, and finally his head. His head bounced off the floor with a crack.

A gasp escaped Ava's mouth, and then her hands covered her face.

Grandpa Jack moaned from the impact. Dennis sank to the floor, cupping her grandfather's head in his hands.

"Go to the front desk. Have them get a doctor."

Chapter Sixteen

It had been a long night. Even before Ava could get to the front desk, the waitress had alerted the manager. The village doctor had visited, declaring that Grandpa Jack was bruised but fine. Ava had stayed up most of the night watching him and somehow also managed to put together the second video, sending it off.

She'd used footage of her grandfather and Grand-Paul talking about the freezing winter, about how many of the towns in this area had been destroyed, and about how it felt good to see them fixed up.

Then, as images of the countryside, the American flags, and the memorials flashed on the screen, she added audio from the letter Dennis read. He'd done a good job of sounding like a young kid lost at war. They'd been together for two days, and he still was a stranger to her—a ghost from the past who haunted her with his presence and turned invisible whenever she tried to get close.

Even with little sleep, Ava roused herself by 7 a.m. to make sure she made it to the town square by 8 a.m. to videotape the chiming of the clock. The May air was cool and the square was quiet. All around her, shopkeepers were getting ready for the day. The only place that was already receiving traffic was the small bakery two doors down from the hotel. Old women, young women with strollers, and small boys holding fresh bread strolled through town. It seemed like such a simple life—so different from Seattle—and a longing tugged at her heart, surprising her. She videotaped some of the town too. Not for the videos, but for her. To remember.

She counted down the time with the clock and turned on her video camera as it got close. When the minute hand clicked to the twelve, the "Star-Spangled Banner" chimed again and emotion filled her throat.

When the chiming stopped, she packed up her things and walked back to the hotel. As she approached, she noticed Dennis leaning against the rental car, his arms folded on the roof and his face buried in his arms. His shoulders shook, as if he was laughing, but from his position, it had to be tears. She quickened her pace, the weariness of the night slipping away.

As she crossed the street, the wind picked up. Ava took a hair tie from her wrist and pulled her hair back. Her heart seemed to double in size at the sight of Dennis—his tan neck and the way his dark hair curled so slightly at the nape. His broad shoulders. His arms. He was strong, but at this moment he looked like a lost little boy.

"Hey there." Ava placed her hand on his arm. "Are you okay?"

He wiped at his face and then patted her hand. His eyes were puffy and bloodshot.

"Dennis, what's wrong?" Her brow furrowed and her heart quickened, knowing what it had to be. "Is it Grand-Paul? Is he all right?"

Dennis rubbed his forehead. "My grandpa hadn't zipped his suitcase all the way and his medication fell out. I'd seen him taking stuff every day, but I didn't know what it was till I picked it up. There were a lot of different things. Not your typical blood pressure stuff. Ava, I came down to the hotel lobby and used their computer—I didn't want to wake him up by getting my computer out. I looked it up and I discovered that the medication he's on is for cancer patients."

Ava's knees weakened. "Cancer?"

"It gets worse. He doesn't want treatment. The doctor has given him less than a year—that's if everything goes well. The medication is just to help with some of the symptoms and for pain."

Dennis opened his arms to her. Looking into his face, she didn't see the man who'd tried so hard to keep her at arm's length. Instead, she saw the eighteen-year-old boy she had fallen in love with. Without hesitation, she stepped into his embrace. His shoulders trembled again.

Her breath stuck in her throat, and she tried to think of something to say. Something to comfort him. There was nothing. She felt his pain, but there was nothing she could do to fix this.

Not counting the quick hug at the airport, this was their first embrace in fifteen years, but it wasn't exactly like she had imagined. She pictured Grand-Paul's face. During this trip, she'd noticed his need for extra help, his pallor, but she couldn't wrap her mind around the idea he didn't have much time. His mind was so sharp. And her grandfather. How would he go on? First losing his wife and now his best friend?

Leaning on Dennis's strength, she felt his chest rise and fall quickly, as if he was trying to hold sobs in. She focused on the beating of his heart, for a time forgetting where they were and the answers she was trying to uncover.

"Oh, Dennis." She wanted to say more but didn't know how. "I'm so sorry."

"I'm sorry too. Why didn't he tell me, Ava?" Dennis's breath was warm on her hair. "Why did he hide it?"

"He didn't want to worry you."

"He said he needed this last trip. He said he was looking for an answer to something but didn't say what. He also said coming here was for me more than him."

"A last trip for the two of you together."

"This can't be happening." Anger laced Dennis's voice. "I can't lose my grandpa. Part of me believed he'd always be here." Dennis blew out a long breath. "I'm glad you're here. I don't know how I could have faced this alone."

Finally, Dennis released her. She stepped back and looked up at him. "I'm glad I could be here too. I just don't know how I'm going to look at him and not burst into tears."

"You gotta try, Ava. *We've* got to try. We need to finish off the trip the best we can. We need to fulfill his last wish to experience the ceremony at Mauthausen concentration camp."

"I'm here. For him, for you." She patted Dennis's cheek with her hand. He hadn't shaved that morning, and his stubble was scratchy. Then, as if he realized their closeness for the first time, he scooted to the side, putting more distance between them.

As she looked into his eyes, Ava could almost see the invisible wall rising as he put distance between them once again.

She took another step back and brushed back the stray hairs blowing against her face. She looked up to the sky, noticing the sun slip behind a cloud and wishing the warmth of just a moment ago had hung around longer.

Ava's cheeks grew warm as they entered the lobby and then made their way to the small restaurant. Grand-Paul and Grandpa Jack were already there. Even though there were plenty of open tables, the elderly men sat at a table set for two—leaning toward each other, talking in low tones. Ava tried not to let her eyes linger on Grand-Paul. She was pleased to see that her grandfather looked fine. Even though he lifted his fork with a shaky hand, he looked no different than he had since they'd been there. There was no evidence of his tumble last night except for a slight scratch at his temple.

Ava and Dennis approached, and Grand-Paul glanced up, as if he was surprised they were there. A Bible was open on the table between them.

"I hope you kids don't mind. I haven't seen my buddy in a few years, and we have some catching up to do—private stuff. Can you get your own table this morning?"

"Sure." Ava looked at Dennis. She didn't like the idea of their grandpas whispering between themselves. What things could be private that they couldn't share?

Dennis scanned the room. "You pick."

She picked a spot four tables away. Far enough that they couldn't hear conversation but close enough to keep an eye on the guys.

Ava spread her napkin on her lap. "That was strange. But I'm glad to see my grandpa's doing okay. I had no idea he would react like that simply from the reference to Chenogne."

"Me neither." Dennis opened his menu and stared at it, yet from the strumming of his fingers on the glass tabletop, there was more going on in his head than deciding what to order for breakfast. His eyes were still bloodshot, but she could tell from his gaze there was something else bothering him.

"Dennis, are you sure you can't fill me in a little about my grandpa's experience in Chenogne? I looked it up last night but didn't find much on the Internet—just that there was fighting there and that it was near Bastogne."

"Ava, when are you just going to let this drop?" He let out a low sigh, and he leaned forward, looking into her eyes.

"Well"—she closed her menu—"maybe it's because you seem to know a lot about all this World War II stuff. I mean you knew something about . . . the girl." She whispered the last two words. "It's obvious you've taken time to learn about your grandfather's experiences. You're doing better than I am."

"Aren't you going to try to earn your grandfather's trust?" It was the same thing Dennis had said before, but this time his voice was gentle, as if he was speaking to a child. If this was him acting nice, she didn't like it much.

"And what if he never brings it up?" Her voice squeaked, and a couple at the other table looked at her, curious. She pressed her lips together and ignored them, placing her red-and-white checkered cloth napkin on her lap. This was too important to try to act nice about.

The waitress approached, and Dennis ordered ham and eggs. Ava ordered the same, just so she didn't have to think about it.

"You didn't answer my question," she said after the waitress left.

"Maybe I don't want to."

"Why not?"

"Well, I had a different reason earlier, but I have a new one now."

She tapped her fork on the table. "And what's that?"

"I don't want to tell you because it makes you mad . . . and you're beautiful when you're angry."

Ava opened her mouth, but no words came out. Her heart pounded in her chest. She smoothed her hands on the napkin on her lap. "Should I say thank you?"

Instead of answering, Dennis glanced back at the grandpas and then looked back at her with a wistful look. "Give your grandfather some time. He'll talk about it when he's ready—everything. I have a feeling that's why he's here. To face the past. To put what pains him to rest."

"And if he doesn't?"

Dennis shrugged. "I have a feeling he will. In his own time."

Their breakfast came and Ava pondered his words as she cut her ham into small pieces.

As they ate, they briefly discussed their travel plans to Prüm, Germany, and the brief stops they would make at the American military cemeteries at Margraten and Henri-Chapelle. They were the last resting place for thousands of American servicemen.

"There's something else I wanted to talk about," Ava said when there was a pause in conversation. "It's you. I'm not sure if you're purposely trying to be aloof, but since we've been on this trip I haven't learned one thing about your life." She tapped her lower lip with her finger. "Tell me about your life, Dennis."

"What do you want to know?" He wore a smirk. He ate European style, with his fork in his left hand and his knife in his right, using both to cut and maneuver his food on his plate.

"Last I heard, you were living in some third world country, India or Uganda or something."

"I've lived in both."

"What were you doing there?"

Dennis shrugged as if what he did wasn't that important, but the intense look in his eyes told her differently. "Hands-on stuff mostly. In the past ten years I've led two dozen groups of people, and we've built a few orphanages overseas. I also oversaw the digging of some wells. It was the folks with me who did the work. They get the credit. I was just honored to organize and help out in my small part."

"You sound like a saint. Like Mother Teresa. I really didn't think there were people out there like that anymore."

"Like what?"

"Willing to put their life on hold to help others."

"It's not like I had a life to put on hold. It's not mine. I surrendered my life to God."

"Right, of course. I mean, as a Christian, that makes sense." Heat rose to her cheeks. She should have expected this conversation, but it caught her off guard.

It's not like she didn't believe in God too. It's just that people who took their faith so seriously made her see all the ways she was falling short. She bit her lip, remembering that it was a conversation almost like this that had started the argument with her grandfather.

"If you love God, maybe you should make sure you're living for Him, Ava. Is getting married to this person God's plan for you . . . or your own idea?" her grandfather had asked.

Her grandfather's questions had bothered her as much as Dennis's statement did now. Wasn't it enough just to love God in whatever you did?

"It sounds like you're really doing great things." She smiled, not knowing what else to say.

From the corner of her eye Ava saw her grandpa rising from his seat, but she wasn't about to end the conversation with this awkwardness. She didn't want to go through another day with this much tension between them. "So how did you end up back in the States? Or are you?" she pressed.

"Do you want the long story or short version?"

Ava shrugged. "Is there something in the middle?"

"Sure." He looked at his grandfather briefly. Seeing he was okay, Dennis turned back to her.

"Let me see. Three years ago I was headed to Uganda to help this young woman who was caring for thirty orphans in a small two-bedroom shack. I got into a conversation at the Amsterdam airport with an American businesswoman. She was interested in helping, and she asked if there was a website so she could check it out further. I didn't have one. These kids were sleeping on a few blankets on the ground, and the woman wondered if they had a website!"

Ava laughed. "I suppose that's a good point, but I have to admit it's a question I'd probably ask."

"Yeah, well, I gave the woman my business card and she said she'd keep in touch. I honestly doubted she would. I mean, she didn't know me from Adam." His eyes brightened as he spoke, and as Ava watched, she saw a different man—one of passion and intensity—reveal himself before her.

"I was bothered by her question, but not because she asked it," he continued. "It was mostly because I figured there had to be a way to bring the needs of people around the world to the attention of those who have the means to help. As I was thinking about this, I happened to look around the airport. It was a small waiting area, and there were twenty people on computers. Others had cell phones and iPods. I'm not really in love with technology. Sometimes machines get more attention than people, but as I looked around, it was as if a light switched on in my mind. Those computers were tools to connect needs with supplies."

Ava nodded. She knew how technology brought people together. Her job, after all, was sharing people's stories with a wider audience. But she wasn't going to bring that up. Just when things were improving between them, she didn't want to throw an I-told-you-so in his face.

"That was my last trip . . . until now. At twenty-nine, I went back to college and learned web design and marketing. It was harder than I thought—at least to turn out something good. I'm heading to the Czech Republic after we finish up in Austria. There's a group doing career training for Roma people who have a hard time finding work. I'm going to get a website set up for them, to connect them with supporters in the States."

Ava couldn't help but smile.

"What?"

"Nothing. I just think it's amazing."

The waitress came and refilled her coffee and she took a sip. "It's funny where your life took you, that's all. We were eighteen when we met. You're so grown up now. So grounded. And it's cool to see your heart. Back then, all you ever talked about was playing college basketball. Whatever happened to that?"

Their grandpas left the dining room, and Dennis scooted back his chair, ready to follow. "I tore my ACL in my knee during a street ball game a week before college. I was able to have surgery, but it took six months before I could play again. It was one of those freak things. I just landed wrong after a jump shot and *poof,* there went my dreams, my scholarship, everything."

"It sounds like God gave you different dreams."

Dennis's eyes brightened. "Yes, I suppose He did."

In the back of her mind, Ava thought about what a wonderful guest Dennis would make on the show. Three million viewers meant more people would be aware of his work—potential donors for the causes he cared about.

She bit her lip, not wanting to bring it up. She didn't want Dennis to think that *everything* centered on her work. There'd be time later when they could discuss the possibility.

He looked like he was about to stand but didn't. Instead he leaned forward, as if wanting to confess a secret.

"It was actually a memory of one of our times together that helped with that transition. My willingness to try a new step started with a memory of you," he finally said.

"Me?"

"Yes." His blue eyes sparkled. "Remember how our grandpas taught us to jitterbug in your grandparents' living room? At first I was so embarrassed, but then I saw you trying. You weren't a pro, but at least you tried. After that, I decided to just learn the steps the best I could. I tell myself now to at least try something."

"I wish I was like that now." She lightly tapped her fork on the side of her plate. "I've swung too far in the opposite direction. I like to have a plan and stick to it. I like to think I'm still adventurous, but I haven't tried new things in a long time. That's why this trip has been so challenging."

A long silence stretched out, and then Dennis's eyes locked on hers.

"You look so different."

"What?" Ava interrupted. "Thanks a lot." She faked a pout.

"I didn't mean that in a bad way. You didn't let me finish." He reached over and placed his hand on hers. The tapping of her fork stopped. "I was going to say that I always thought you were pretty, but now you're downright beautiful. No wonder you're working on television."

Heat rose to her cheeks. "I work behind the scenes, mostly. Except for this week. But really, I don't feel beautiful. I—"

Dennis shook his head. "Ava, honestly, after all these years I'd thought you would have learned—when someone gives you a compliment, all you have to say is thank you."

She looked at him, surprised. Partly because they'd made it through a whole conversation without fighting. And also because he seemed to mean it.

"Thank you," she whispered, not knowing what else to say.

Ava rode along in silence, flipping through the other letters her grandpa had given her to read. For some reason, the letters jumped from December 24 to April 7. From the Belgian battlefield to somewhere in Germany. She knew better than to ask her grandpa about the missing letters. As much as she didn't like it, Dennis was right—he'd share when he wanted to.

From the front seat, Grand-Paul was directing Dennis to their "side trip," she supposed. They'd gotten off the main road, and she guessed they were visiting yet another battle spot. They drove on a country road with vast fields on either side. Small farmhouses popped up here and there. As pretty as it was, Ava returned her attention to the letters, trying to figure out a plan for this night's video.

April 7, Germany
Dear Mom and Dad,

Looks like I'm getting lax in writing, but if you could have been with me the last few days, you'd know the reason why. Let me just say, I'd like to settle down in some quiet place, eat a good meal, not C or K rations or something we've cooked ourselves, and sleep for forty-eight hours. Some out-of-the-way place where there are no tanks, trucks, tracks, airplanes, or uniforms.

Our outfit liberated some American and English POWs, and that was a wonderful feeling—seeing them as they were freed and rejoicing with them. One of the prisoners was a chaplain from Mississippi. He told us we were an answer to many prayers. I'd like to think that was true, but what about those who weren't rescued? Didn't they pray?

Love,
Jack

Ava paused, amazed that her grandfather had been so open with his thoughts. The pain of his last few sentences countered the joy just a few sentences higher: "Our outfit liberated some American and English POWs."

She closed her eyes and tried to picture the scene. Rejoicing. Freedom. She wondered if those prisoners of war had questioned whether they'd ever be free. She wondered if they truly believed it when help finally came.

April 21, Germany
Dear Mom and Dad,

The apple trees are budding here in Germany. It would be pretty if there wasn't a war going on. Last night, we were supposed to sleep in two rooms of a house, but a drunken lieutenant came in and said we were fraternizing. We had to move out into the yard.

I read in the *Stars and Stripes* that Ernie Pyle was killed in an ambush in the Pacific. We were all sorry to hear of his death, for he was the only civilian who knew exactly what we go through in the infantry.

Yet, it's hard to be sad for one man when there are so many to be sad for. I feel numb sometimes. Maybe because what happened in Belgium haunts me in my sleep.

Keep on writing. I'll get your letters

sometime next September. I need news of home. I need to remember it's still there.
Love,
Jack

Ava paused, again wondering about the trouble in Belgium. Even though she'd decided not to ask her grandfather again until he was ready, she'd still keep looking to see if she could find more on the Internet any chance she got.

May 7, Somewhere in Austria
This makes the sixth foreign country I've traveled in, and the fourth I've fought in. I've seen enough now to last a long, long time. I'm ready to see the USA. Because of security regulations, I cannot tell you just where I've been, but I can say it's been a long and tough drive. I don't think I could put to words what's been going on even if the censors would let me. Pray for me. I'm not only haunted by all I've done, but what I refused to do.
Love,
Jack

May 9, 1945, Austria
We've heard the news that we (and the world) have been awaiting for so long. The news came to us in a small Austrian village north of Linz. The war in Europe is over!

Even today, I find it hard to believe that this phase of the war is done. There were no celebrations or parties where we were. Instead, we're wondering what the next move will be. I hope that our last drive is history and that we can settle down to somewhat of a normal life, but no one knows.

I'll write more later. I'm thinking about too many things. I'm also seeing what no one ever thought we'd see. I'll tell you someday about how Austria welcomed us.

Love,
Jack

Ava tucked the letter into the envelope.

The guys up front were quiet now. It looked as if Grand-Paul was taking a nap.

Quaint countryside passed outside the window. Dennis's window was rolled down slightly, letting in a cool breeze that ruffled Ava's hair.

"Grandpa?"

"Hmm?"

Her grandfather had his favorite map opened on his lap, and she wondered if he thought Dennis needed a second navigator. She didn't want to ask, though. She was more concerned with his stories—his words.

"Did you see a lot going through Germany?" she asked, realizing they'd be there today.

"Yes, but our goal was to take over as much of

the country as possible. We weren't there as tourists. When we made it to Austria, I was more than ready to see home. But we had to go through the last gate before that was possible. That's when we came to the concentration camps. I know now what the Bible means when it talks about the valley of the shadow of death."

As he said the words, Ava thought again about the letters she'd just read, and she realized that although he had talked about many things, the letters had a common thread. The battle was more than just a physical fight. There was a fight in his heart too. A fight over his faith.

How did someone experience so much and still believe in God? It was a question she wanted to ask but didn't. Maybe because, unlike her grandfather and Dennis, she still struggled with the faith they seemed to grasp so easily.

Chapter Seventeen

When Ava opened her eyes, they were no longer on the paved country road. Instead, they were on a dirt and gravel one. She looked around, sure they were lost. She was also certain they were traveling down a path most American tourists had never stumbled upon.

"What's going on?" Her voice sounded like she'd swallowed gravel, and from the heaviness in her head, she'd been sleeping deeply. She rubbed her eyes and then yawned wide.

"There's a place your grandpa wants to see," Dennis answered. "A farmhouse he remembers."

Ava glanced at her watch. *He didn't want to go to Chenogne but wants to visit a farmhouse in the middle of nowhere?*

"Are we going to be able to get to the American cemeteries today?" she asked. A sweeping shot of the cemetery with close-ups of several graves would make for some powerful video.

Dennis shook his head. "I'm not sure we'll make it, but I have to say I never thought I'd see this part of Belgium. This isn't Kansas anymore, huh, Jack?" Dennis glanced over his shoulder.

Her grandfather didn't answer. Instead, he stared intently out the window, his eyes searching, his hands folding and unfolding in his lap.

Ava looked around and blew out a deep breath, reminding herself this was about her grandpa and hoping that wherever they ended up, she'd be able to get some good footage and some interviews. After the night before, she worried her grandfather would once again resist being videotaped. She hoped not.

They passed a small cottage. A woman in a faded dress and apron swept her front step. Chickens clustered around her feet. This didn't look like promising footage.

"Is there really something out here worth

looking at? I don't remember anything like this on the brochure. Do you remember the name of the last town?" Ava dug through her satchel, hoping she'd packed the brochure. It was times like this when she wished she or Dennis had brought a GPS. They hadn't planned on driving, or she was sure they both would have thought of bringing theirs from home. They weren't standard in European rentals. *Maybe helping lost American tourists is entertaining for Europeans.*

"We're somewhere in Belgium, Ava. I really don't know where we are." Dennis's voice was curt, and she could tell he wasn't thrilled about this side trip either.

"I know exactly where we are," Grandpa Jack snapped. "We're getting close, slow down." He leaned forward in his seat and patted Paul's shoulder. "Do you remember, Paul? There was a Y in the road. Our map wasn't that great, but we studied the mountains. Look." He pointed to the Y in front of them and then flicked the map on his lap. "Yes, we're exactly where we're supposed to be."

Her grandfather's voice quivered. He swallowed hard. He placed a hand on the window and then pressed his forehead against the glass, like a child peering out. His cheeks were flushed.

"Do you need some water?" She held up her half-full water bottle.

"I think you better slow down, Dennis." Grand-

Paul leaned forward and gripped the dashboard.

"Jack, are you okay?" Dennis sounded confused.

"Jack's fine. There's just something we need to see. Slow down." Grand-Paul's voice was firm. "See how the road splits? Go to the right."

"But that will take us south. Germany's east."

"Dennis, my boy, don't pick now to rebel!" Grand-Paul said.

Dennis didn't answer, and Ava could tell it took all his willpower to head down an even smaller dirt road that looked like an ox path winding through the trees.

They drove another mile, and Ava was sure they'd hit a dead end any minute. Yet the road kept going, and up ahead she noticed a small house nestled in the trees.

"There." Grand-Paul pointed.

"It's somebody's house. We can't go tromping around private property." Ava saw Dennis's jaw tighten.

Even though he protested, Dennis still did as he was asked and parked the car on the dirt area in front of the house. It was two stories but small. Ava thought it was abandoned. The paint was chipped and faded, and a fenced-off area near the side was only half erect. Then Ava noticed the clothesline to the side of the house and the clothes that fluttered in the breeze.

"Someone still lives here. Are you going to try

to talk to them? Did you know the family?" Her heart pounded. What was her grandfather looking for? He ignored her questions. Instead, he got out of the car. As Dennis helped Grand-Paul out, Grandpa Jack walked, with shaky steps, to the front of the car and leaned against the hood. Ava joined him.

"They used to keep their animals on the ground floor, but when the Germans moved in, that's where the family hid. And that's where I found her."

"Her?" Ava touched his arm, reminding her grandfather that she was there, standing next to him.

"Do you want me to see if anyone's home?" Dennis asked.

Ava could tell that Dennis was also confused about what was happening.

"Go ahead." It was Grand-Paul who answered.

Dennis took the steps two at a time, and when he reached the door, he knocked. Ava wasn't sure what he'd do if someone answered. He knocked three more times, and when still no one answered, he returned to the car.

"Who was she?" Ava repeated. "Who did you find?" She wondered if she should mention Angeline again.

Grandpa Jack still didn't acknowledge Ava. Instead, he pointed to the woods. "We saw some Germans taking off after they saw us coming. My buddy Bill and I got orders to go check the house to make sure there weren't any Germans left inside.

"Bill headed upstairs, to check things out. I took the bottom story." He paused. "When I approached the door, I saw movement. I fired into the room—" A sob erupted from his throat.

"Grandpa, are you okay?" Ava wrapped an arm around his shoulders. Then she looked at Paul. She didn't want to ask what had happened, but she had to know. Paul must have read the questions on her face.

"There were civilians—a couple with a baby," Paul said. "Jack told me he also saw a woman and a little girl who were dead."

This wasn't the story she'd expected. Her heart ached as she imagined it. She looked at Dennis. His eyes were wide. He wondered the same thing: had her grandfather's gunfire killed them?

Grand-Paul approached his friend. "Jack, I think she needs to hear the rest from you."

Grandpa Jack stood silent, and just when Ava was sure she'd never know, he lifted his head.

"I checked their pulses. The woman first. She had none, but when I checked the girl, she had the faintest pulse."

Ava covered her mouth with her hands and for the first time realized they were trembling.

Sobs shook her grandfather's shoulders. He lowered his head when he talked. "The girl wasn't breathing, and so I turned her head. We'd learned in training that often breathing stops because the tongue blocks the airway and that turning the head can fix it."

"Did she start breathing?" Dennis leaned closer, waiting.

Grandpa Jack nodded. "Then she cried, and it was one of the most beautiful sounds I'd ever heard."

"Was she injured?" Ava touched her grand-father's shoulder.

"Yes. I found the wound. The shot had gone through the back of her leg. The dirty straw under her leg had a puddle of blood."

The shot. The shot that he had fired. No wonder he didn't want to tell the story. She was surprised he'd wanted to come here. Ava looked at him, feeling prouder of her grandfather than she ever had before. *He faced his past. He shared his heart.*

"Was the wound bad?" Dennis asked.

Grandpa Jack didn't answer right away, so Dennis turned to Grand-Paul. But this time Paul didn't speak for his friend. Instead his gaze was one of patience and understanding.

Grandpa Jack lowered his head. "It hit an artery. I applied direct pressure to stop the bleeding, and then I put sulfa powder on it and wrapped the wound. And . . ."

"And then what? Was she okay?" Ava crossed her arms and pulled them tightly to her, almost afraid for him to answer that question.

"Bill went to tell the others that the house was clear, and I went for help. . . ."

Ava watched Grandpa Jack as he talked about running back to the sergeant, begging him to send a medic. She watched his face and listened to his shaky voice. She could tell this was hard. His eyes were wild, and he had a look of fear.

"They said the medics were busy. They couldn't do anything." Grandpa Jack stopped. He pressed his lips together, and she worried he was going to end the story there. Seeing him like this was like discovering a different person.

Grandpa Jack was the neighbor who helped everyone. He prided himself on being a solid rock of dependability. But that was at home. Here, he struggled to stay one step ahead of the memories, but he couldn't keep up. He was holding back his emotions. *He's probably spent all these years keeping the sadness at bay, holding it all inside.*

Grandpa Jack pressed his fingers to his eyes, as if willing himself not to cry. Finally, he took in a deep breath, and even though his eyes watered, he smiled.

"I refused to allow them to let her die in that place."

As he said those words, a new emotion transformed his face. Love. She'd seen that look in his eye as he looked at her mom, at her, and at her grandmother too—when she was still alive.

But she'd never seen him react in such a way to people outside their family.

Her grandpa paused, and he turned to Ava, searching her face. "She was so small. I didn't know where to take her. I couldn't just leave her there. After all, I had done that to her. . . .

"I was looking around, trying to figure out what to do next, and then I knew what to do. I prayed. I prayed that God would save the girl.

"Then I heard a truck coming down the road. The girl was crying louder, and she was shivering from the cold. I picked her up and carried her to the road."

"But it could have been the Germans coming," Dennis said. "The area wasn't secure yet."

"But it wasn't the enemy, it was one of our ambulances. I flagged them down, ran to the back, and put the girl inside. Then I ran off—"

"Oh, you did something else too," Grand-Paul's voice interrupted. "Before you ran away."

All eyes turned to her grandfather.

He shrugged. "I had a necklace that my sister gave me. It had a small pearl and a silver bird. I carried it in my pocket through training and the war. Alice said it was to remember her, but at that moment I had a feeling the necklace was for the girl. I took it from my pocket and clasped it around her neck before I turned and hurried away."

The scene around Ava blurred as tears rimmed

her eyes. She swallowed hard and lowered her head. "And then what happened?"

"Realizing the Germans were gone, I returned to our commander, waiting to hear what I was to do next." A thousand questions seemed to fill Grandpa Jack's eyes. Questions he'd had for decades.

"Did you ever check on her? Was there a way to find out if she made it?" Ava asked.

Paul shook his head, jumping in. "We were on the front line. We had to keep going. Patton wanted his troops to get to Germany first. There was no looking back, no asking. After the area was secured, we moved on."

"What about the people in the house?" Dennis asked.

"As I carried her away, the people were saying her name. It sounded like they were praying for her."

"What was her name?" Dennis asked.

"Angeline."

Chapter Eighteen

Ava had to think of a way to find her.

"I could call the museum in Bastogne again and look online—"

"A first name isn't much to go on. It would take a miracle to find the right person with the right information. . . ." Dennis let his voice trail off.

"Just like it took a miracle to find this place?" She lifted her chin and focused on his gaze, and she saw something there—protection. He was afraid to get their hopes up.

Or he was worried that they'd find her, only to discover she'd died. Could her grandfather carry that pain? *Wouldn't it be better to have even a small hope?* Dennis's eyes seemed to say.

"Don't you think we should just head to Darmstadt? That's the next town on the tour." Dennis's voice was low, soft—the same tone her mother used to use when trying to direct Ava's decision.

Ava didn't know what to think. She looked at her grandfather. He did look tired. She looked at Paul, who leaned heavily on his cane. They needed to rest. They needed to move on. She looked at the sky, wishing the right answer was written in the clouds.

She turned back to Dennis and nodded, resigning herself to the fact that this trip was producing more questions than answers.

They looked around the farm for a few minutes. Grandpa Jack and Paul pointed out bullet holes and even small craters in the yard behind the home—proof of the battle that had taken place so long ago. After fifteen minutes, they returned to the car.

They were just pulling out when Ava spotted

movement in the trees. It was a woman, and she was walking out of the woods with a handful of wildflowers. She looked older than Ava's mom, but not by much.

Ava's heart pounded. "Wait."

Dennis slowed the car. When it stopped, Ava opened the door.

"Ava, what are you doing?" Then he spotted the woman. "Ava, she's too young, that can't be her."

"I know. I'm just going to ask the woman if she knows anything."

"Do you think she'll understand?"

Ava paused. "You're right. I don't speak French." But even as she said the words, she remembered someone who did.

Ava climbed out of the car, pushed speed dial on her cell phone, and smiled as she approached the older woman.

The woman seemed curious but not alarmed. She smiled back and said something Ava didn't understand.

"Hello." Ava extended her hand. The woman took it, but her smile faded.

"No English." The woman shrugged. She had dark hair and wore it on top of her head in a loose bun. She looked curiously at the cell phone in Ava's hand, and her eyebrows V'd. Ava's guess was she didn't get many visitors, especially foreigners.

Just then Tana answered the phone.

"Thank goodness you answered."

"Ava, are you lost, broke down, in the middle of nowhere?" Tana said.

The older woman before her said something else Ava didn't understand.

"One minute." Ava held up one finger to the woman, unsure if she understood, and then she turned her attention to the phone.

"Tana, I'm okay, really. I am in the middle of nowhere, but I'm with Dennis, and I really need your help. We're at a farm in Belgium and there's a woman I need you to talk to."

"A woman? Okay, what do you want me to say?"

"I need you to tell her that my grandfather knew someone here, and I want you to ask her if she's related to the people who used to live in this house."

Ava smiled at the woman, who curiously eyed the men in the car and was becoming increasingly wary. Ava was glad they were staying put. The last thing she wanted was to scare this woman away.

Ava explained the whole situation to Tana—how they came upon the house, the battle, and even about the young girl.

"I think I got it. Okay, put the lady on the line. I've never spoken French with anyone from Belgium before—I hope we can understand each other. I think their language has a little bit of Dutch worked in."

Ava handed the woman the phone. She seemed

surprised, but she put it up to her ear. "Bonjour?"

For the next few minutes Ava watched the woman talk on the phone. As the woman talked, she pointed to her house, then to the car, then to herself, nodding at Ava as if Ava could also understand it all.

The woman's face filled with excitement, and then she approached the car, motioning that it was okay for the men to get out. She smiled at Grandpa Jack and Grand-Paul, and then she waved and motioned them to follow her to the bottom story of the house.

"What's going on?" Dennis approached, placing his hand on Ava's back.

"I asked Tana to tell the woman the story and to ask if she knows anything."

They watched the woman, whose head was nodding like the bobblehead dachshund that Ava used to have in her car when she was in high school.

"Well, it looks like she knows something." Dennis's jaw dropped and he patted Ava's back. "Quick thinking. I like that."

"Yes, I'm excited. I'll be more excited if we can figure out what she's saying." Ava chuckled. Joy over the possibility of getting an answer overwhelmed her.

Finally, after fifteen minutes, the woman approached Ava with a smile and handed her the phone.

Ava chuckled. "I suppose you understood each other . . . what did she say?"

"I have good news and not so good news. Which do you want first?"

"The good news."

"The good news is she knows the story. The not-so-good news is that the girl who was shot didn't live there. The woman's family had taken them in. I think their own house had been destroyed by the Germans. The mother, of course, didn't survive, and she doesn't know how to find the girl," Tana continued.

"Find her? Does that mean the girl survived?"

Tana's voice was hesitant. "The woman doesn't know."

Ava looked at her grandfather, noticing the hope in his eyes. "I'm sorry, Grandpa. The woman isn't sure if the girl made it."

He didn't say a word, and he didn't need to. The expression on his face—and the tears—made it clear how much this meant to him.

Ava asked Tana to do one more thing—get the woman's permission to videotape the house. Then, with an I-owe-you-one, she hung up.

Slipping her phone into the pocket of her jeans, Ava looked at Dennis. "Can you pop the trunk?"

A puzzled expression filled his face. "You're not serious, are you?"

"Dennis, we need to record this. The woman said it was okay. This is going to mean something to my grandfather. I'm sure he's going to want to look back on this day."

"Is that what you're really concerned about, Ava?" he spat, walking to the back of the car.

"Listen, I don't need you to judge me here. I know what I'm doing. I know what's important."

Dennis held the keys in his hand, but he didn't pop the trunk. "Do you, Ava? Do you really?"

She walked around to the driver's side door, reaching inside the open door, and pulled the lever for the trunk. But even as she walked back to get her things, the excitement of capturing this moment dissipated. She felt like a traitor.

Dennis placed a hand on her arm. "Ava, now is not the time." His tone was more gentle, but she could see in his eyes that he was serious. He forced a smile, looking at Grandpa Jack out of the corner of his eye.

With shuffling steps, her grandfather approached. Ava glanced at Dennis and then pulled the rest of her things out of the trunk.

Ava set up the video camera and filmed the woods and fields and then a little of the house. The woman approached and smiled at Ava, and then she pointed toward the ground-level door, which Ava guessed was now used for a basement, rather than a barn area for animals.

"I'm sorry. I don't understand."

With a smile, the woman took Ava's hand, leading her to the door. Ava was afraid to look back at her grandfather. Should she follow? Would he be upset if she went in? The woman seemed to have something she wanted to show Ava.

The heavy wooden door opened with a squeak. The woman grabbed a flashlight and motioned for Ava to follow her in. Ava's heart pounded, and suddenly fear coursed through her. She wondered if they would find something that would break her grandfather's heart. Or—perhaps worse—find nothing at all. She tentatively stepped in.

The room smelled of wet dirt. Cobwebs covered the lone, dingy window. Various yard tools were stacked in one corner. And even though there was no sign of animals, it smelled of them.

In one corner of the room, there was a wall that looked like it had been painted by a child's hand. The art was all one color—white—as if someone had given her a pail of paint and a brush. Ava placed a hand over her heart as she looked at simplistic drawings of trees, birds, and something that looked to be a horse. She bit her lip, trying to picture a five-year-old painting with the sound of artillery outside.

Ava pulled her camera out of her pocket and snapped a few shots. She was surprised that no one had followed her—not her grandfather, not Paul, not Dennis. Maybe they worried the memories would be too much.

Ava turned to leave when the woman grabbed

her arm and then pointed. Ava could see something painted behind a small metal shelf. She moved it to the side, realizing the shelf hadn't been there in 1945. The young girl had used that part of the wall as her canvas too. And when the shelf was moved, tears sprang to Ava's eyes. Like every artist, the girl had signed her name. The letters tilted down to the right and a few were backwards, but Ava could make it out: Angeline Pirard.

Ava looked at the woman and smiled. Angeline now had a last name. It could be the key to finding her.

Chapter Nineteen

Mud from the farmhouse clung to Ava's shoes, and she kicked them off, pushing them under the bed with her foot.

Ava set the suitcase on the bed and unzipped it with a flourish. She pulled out a pair of sweatpants and a T-shirt and tossed them on the bed, wrinkling her nose as she glanced around. She didn't like the hotel one bit. It was part of an American chain, and stepping into the room was like stepping into any hotel in Chicago, Dallas, or LA. There was a brown-and-orange floral bedspread, flower prints on the wall, and brown carpeting that looked like it had been there since the eighties.

"You should have let Dennis help you with those suitcases." Grandpa Jack sat down on his bed with a weary grunt.

"I'm sure the bellboy liked the tip."

"Dennis doesn't mean to be so bossy, you know. He was trying to make it up to you." Her grandpa removed his baseball cap and placed it on the side table.

Ava bit her lip. She hadn't said a word to Dennis after she showed him Angeline's paintings, even though he had tried to start a dozen conversations on the drive into Germany. She had refused to be charmed. She would try to be compassionate as he dealt with the news of his grandfather's cancer, but she was tired of his charming act only to have him turn into bad cop once more. She plugged in her computer, preparing to download her video— mostly footage she couldn't use for the show.

Dennis had been so great this morning as he told her about his grandfather and held her in his arms. He'd also talked about his new career path, sharing his dreams. Then, this afternoon it was like he was a different person. Someone who treated her filming on the farm as if she were a Nazi sent from the past to ruin everything her grandfather cared about.

She looked at her grandfather, noticing the weary way he looked down at his boots.

"Here, let me help you get them off." She kneeled before him, and he lifted his foot slightly.

From the grimace on his face, one would think he was lifting a two-hundred-pound weight. She grabbed the boot right above the heel and pulled. The boot slid off, revealing his white sock with a hole in the toe. A soft smile touched her lips, and then she took off the other boot. That sock was gray, and there was a hole in the heel.

Tears sprang to her eyes. She quickly brushed them away. Grammy would never have let him get away with wearing mismatched socks, let alone ones with holes in them.

She pulled back the polyester comforter on the double-sized bed. "There you go. Get some rest before dinner."

He lay down and was asleep nearly as soon as his head hit the pillow.

Ava finished connecting her camera to the computer as quietly as she could. It was only 4:00 p.m., and she didn't know if the drive or the emotions of the day had worn him out. Probably both.

As Ava started downloading the day's video-taping of the town of Bastogne, the clock, and the farmhouse, more tears came on. Maybe it was finally hitting her how frail her grandfather was. While she was in Seattle, she just assumed he was as healthy as he'd always been. He wasn't. He needed help walking and getting his boots off. Did her mother know? Her uncle? Ava couldn't imagine taking Grandpa home, dropping him off, and then not worrying every day whether he would be okay walking down his porch steps or carrying wood to his stove.

As Ava looked through her notes, she wondered if the woman at the farmhouse would follow through with trying to get more information about Angeline. The woman had written down Tana's number. She said she'd ask around and would let Tana know what she found out.

But Ava couldn't just wait around. Her grandfather wasn't getting any younger. He'd cared enough to spend his money coming here, and then he and Grand-Paul had organized the side trip. He'd done what he could; now she needed to do her part.

She tried to picture what it would be like for her grandpa to see Angeline again. To know he'd made a difference in one life. Just thinking about a reunion caused her whole body to feel as if it had been inflated with helium. Her grandfather had faced a lot. He'd been injured, and he'd seen friends die. He had painful memories tucked deep inside—things so hard and harsh that he found it difficult to share. He needed this. He needed to see that he'd done a good thing. That he'd made a difference.

Besides, their reunion would make for some great TV.

Tomorrow the plan was to visit the sites around the city of Darmstadt, where the Eleventh

Armored Division fought to get across the Siegfried line—a line of barriers and gun towers that protected Germany and that Hitler deemed impenetrable.

Tomorrow they would talk about more conflicts. Tomorrow she'd videotape the battle stuff, but today she'd let her mind dream about finding Angeline.

Ava logged in to her computer and then started searching for key words in her search engine.

"Angeline Pirard, child saved, World War II . . ."

Nothing popped up. She honestly hadn't thought it would be that easy, but it was worth a shot. At work she sometimes got lucky when the person being sought was also seeking. Those were always nice.

When she searched the first and last name, fewer than fifty websites came up and all of them were in French . . . or some other language, she really couldn't tell. Ava did note that one of the Angeline Pirards was in Linz, Austria. Excitement filled her. Linz was one of the places they'd be visiting. It wasn't far from Mauthausen concentration camp. Ava thought about calling the phone number now, but they spoke German in Austria.

Instead, she wrote down the name, address, and number, determined to find someone in Linz to help her when she got there. Until then, she'd try to get help reading these other websites, just in case one of them mentioned Angeline's experiences in the war. She tried to call Tana, to ask for more help, but Ava got her voice mail. After today, Tana was probably screening her calls.

Ava glanced at her watch. It wasn't long until dinner, and after eating she'd get her next segment done. She just hoped that with the footage she'd taken at the museum, she'd have enough. She also had the chiming of the clock in Bastogne. But first she needed help finding Angeline. If she could accomplish only one thing on the trip, she wanted that to be it.

Her first attempt was to call the museum in Bastogne. She found the number on the Internet. The phone rang once and a woman answered in French.

"Camille?" she asked.

The person didn't respond. Instead the phone beeped once and then voice mail picked up. She recognized Camille's voice on the message, but she still didn't understand the words. After the beep, Ava left a message.

"Hello, Camille. This is Ava Ellington. I need information about Angeline from the file you showed me. I was mistaken. Angeline was the young girl. Or at least I think she was the young girl in your file. Her last name is Pirard. If you can find any information please call me." She rattled off the European cell phone number. "Thank you."

Next, she searched for almost an hour, scouring Internet sites for any stories about children helped by soldiers in World War II, but she could find nothing that came even remotely close to her grandfather's story. When her stomach growled, reminding Ava that it was nearly time for dinner, she panicked. She still didn't have a definite plan for tonight's video.

Ava looked at the time. It was nearing 5:00 p.m. She had many research friends back home— librarians, friends at the various historical museums. There were many people she could enlist to help her with research. She did the math and realized it was 8:00 a.m. in Seattle. She could get plenty of help, but if she started making calls she'd be on the phone for hours. If she did that she'd never get her video done. Maybe she could get Jill to recruit help for her. She dialed her friend's cell.

Jill's phone rang four times, and Ava began to worry. Jill always answered. She was like the mailman who made it through snow, hail, and sleet. Where was she? After six rings, Jill's voice mail picked up.

"Hey, Jill. I need your help. I would call around myself but I prepaid only a certain number of minutes on this phone. Also, I have a video to work on . . ."

For the next few minutes, Ava rattled off all the information she had about Angeline. She also left

Tana's number for Jill to contact if needed. She also left Camille's contact information.

Just as she was finishing up, she heard a knock on the door. Her heart raced and she guessed it was Dennis—most likely with his feathers ruffled about something else.

"Hey Jill, I have to go, but . . ." She bit her lip, trying to decide if she should ask for one last thing. "But can you also look up something else? Chenogne, Belgium. C-h-e-n-o-g-n-e. I did some Internet searches, but I'm looking for something —I don't know—impacting. Maybe Judy at the library can help? Something happened there near the end of December or beginning of January that my grandpa was involved in. Okay, love ya. Thanks." She hung up and then hurried to the door, hoping the knocking wasn't going to wake up her grandfather. A dozen different greetings for Dennis came to mind. None of them good.

"Yes?" She swung open the door and was greeted by the scent of flowers. Then she saw them. A small bouquet, and behind the mix of colors, Dennis's apologetic smile. The flowers stuck out of an old bottle and looked handpicked. In his other hand was a paper bag.

Ava sucked in a deep breath and blew it out. She was tired of this. Mr. Nice Guy one minute and then receiving a lecture from him the next. She lifted her chin and narrowed her gaze. Then she stepped into the hall, shutting the door behind her. If she was going to give Dennis a piece of her mind, she didn't want to wake her grandfather.

His eyebrows furrowed. "After such a great morning, I really messed things up."

"Yes, you did." She placed a hand on her hip.

"Would it help if I told you I was walking by a field and thought of you?"

"I feel like I'm on a roller coaster. Can we just deal with each other over the next couple of days and get through it? Besides, those weeds are a poor excuse for a peace offering."

The elevator opened and a couple exited. They eyed Dennis and Ava suspiciously and then hurried past. Dennis held the bag up. "Actually, this is the peace offering—sandwiches from a bistro down the street."

She shook her head and thought about walking back inside and slamming the door, but her stomach growled. The food did smell good.

Dennis extended the bag, and she took it.

"I was also going to offer to read more letters for you if you need some for your video. There's a nice patio out back. We can leave food for your grandpa and eat back there."

Ava rubbed her hand across her forehead. Why did he have to do this? The flowers were just a warm-up, she now knew. The food was nice, but she really needed help with the videos. He knew that. She hated that he knew.

"It's amazing how quickly things change. Back

at the farmhouse, I thought you were going to tackle me as I pulled my camera from the car, and now you want to help?"

Dennis looked to his side, as if there was someone there holding cue cards, telling him what to say, and then turned back to her. "Yes?"

"Fine." Ava pulled the hotel key card from her pocket and turned back to the door. "I'll accept your help, but I'm not happy about it. My deadline's got me in a chokehold, and you just happen to be a slight breath of air. Slight. Very slight."

Chapter Twenty

Ava woke with a smile. Her first thoughts were of Dennis reading the letters about her grandfather's fight through Germany. He'd done his best to let his emotions come through his words, and it had made her job easier. She'd finished the video by 11:00 p.m., sent it off, and gotten some much-needed sleep.

Dennis hadn't tried to flirt. She hadn't pushed him away. It had been enough to just record and go their separate ways.

Her grandfather was gone. She guessed he was already downstairs enjoying breakfast with his friend.

After rising and dressing, she checked her voice mail, hoping for news from Jill or Camille. There wasn't any. She checked her e-mail too. There was nothing from Jill or from Jay either—not that she should be surprised. He'd been such a charmer, but no one could wear a mask forever. Her grandfather had seen the truth. He'd told her about it. He'd warned her, and what had she done? She'd yelled at him. Ava bit her lip, realizing she still hadn't apologized for that. She needed to make amends to her grandfather.

Heading downstairs, she discovered Grandpa Jack sitting in the small hotel breakfast room with a cup of coffee. His Bible was open on the table, and it reminded Ava of her grandparents' house as a child. She would wake to find them reading the Bible together most mornings.

Even though he wasn't a big man, Grandpa looked large at the small café table. Ava paused, seeing him there. She was still sometimes struck with the reality that she was in Europe with her grandfather. He was the grandpa who ate bologna on white bread for lunch and found joy in writing down each day's high and low temperatures on the free calendar he'd gotten from the bank.

He was really here way back when. This is part of him.

She crossed her arms over her chest and tucked in her lower lip, realizing that all the times she'd visited, gone fishing, and joked around with him, she'd never asked about the war. He always asked her about her work and life and friends. How come she'd never thought about getting to know his life better or learn about his experiences? She thought about offering the apology she'd wanted to give since before they started. The other guys weren't around, and this seemed to be her chance. Yet her chest grew heavy just thinking about it. Not only had he been right about Jay, the truth was, she didn't have many more answers than she had six months ago. If anything, she was more confused about her life, her faith, her everything.

She approached with quiet steps. He was looking out the window. His eyes were focused on the narrow road leading out of town.

"Good mornin', sweetheart. How are you today?"

She pulled out a chair. "Good."

He lifted his cup. "Good coffee here."

A waitress approached, and Ava ordered coffee, sausage, and toast.

The waitress returned and poured her coffee. Ava took a sip. "You're right. It is good coffee. Reminds me of Starbucks."

"Four dollars for a cup of coffee?" He shook his head.

Ava smiled. Four dollars probably fed his family for a week before the war, maybe longer. She wondered if he was thinking about that, or thinking about something else. It was clear his mind wasn't on this café or the coffee.

"There's something that's really stuck with me

216

from the war." He had a contemplative look on his face. The wrinkles on his forehead deepened. He wore a half smile as he talked. It was a sad smile. Ava wished she could capture that smile on camera, but he was never this relaxed when she had her equipment out.

"I don't know if it was this town or another one like it, but I remember when we entered," he continued. "It was just piles of rubble. Old piles from the bombers. New rubble from the artillery. There didn't seem to be one building that was whole."

She looked outside at the brick buildings—the painted window frames and flower boxes that were just beginning to show their first buds. "I bet it's different seeing the buildings standing, not crumbling."

"It is different, but what was even more troubling were all the people. I keep thinking about the refugees. They were walking out of town, stumbling along the road. They were leaving the city—old people, small children. Mothers carrying babies in pouches across their fronts. Some had wagons or baby carriages filled with things. And they didn't look back. I could see it on their faces. It was too hard for them to look back. They didn't really look ahead. Mostly, they just watched their feet. The children, not knowing any better, sneaked glances at us."

Ava could picture that. She felt the same way.

Not looking back because of the pain. Afraid to look ahead. Maybe she was just watching her feet too.

They sat a few more minutes in silence, sipping their coffee and watching people pass on the street. It seemed right, in a way, to enjoy being together without an agenda. She breathed out a soft breath, taking in the sight of an old woman riding down the street on a bicycle, of a younger woman pushing her baby in a pram.

A family walked by, and Ava could tell where they were from by their Texas T-shirts and guidebooks. The dad led them, video camera in hand. The mother followed with a guidebook, reading as they walked along. Behind them were two girls, around seven and ten. They held hands as they trailed behind, singing. Joy filled their faces, and seeing them warmed her heart. Ava looked again at the dad, and she wished she could call to him—to tell him to look back at his daughters. He was missing so much—missing the joy of the moment, in search of the next site.

Thinking of this, her heartbeat quickened.

Is that what I've been doing? Missing the joy of being here in search of the perfect shot?

She turned her attention to her grandfather as he watched the passersby. She took in his pale eyes, the slight smile on his lips. She appreciated the sight of his age-spotted hands wrapped around his coffee cup and tried to capture the moment—not with a camera but in her memory. Tears welled when she realized this was what she wanted to share with her children someday—moments exactly like this.

"Grandpa." She looked down into the coffee cup. "Remember that conversation we had just after Thanksgiving? I've been wanting to apologize. . . ." Ava paused when she heard footsteps behind her, and then hands squeezed her shoulders.

"All packed up and ready to go?" It sounded like Dennis wore a smile, but she resisted the urge to turn and look at him, lest he see the heat rising to her cheeks.

"Mm-hmm." Ava closed her eyes. Dennis's hands felt warm and strong. She tried to stay mad at him, but it was hard.

She opened her eyes and looked at her grandfather, trying to remember what she was saying before being interrupted. Grand-Paul watched with a large grin. An ache circled in her chest. This was his last year. What an honor it was for her to have this time with him. To see his smile. She captured the smile in her memory.

"Dennis, have you told Ava about your date tonight?" Grand-Paul asked.

Dennis released his hands then stepped back.

The last word dropped from his lips, and Ava felt as if cold water had been splashed in her face. *Date?*

She shrugged, trying to pretend it didn't bother her. He traveled the world. He knew lots of people. It only made sense he had a girlfriend in Germany.

Dennis cleared his throat, and Ava looked up.

"It's not confirmed yet, though. Ava, would you like to go out with me tonight?"

From the corner of her eye, Ava noticed a smile fill Grandpa Jack's face.

Dennis quickly added, "As friends of course. It might be good for us young folk to get out and see the city."

Ava cleared her throat and looked down. "I don't know. There's the video. I'm going to have to edit and send it in on time."

"Don't worry about that. We'll give you good stuff today and make it easy, right, Jackson?" Grand-Paul elbowed Grandpa Jack. Grandpa Jack's smile didn't fade as she expected it to. Maybe it was going to be a good day after all.

An hour later, Ava had already set up her video camera, and the guys sat on two folding chairs they'd picked up at a small hardware store before heading out to the countryside. Behind them was a small portion of the Siegfried line, a line of concrete "teeth" that had once protected the border of Germany for hundreds of miles in both directions. The line had been there to protect Germany from an invasion from a foreign enemy, but Ava happened to be talking to some of the first soldiers to get through.

Ava looked at the steel and concrete triangles. They reminded her of the Egyptian pyramids with their tops lopped off, only these were small—knee high—and they were lined up in a wide, zigzag pattern, six deep and stretched across the fields in both directions.

The triangles were covered with moss and worn down slightly from age, but she could see how challenging it would be for tanks or trucks to break through them.

Grand-Paul wore a large smile. Grandpa Jack sat perched on the edge of his seat, and until this moment, Ava hadn't been sure he would really go through with it. He looked at the camera and then looked at Paul with a narrow gaze. Her grandfather was doing this for his friend, which was fine with her. If it meant she'd get good footage, she'd take it.

Dennis was also silent as she prepared to videotape, and she wondered what had gotten into him. She especially wondered about his proposed date. Why was he being so nice? Ava shook her head to refocus.

"Okay, feel free to start whenever," Ava told them. "Just talk like you're explaining what took place here—as if the viewers had never heard of the Siegfried line." She laughed. "And since I really haven't heard much except for what I studied on the Internet, you can just talk to me."

She turned on the camera. "How did you two feel, waking up and realizing you were going to try to break through the line?"

"Scared. We were heading into unknown territory. But it all turned out. Intelligence had gotten us accurate information on the pillboxes, and we completely surprised them," Grand-Paul said.

"Pillboxes?" Ava shook her head. "I'm not sure I follow."

"Mini fortresses," Grand-Paul explained. "Concrete huts with machine guns. They were spaced out along the whole Siegfried line and were manned by German soldiers. You can't see them now, but they're up in those hills behind you. It wasn't us just trying to get over these teeth. There were fortifications filled with enemy soldiers on the other side."

Grandpa Jack looked at Paul. Then he looked at the camera. Ava cast him a reassuring smile. "We snuck up on them on foot. Paul here was our unit commander and he watched out for me. He told me he didn't want to have to write a letter home to my mom. The commanders always got the job of writing to the parents if they lost a guy."

"Yeah, but if I had known then what type of guy you were I would've let the Germans get in a shot or two before I covered you." Grand-Paul held up a playful fist, and Ava got a glimpse of the nineteen-year-old kids they'd been. "Yes, I was the lucky cuss who got to lead these men through the dragon's teeth."

Grand-Paul continued talking about how fearful they were the night before the attack. Ava listened, but only partly. She mostly watched Dennis from the corner of her eye. Watched him watching their grandpas. It warmed her heart to see his pride.

Laughter carried on throughout the day, and after the videotaping was done, she packed up her things. Dennis pulled her grandfather to the side, to ask him more questions about what it was like serving under his friend, and Ava saw her opportunity to talk to Grand-Paul.

"Thanks so much for doing that."

"Oh, Ava-gal, I'm always eager to tell the stories." He remained in the chair, his palms on his knees. A cough shook his body.

"I don't mean only that. I mean talking my grandpa into this."

He shook his head. "I didn't talk him into it."

"Really?" She glanced over her shoulder at her grandfather. "I thought for sure."

"No, but I've been praying about it," Grand-Paul said.

Ava cocked an eyebrow. "I thought you didn't believe in prayer—in telling God what to do."

"Dennis explained that it's about letting God know what's on your mind." He rubbed his chin, his fingers quivering. "I let God know it would be easier on you if your stubborn grandfather would just tell his stories. God must have agreed."

She hugged Grand-Paul again, clinging to him a few extra seconds. "Thank you," she said with a smile. "Keep praying, it's working."

Ava was still smiling as she finished the video before dinner and e-mailed it off long before it was due.

She still hadn't heard back from Jill about the research, and as time passed she almost didn't expect to. Jill was most likely running around trying to do her job, and Ava's job too. Ava resigned herself to the fact that she'd dig in when she got back to Seattle. If Angeline was out there, Ava was determined to find her, even if it took a week, a month, or a year.

She'd try to get in touch with Jill again—just to see how things were going at the studio—but not tonight. Tonight she'd forget about what happened sixty-seven years ago. Tonight she'd just enjoy seeing a new place with an old friend.

Dennis met her in the hotel lobby at six o'clock sharp. The lobby was small and quaint, just like the city street outside.

"Hope you don't mind walking. The restaurant's a few blocks away." He held up a pamphlet in English. "The lady at the visitor's center down the street recommended it."

"I don't mind." She wrapped a baby-blue scarf

around her neck. "In fact, I hope it's not too nice of a place." She kicked up her plain black Danskos. "I really didn't pack for elegant dining."

"You look fine, Ava. And it's not *that* nice. I just got out of college, remember? My career hasn't taken off yet."

A cool breeze stirred the air, and Ava looked around the large square. Even though most of the town looked modern and plain—most likely because it had been bombed and rebuilt after the war—the square gave her a sense of what the town had been like before the war.

"So this is Darmstadt?" She sighed and placed a hand against her chest. "I've always dreamed of coming here and seeing those dragon's teeth."

"Really?" Dennis paused and eyed her.

She quickened her pace. "No." She laughed. "I've never heard of this place before, but it's nice. I'll give it that. Germany has been very beautiful so far."

He caught up with her. "You sound surprised."

"Maybe I was expecting the people in the old film reels. Strict and stern. I'm pleasantly surprised by the diversity of the people. Seeing this is like throwing all the narrow-mindedness and hate back in Hitler's face."

They turned a corner and the buildings rose up, square and modern. In the center of the business area, there was a large tower. It looked like a tall, brick arm with five curves at the top that resembled fingers. She tilted her head, picturing a giant reaching into the sky.

"Wow." Ava glanced up again.

"It talks all about it in this pamphlet. I don't know how to pronounce it in German but it's translated as the Marriage Tower."

"You're just making that up. It looks more like a hand . . . with those five spires that look like fingers. I don't see any wedding ring." She smirked.

"It's no joke. It says here it was built in the memory of the wedding of the Grand Duke Ernst Ludwig in 1905."

"I like it. Especially the wedding part."

As soon as the words were out of Ava's mouth, she wished she could take them back, just in case Dennis had heard about her failed wedding plans.

If Dennis was having any of those thoughts, he didn't voice them. Instead, they walked a few more blocks in silence, taking in the picturesque scene of old men and women, teens and young couples strolling along the avenues.

She knew they were getting close to the restaurant when he placed his hand on the small of her back. She slowed her steps, and he led her to the door. Above it a sign read *Braustub'l*.

"I hope you're hungry."

Warm scents of comfort food met her as they entered. Dennis gave his name to the hostess, and they were led to a table shared by another couple. At first Ava was confused.

They sat, and Dennis leaned in close. "A fine example of German efficiency." He smiled. "Waste no room with empty seats and half-filled tables."

The other couple knew quite a bit of English, and they chatted about the weather and the best sites to visit in the area. Dennis and Ava listened politely and made small talk, but neither had the heart to tell the other couple that they would be staying only one night. Tomorrow they'd be off to a new German town and off to discover more stories of war.

Ava ordered the *rosti pfifferlinge*, a potato cake with a creamy sauce, loaded with chanterelle mushrooms. When it arrived, the portion was bigger than she expected—the complete opposite of the small portions from France.

She breathed a sigh of relief as the other couple finished their dinner and left with a warm good-bye.

"Finally." Dennis swirled his fork in the leftover gravy on his plate. "We're alone. I mean without the grandpas in arm's reach."

"I think it's the first time on this trip." She smiled, and all the questions she'd been waiting to ask escaped her mind. It was easy to have a conversation when the grandpas were around. They were always quick to share their opinions.

Dennis and Ava chatted about some of the things they'd seen and about the amazement of coming upon that farm and learning about Angeline.

After the waitress brought them *apfelkuchen*—apple cake—and coffee, Dennis's voice softened. "Do you remember when we went up to the ski park on Mount Shasta and got in that accident on the way down?"

"That bear ran into my grandpa's car." Laughter bubbled from her lips. "Grandpa didn't believe us!"

"Not until he saw those hairs stuck in the door panel. Poor thing, the way the bear staggered into the woods after that. I bet his head ached for days."

She turned to Dennis and studied his face. "I also remember swimming in Lake Siskiyou. Remember the day we timed ourselves to see how long we could float? I think it was an hour."

"Two at least." He took another bite of his cake.

"We heard some of these same war stories from our grandpas back then, but they didn't seem as interesting then as they are now."

Dennis looked down at his plate. "Maybe I was a little distracted." He rested his elbow on the table, and then placed his chin in his hand.

"You know you're the first girl I ever kissed, right?"

Ava had been taking a sip from her mineral water, and she nearly spit it out all over the table. As soon as she swallowed, laughter burst from her lips. "You should warn a girl before talking like that."

"Yes, well, I can't stop thinking about that summer. Especially our hikes. Remember when we tried to climb the back side of Mount Shasta?"

"I remember we packed more food than we'd need in three days, and I nearly froze because I didn't realize we were walking all the way up to the snow." Ava sighed. "Remembering those days—talking about them now—makes it seem like they happened just last week."

"I remember your telling me how excited you were about college, and all your friends, and everything you'd already bought for your dorm room."

"I'd been planning it for a long time."

He smiled. "I know. You must have told me that twenty times on that hike."

The waitress cleared their plates. In the next room a group sang in German, and she wondered what they were celebrating. The birth of a baby? A birthday? A wedding?

Dennis wasn't paying attention. She could tell he was still thinking more about then than now. If they kept going, they'd get to the subject of their last night together, and she didn't want to ruin their evening by bringing up that.

"I wonder what's next. What will the rest of the week hold?"

Dennis looked at her. "You're trying to change the subject."

"Wouldn't you want to change the subject if you had acted like I did?"

"We're going to have to talk about it sometime, Ava. That night—that fight—changed the course of our lives."

Chapter Twenty-One

The next morning, Ava hummed as she hurriedly showered, dressed, packed, and made her way to the hotel lobby with her tripod and camera, just in case there was something around the hotel she wanted to videotape. Yet, instead of joining the two grandpas outside on the patio, she chose a table inside with a view of the elevator and ordered breakfast. Taking a sip of her orange juice, she heard the elevator ding and watched the doors open, a smile on her face. Three college-aged students exited, and she bit her lip, disappointed. The next time it dinged it was a businessman in a suit, followed by a young woman carrying a baby.

Ava cut her ham into small pieces and told herself not to watch the doors anymore. On the next ding, a couple exited, holding hands. She sighed and pushed her plate back, no longer feeling hungry. Nervous tension caused her stomach to rumble, and she rose and hurried to join the grandpas, motioning to the extra seat.

"Can I sit here? Dennis isn't using it, is he?"

"It's all yours," Grand-Paul commented. "Dennis went to gas up the car. He also mentioned he's working on a surprise for tonight, so it might take a little while to get back."

"You weren't supposed to say anything," Grandpa Jack grumbled.

"Now that's just foolishness. I need to teach my grandson a thing or two. Doesn't he know the rule of surprises?" Grand-Paul turned to her. "Do you know, Ava?"

"I'm not sure if I do . . ."

His face grew serious, and he leaned forward with his elbows on the table, as if preparing for a lecture. "The rule of surprises is that there's a measure of joy and excitement when a surprise is revealed . . . but the same happens when someone *hears* that a surprise is coming. *Because* they know, the happiness is spread out. So, in the end, the sum joy is far greater if you just spill the beans that you're up to something."

Ava laughed. "Yes, I suppose that's right. It's like Christmas. There's the excitement over the surprise of the gifts, and there's the excitement that builds over knowing Christmas Day is nearing."

She looked around and noticed how quiet this outside patio was. Perfect for videotaping. "I suppose while we wait I can get my camera out." She set up her tripod. "I know we have a long day on the road to get to Bayreuth. Will it be okay if we talk a little bit?"

"Sure, might as well." Grand-Paul dabbed his face, making sure there were no breakfast crumbs tucked in the wrinkles.

"Great." Ava unzipped her camera bag. She glanced over at her grandfather to see his response and her heart sank. The smile and bright eyes of a moment before were gone. He lowered his head and was looking at his lap. Something inside told her to stop—to put the camera away and just enjoy the sunshine and conversation—but the more practical part of her nagged about the work she had to do.

As she checked the battery in the camera, she remembered Dennis's comment from the previous night—the closer to Austria and the concentration camp they got, the more emotions would come out. The sorrowful look on her grandfather's face was evidence of that.

Emotions are good on camera, she reminded herself. *They draw the viewers in.*

She set up the camera to capture both men as they sat side-by-side sipping coffee. When everything was in place, Ava locked eyes with Grand-Paul and he winked at her. She hoped he'd still been praying.

Pushing RECORD on the camera, Ava began. "Tell me about what you saw on your way to Austria."

"The thing I remember the most are the white sheets hanging from the windows," Grand-Paul started.

"People were surrendering?" Ava asked.

"They wanted us to think they were," Grand-Paul explained. "Sometimes we'd get close, and then we'd get shot at with sniper fire. If that happened, we'd tell the mayor he had an hour to clear the town of civilians. Then if we got shot at again, we'd level the town. We leveled several towns that way." He spoke the fact simply. It was part of his job, part of his life.

She looked at her grandpa, seeing sadness in his gaze. "Is there one event that sticks out most in your mind, Grandpa?"

It took him a moment to answer. "I remember one town so vividly because our buddy got killed there." Grandpa Jack's words caught in his throat. He covered his face with his hands.

Ava looked at his fingers. His knuckles were like knots under the red patchy skin. She imagined those hands young. Pictured them covering his face in such a way, trying to hide the pain of losing a friend.

A sound escaped her grandfather's lips, but it wasn't a cry. It was more like an utterance. She strained to listened and finally made out his repeated word.

"Why? Why?"

After all these years.

Tears sprang to her eyes, and silent gasps vibrated her chest. She didn't know why she was asking him to do this. Dennis had known all along the pain they carried. The pain of sharing.

"Grandpa?" She leaned forward and touched the checkered sleeve of his shirt. "You don't have to do this. I'm sorry." A sob escaped. "I'm sorry I pushed this on you. I'm sorry I didn't understand." She pinched the fabric between her fingers, realizing these men never left 1945. This trip wasn't about remembering. It was about returning to the place that was always with them.

Ava released his sleeve. Moments like this were exactly what would make for good television, but her heart was heavy. She didn't want to gain viewers at her grandfather's expense.

"You don't need to do this," she repeated.

He lowered his hands and looked at his lap.

"I'm proud of you, Grandpa. Proud of who you were then and who you are now. I've always been proud of you, and if you never sit in front of this camera again, I'll love you just the same." There would always be another job. She'd deal with that. But this day with this amazing man was something that would never come again.

He nodded and attempted to stop his trembling chin. After a minute passed, she turned off the camera. Her grandfather's eyes met hers. "I'm sorry, Ava. I can't do this now, but I'd like to finish stronger. I know I didn't play a big part in the first videos, but as we continue . . . I have some things to say."

Ava tilted her head, surprised. "Really? Are you sure? It's okay if the camera sits in the trunk the rest of this trip."

"I have a story I need to tell. I didn't realize it until I started reading through my old letters." He lifted his head and looked at her. "You know, Ava, I wasn't kind to you. At Thanksgiving I challenged your upcoming marriage, but I didn't tell you what troubled me. I see something in you that reminds me of myself. For so long, I worked to do everything right, while missing the whole point of life. At Mauthausen concentration camp I learned that I was just as imprisoned as the prisoners there—but the brick walls were inside me. I thought I'd built them for protection, but I was the one enslaved. And on this trip I did the same thing—trying to protect myself from the pain. I'd like to tell you about the concentration camp, not now, but when we get to Austria." He cleared his throat. "And if I'm willing to do that, I think my friend here needs to face something too."

Her grandfather turned to Paul. "You're afraid to pray because you don't want to be disappointed, but prayer is more about being willing to change ourselves. To know God has the answers."

"You're sounding like a preacher," Grand-Paul said with a huff. Then he lowered his chin. "And it's a sermon I've needed to hear."

They sat in silence for several minutes.

"I like what you're saying about the walls coming down too." Grand-Paul cocked an eyebrow at Grandpa Jack. "So are you going to talk about *everything* now?" Even though Grand-Paul didn't mention Chenogne, they all knew what he was talking about.

"That's different." Grandpa's chin jerked upward like a yo-yo on a string.

Grand-Paul crossed his arms over his chest. "Is it?"

"I was talking about allowing Ava to videotape me talking about the camps."

Grand-Paul nodded but didn't say a word. Ava felt like her heart was going to break. Whatever happened in Chenogne impacted her grandfather even more than discovering the piles of bodies, the half-dead prisoners.

Ava didn't know Dennis had approached and was standing behind her. She didn't know that she was crying, until Dennis gently wiped her cheek with his curled finger. His touch was gentle. She glanced up at him and offered a sad smile.

Deep inside she realized she really would never know her grandfather until she knew what happened in Chenogne. She looked at Dennis, and his eyes attempted to see inside her as if challenging her walls too.

Was it worth sharing everything?

Chapter Twenty-Two

Ava was buckling up her seatbelt when the cell phone in her pocket vibrated. She pulled it out and saw that it was Jill calling.

"Dennis, can you hold on? I'm getting a call from work that I need to take."

Dennis nodded and turned off the car engine, but he didn't seem happy about it. They'd all experienced a powerful, emotional connection as her grandpa Jack shared about the walls he'd built up—the ones he was still trying to break down. The mention of work pulled them back to reality like loose change being sucked up into a vacuum cleaner.

Ava climbed from the car, walking toward the sidewalk with long strides. "Jill, thanks for calling! Did Todd like the latest video?"

"Oh, the video. Yeah, it was great." Jill's voice sounded far off, and it wasn't just from the distance of the call. "We're already getting e-mails on our website. Everyone loves it."

"Good news. But something's wrong." She slowed her pace. "I can hear it in your voice."

The line was silent for a moment, and Ava was trying to decide if she'd dropped the call when Jill spoke.

"I wasn't really calling about the videos or the

ratings. It's something you asked me to research."

Ava glanced back to the car. Three sets of eyes were on her. She forced a smile and then walked a little way farther down the sidewalk. Her shoulders tightened with every step.

"What is it?" She bit her lip, thinking of the two things she'd asked Jill to help with—finding Angeline and Chenogne. She didn't want bad news about either.

"Do you want bad news . . . or worse news first?"

"I don't like the sound of that, Jill. Don't you have some good news to throw in?"

"You already got the good news. Everyone likes the videos."

"The bad news then."

"Okay, I've done a ton of research, but I can't find anything about that woman Angeline Pirard."

Ava approached a small brick wall and sat. She didn't want to look back at the car. She didn't want to see the guys watching her. "Well, I found something. It's a woman by the same name in Linz, Austria. I'm going to look her up when I get there."

"Oh, that's good." Jill's voice sounded hesitant. Then she continued. "I discovered information about Chenogne. You're right, there wasn't much on the Internet, but I went to the library. Marge, in the reference department, found an old book. In it were soldiers' stories and one talking about

Chenogne. She's supposed to scan the page and e-mail it to you."

"Can you give me a quick rundown? I won't be on e-mail until tonight."

Ava dared to glance at their car still parked in front of the hotel. The guys had gotten out of the car and were now standing in the sunshine. As she watched them, Dennis glanced over. Ava quickly looked away, turning her attention to the cobblestone sidewalk.

"The e-mail has more information, but something happened in Chenogne. Something to do with prisoners of war on New Year's Day 1945. But maybe it wasn't even your grandpa's unit."

"Thank you for looking," Ava said, not feeling thankful at all.

"I'll let you know if I find out about that girl."

"Oh yes, that would be great. I'll let you know if I find out something too."

Ava hung up the phone. It wasn't until after she'd tucked it back into her jean pocket that she realized she hadn't asked Jill about how things were going at the station and with the morning show. She hardly had the strength to walk back to the car and pretend to enjoy the day. All her mind could focus on was that something happened on New Year's Day 1945. Something that her grandfather could have been a part of.

Ava forced a smile as she hurried back to the car. "I'm so sorry to keep you waiting."

Dennis's eyes scanned her face and he frowned. "Is everything okay? You're a little pale."

"Am I?" Ava patted her cheeks. "I hope I'm not coming down with something." She stressed the last word. "Just work stuff—things I can take care of when I get home." She waved off his concerns and then climbed into the backseat of the car next to her grandfather.

The others got in the car.

"You sure everything's all right?" Grandpa Jack patted her hand, and she winced slightly.

"Yes." She rubbed her forehead. "It's just a little problem, but it'll all work out. The good news is Jill said they liked the videos."

Dennis started the car, and Ava was ready to leave this place. To move on to a different city with other stories.

Ava looked out the window, watching the buildings as they passed, seeing the German people walking by. Some in ordinary clothes, some in business suits, mothers pushing prams.

In the front seats, Grand-Paul and Dennis talked about their flights home and a family reunion they were planning with Dennis's family for that summer.

Beside Ava, Grandpa Jack sat silently, looking out the window, taking in the view of the German countryside. Did he think about his friends who had been captured near Chenogne? Did they all make it out, or did some die in the prison camps?

Ava pushed those thoughts out of her mind. Or at least tried to. Then she pulled out the last of the letters her grandfather had given her. They were the ones he hadn't wanted her to read, and she guessed that perhaps some of the events of Chenogne were within these pages.

February 5, 1945
Dear Mom and Dad,

I have to say I'm thankful January is over. We're leaving Belgium behind—or at least that's our plan. We're parked outside in a little village, waiting for what's to come. There's a stream that runs through the village, and at night all the villagers come down to water their cattle. I want to hate the enemy, but these people don't seem like they're the enemy. It's hard figuring out what to think. It's hard to deal with what we must do. What we have done.

I've been having nightmares again. But can they be called nightmares if the events really happened? Over and over I see the soldiers being lined up. I try to scream, to tell them to run, but no words come out. I try to run, so I don't have to watch, but my feet won't move. They look at me with trust in their eyes, and I just look away.

With my love,
Jack

Ava paused. She folded up the letter and held it tightly between her fingers. She didn't want to believe what Jill had revealed was true, but now she knew it was. She closed her eyes and tried to picture it—having good friends rounded up by the Germans.

Ava wished her grandma was still around. It would have been great to talk to her about all this—to see how Grandma Maggie had handled her husband's memories and experiences of the war. Grandma might have been able to advise her when to listen and when to prod. Or Grandma might have just said it was enough to hold the knowledge inside and trust that love and respect for her grandfather would go further than words ever could.

God, help me here. I don't know what to do . . . what to say. How to say it. Help me to promote healing and not pain. Help me not to judge or jump to conclusions.

Ava glanced up and studied the back of Dennis's head. She noted the way his dark hair curled on his neck, and she was suddenly flooded with a new gratefulness that he was here and she didn't have to do this—the trip, the driving, the talking, the remembering—without him. She also wondered if she should talk to Dennis about what she knew. She wondered if she'd be able to continue her work. Her videos seemed so shallow now. They merely scratched the surface.

She'd try to do better, but she didn't have much time. There would only be two more videos, and then they'd be at Mauthausen. The experience there would speak for itself as survivors joined with liberators. It would be good to celebrate the freedom some found despite Hitler's attempts to steal, kill, and destroy.

Ava tucked the letters back in her bag. She couldn't read more now. She leaned back against her seat—trying to take it all in, attempting to make sense of everything she was learning.

Grand-Paul turned to her. "So, you find out anything interesting?"

She looked at her grandfather, and the sadness of this morning was gone. A new emotion was there—worry.

"Not much." She offered her grandfather a smile.

Grandpa Jack squeezed her hand and then released it, and for the first time on this trip, she wished she didn't know so much. Because deep down, she'd never look at her grandfather the same again.

Was there something he could have done to help those men?

Chapter Twenty-Three

The fading sun descended on one of Germany's most famous buildings, the Festspielhaus— Festival Hall—opened in 1876.

Ava crossed her arms as she looked around the manicured grounds in front of the famous opera house designed by Richard Wagner. A picture she'd seen on the Internet had shown scowling brownshirts with rifles on their shoulders, guarding the entrance. It also showed Hitler, standing at a podium near the front steps, wooing the crowd with his words and SS troops marching down the road. She shuddered.

Grandpa Jack and Grand-Paul had shared more of their stories at the hotel in Bayreuth and then asked if they could wait there to rest. She and Dennis had come to the Festspielhaus together, and while she was drawn to the front of the building, taking in the sight of the tall steps that Hitler had strode up hundreds of times, Dennis had walked just down the road to the Richard Wagner gardens to stretch his legs.

Ava had just returned her camera to its case when a young man approached, carrying a frayed knapsack over his shoulder and a digital camera in his hand. He smiled as he walked up to her—a flirty smile—and Ava felt heat rising to her cheeks. He reminded her of Brad Pitt in his younger years, only cuter.

"Excuse me." He had a bit of an accent, Scottish maybe.

"Yes?"

"I was wondering if you wouldna mind taking my photo. Maybe over here on the steps."

"Sure." She took the camera from him, and his fingers brushed hers.

"Beautiful evening." He smiled.

"Yes, it is." She lifted the camera and looked into the viewfinder.

"It seems like we are the last ones." He smiled slightly as she captured the shot.

Ava's stomach fell, and her grip tightened on his camera. She glanced around, looking for Dennis. "No, we're not the only ones. I'm with someone. He's still around. In fact, he should be here any second."

She snapped another shot and then held it out to the guy.

"I feel criminal having my photo taken here. It's not a happy place. I mean, the music of Wagner was beautiful, but I canna think of it without considering Hitler."

"I know what you mean. I had the same thought." Her shoulders relaxed slightly, realizing he only wanted to talk.

They stood in silence for a few moments looking at the opera house. From the corner of her eye she noticed his hand cover his heart, as if overcome with emotion.

"I wish more had been done to stop Hitler sooner," the man said.

She thought about telling him about her grandfather but changed her mind. Those stories seemed easy to share on video—to thousands of viewers—but not so easy to talk about one-on-one. She wouldn't know where to start.

He turned, catching her looking at him, and smiled. "Will you be here long? In the area?"

"No, we're heading out in the morning."

"Do you have dinner plans? I—"

"Yes, she does, actually."

Ava jumped at the voice. It was Dennis. She turned and her face grew warm. Though Dennis spoke to the man, his eyes were on her. "We have dinner reservations. Just the two of us."

She felt his hand on the small of her back. She'd enjoyed their other dinner, but she didn't know it would be repeated. *This must be the surprise.*

"Someplace really nice too." Dennis glanced at his watch. "And we should get going."

The man looked from Dennis to her, as if hoping Ava would offer a different story.

"I do have plans, like my friend said. But it was nice to meet you."

Dennis's hand stayed on her back as they walked away. The guy stayed behind, snapping photos.

When they approached the car, Ava looked up into his face. "So where are we going to dinner?"

Dennis paused. "I had to find a way to get you out of there."

"Excuse me?" Ava turned to him.

"You're not in Kansas anymore, Ava." His tone softened. "I don't want anything to happen to you."

"I don't live in Kansas. I live in Seattle. I work downtown. I deal with people far scarier than that guy nearly every day."

Dennis refused to meet her gaze. "That's the problem. It's the safe-looking guys you need to watch out for."

Ava's stomach knotted, and she imagined the waist belt being snapped over her lap as she prepared for the roller-coaster ride again. An older woman—hunched over with a scarf around her hair—walked past, toward the opera house. She looked at them curiously.

Ava didn't know what to think. Mostly she was frustrated by the fact that he'd lied about dinner, and she was a little perturbed at the old guys for setting her up for a surprise that wasn't going to happen.

He blew out a soft breath. "What if I *were* trying to rescue you?" Dennis's voice faltered. He ran a hand through his short-cropped hair.

Ava tried to hide her smile. It wasn't just that he'd admitted that, it was the sweet, shy way he said it. "You were?"

"You were standing sort of close, and it's not the first time I rescued you. Remember Tom Stein when he was teaching you to foxtrot?"

Laughter burst from Ava's lips. "Tom was like ninety years old!"

"Yes, but you never thanked me for cutting in."

In the graying sky above, the sun was starting to dip behind the horizon. A cold breeze picked up, and Ava pulled her arms tight to her.

"Your mom sent my grandpa a copy of that video. She caught it on tape. Tom was not letting you leave the dance floor, and you were relieved when I cut in. I must have watched it over fifty times."

"Why?"

"Because that's what you do when it's the only video you have of the girl you always thought you'd marry."

The smile on her face faded. "What?"

He stepped back from her and walked around to the car. "Never mind. Forget it."

"You can't do that." She waited for him to unlock the car, and then she got inside. "You can't just say something like that without clarifying it."

"This really isn't the best time to talk about it, Ava. Not when you're angry."

Ava took in a deep breath and then released it slowly. The headache that had been building all day now pounded, knocking at her temples with force. She placed two fingers to her forehead.

"You know, you're right. This isn't the best time to talk about it. Besides, what does it matter now?"

"You're right. It doesn't matter." Dennis looked away. "I don't know why I thought it would."

Chapter Twenty-Four

When they got back to the hotel, they discovered the grandpas had found a place for dinner.

"We went for a walk and saw a nice restaurant down the street. Are you ready?" Grand-Paul asked.

Dennis looked to Ava. "Is that okay?" His voice was tight. "We wouldn't want you to miss a deadline." It was more of an accusation than a statement.

She forced a grin. "There's more to life than work, right?" She looked at Dennis to see his response. He didn't give her a chance to gauge his reaction; instead he walked to the door.

It was only a short walk down the block to a large structure that looked like an old hunting lodge. The lights were low when they entered, and laughter met them as they stepped inside. Ava felt as if she'd stepped into a medieval hunting lodge, with animal mounts, heavy wooden tables, and buxom waitresses in peasant blouses carrying large trays.

A waiter noticed them enter and approached. "*Ja*, my friends are back. Come, I have saved the best table for you." The waiter hurried forward with quick steps and led them to a large round table in the center of the room. Ava wasn't surprised to see that other people were already sitting there.

Grand-Paul sat first, taking the seat closer to an older gentleman. Two other German men were seated next to the older man. Paul sat next to them, then Ava, then Grandpa Jack. There were two empty chairs between Grandpa Jack and the Germans, and Ava wondered if those seats would also be filled. Ava's chest was tense as she sat. Whether she turned to her left or her right she'd need to figure out how to hide her true emotions.

The chairs were thick, heavy, and wood. And tall too. Her toes barely touched the floor. It took an extra boost from the waiter for Ava to push in her seat.

"You Americans?" The elderly man sitting next to Grand-Paul asked. He was hard to hear over the noise of the other diners in the room, and Ava leaned closer to Dennis so she could hear him better.

"Yes, have you been to the States?" Grand-Paul asked.

"Many times. My son lives there. He marries American woman. I visit winters in Florida."

They talked for a while about Florida, the sun, and long plane rides, and then Ava noticed the man's gaze focus across the table at Grandpa Jack's hat.

"What part you fight here?" the German asked.

Ava waited, but her grandfather didn't answer. Instead, he looked at her with a furrowed brow. "What did he say?" Grandpa Jack asked.

"He wanted to know where you fought in the war. He saw your hat."

Grandpa Jack locked eyes with the man. He leaned forward and spoke loudly. "In the Bulge, near Bastogne. Was the coldest winter I ever faced."

"Yes, *ja*," the German man answered. "De tanks." The man's eyes narrowed slightly as if he was remembering something. His lips pressed together, and he nodded. "I was there too."

Ava's fork paused midway to her mouth.

Grandpa Jack didn't seem surprised. He looked at Paul, and Paul turned, meeting his gaze. What emotions were going through them? She studied her grandfather's face—curiosity, sadness, a hint of shame. Then they both looked at the man with worry. Was he angry at them? Would he make a big deal out of this?

The man's face relaxed and he smiled. "I hope you enjoy Germany more dis trip."

"I would say so." Grandpa Jack chuckled. "Better food. Better accommodations."

The German laughed, and Grandpa Jack and Grand-Paul joined in.

For the rest of the dinner they talked about the winter weather of '45, tanks, and the horrible food they had lived on. Dennis joined in, asking questions about German airplanes, but Ava remained silent, listening, amazed. It seemed strange they were able to talk like this. This morning, before they headed out, Grandpa Jack and Grand-Paul had told her a few stories about the concentration camps. She saw the monuments that listed American losses. She knew without a doubt that if they'd faced each other in the war they wouldn't have hesitated to shoot. Guilt pinpricked her heart.

Ava glanced first at Grandpa Jack and then at Dennis. Neither had set out to hurt her. Neither could be considered her enemy, still she held tightly to their faults.

She thought about how stressful it was trying to do everything right, make everyone happy, keep the show—and her life—on schedule. She got exhausted trying to keep up. Now, she was placing the same unrealistic expectations on those she cared about. Her hands played with the napkin on her lap, and the discomfort from a moment before faded.

If old enemies can forgive, how could I do any less?

She placed a hand on Dennis's arm. Feeling the

touch, he glanced at her, his eyebrows lifting in surprise.

"These are my brothers," the older German man continued, pointing to the men sitting with him. "They did not fight in war. Hitler Youth. Their hatred is greater. Never come to America."

Ava thought it was a strange thing for the man to say. She didn't know much about Hitler Youth, but she didn't understand how they could have more hatred than those who actually fought on the battlefield. Perhaps on the battlefield your own humanity helped you to understand the enemy better?

She studied the German brothers as they ate, and the more she watched them, the more she felt their tension over sharing a table with Americans. The two men's gazes were on their plates. They ate quickly without talking, without emotion.

After dinner everyone was too full for dessert, so the waiter brought the two groups the check. Ava paid for her and her grandfather with her credit card, tucking the receipt inside her purse, reminding herself she needed to make sure to separate the expenses.

"Your son and his wife?" the German man asked Grand-Paul, pointing to Dennis and Ava.

"I'm his grandson," Dennis answered for his grandfather. Dennis wiped his face with his napkin and then leaned forward, resting his forearm on the table. "And this beautiful woman is Jack's granddaughter." He gestured toward Jack. "She's a friend, not my wife. Although . . ."

Ava ribbed him. "It's not fair bringing that up here." She wiped her face with her cloth napkin to hide her grin. "Especially since you said we had to wait to talk about it."

Ava couldn't help but notice Grand-Paul's face light up. "Yes, well now, there's a good topic to talk about," he said as he rose.

As they walked back to the hotel, Grand-Paul and Dennis walked in front, and Ava stayed back with her grandfather. She was surprised by the number of people on the streets, but her mind was still on the dinner, or rather their company. From the look on his face, Ava could tell her grandfather was thinking about it too.

"How did you feel about our dinner companion?" she asked. "Was it hard, sharing a table with someone, you know—someone you likely fought at the Bulge? Or maybe even Chenogne?"

At the mention of that name, something flashed in his eyes. Sadness? Or maybe regret?

"The German wasn't at Chenogne." Grandpa Jack's jaw twitched. "Is that what you have questions about, Ava? About the POWs?"

"How did you know I knew?"

Grandpa Jack paused, looking at her. Then he lowered his gaze in sadness. "Sweetheart, I can see it in your eyes."

Ava bit her lip and realized that the secret was out—or at least *that* secret.

"Whenever you're ready," she said, taking his arm and leading him. "If you ever are."

Chapter Twenty-Five

The moonlight gave the room a soft glow. There were only a few more nights until she was back at home, in her own apartment, and in her own life.

Her life seemed so far away. It was amazing how quickly this had become the norm—living out of a suitcase, sharing a room with her grandfather, waking to the sounds of a different world filtering through the window, listening to stories, trying to capture the most meaningful parts in video, spending time with Dennis.

She slid underneath the down comforter and let her head rest on the soft pillow. She should get some bedding like this when she returned home.

Ava felt sad as she considered her life going back to normal. She wondered if Dennis would write or visit. She wondered if they'd ever get around to talking about his hopes that he'd marry her someday. She turned to her side and pressed her fingers to her temple. He'd lied about the surprise—about going someplace special. His mind changed with his moods. It was better, she decided, not to trust Dennis. She could forgive him concerning everything in the past, but she would be cautious about the future.

Ava also wished she'd hear more from Jill. Jill never did let her know if that second contact had any information. Even though it had only been a day, she'd hoped to hear something. Maybe she could just face the fact that most likely nothing would come out of their wild-goose chase. Her grandfather's experience with Angeline had happened over a half century ago. The world had been in an upheaval during the war and afterward. Families had lost touch. Some never went home or went back to the place where there were so many memories.

Maybe, even if they didn't find the girl, Ava could tell the story in a follow-up video. Just knowing that her grandpa remembered and cared all these years was a wonderful story in itself. Then again, she couldn't tell the story without relating that he'd been the one who'd fired the shots and that an innocent woman had died. Her stomach ached thinking of it.

She rolled to her back again and thought instead about the video she'd just finished up and sent. For some reason, it didn't seem as strong as the previous ones. Actually, the stories Grand-Paul and Grandpa Jack shared were interesting. She was sure viewers would be enthralled. It was her commentary that had bothered her. Looking at her captured image, she seemed older. It was clear that the trip was no vacation. It was also clear in the waver of her voice that she seemed more uncertain than she'd been at the beginning. The more she found out, the less she seemed to know—about her grandfather, about Dennis. About herself.

She was exhausted, but as the minutes ticked by, her mind didn't stop. Ava tossed and turned, thinking about all her grandfather had told her about the camp. It was hard for him to tell those stories, but he at least told them. He hadn't clammed up like he did every time Chenogne was mentioned. Which reminded her that she hadn't gotten an e-mail with the scanned page from that book either.

Ava flipped to her back and stared at the ceiling, listening to her grandfather's snores. Whatever happened in Chenogne must still weigh on his mind. On his heart. Did he ever forget? Did he ever have peace from the memories?

Muted sunlight broke through the clouds and shined down onto the car. Both her grandfather and Grand-Paul had mischievous looks on their faces, and when Dennis stepped out of the hotel with a big smile, she knew something was up.

"The surprise is that we aren't going all the way to Linz—at least not this morning," Dennis said, jingling the car keys in his hand.

"I don't understand." She held up the brochure.

"Linz is supposed to be next on the trip." The other veterans had been there nearly a week, and she was eager to meet up with them again. While she'd greatly enjoyed her grandfather and Grand-Paul's stories, she also hoped to videotape some of the other guys. More than that, she wanted to find Angeline Pirard. Her heart beat faster, thinking she could be the one.

"We've made arrangements." Grand-Paul stepped forward, pointing his cane at Ava. "There's a glass museum in Passau Jack and I want to go to. We thought it would give you and Dennis a chance to spend some time together without us underfoot."

"I was hoping we could spend the day together. Just you and me." Dennis didn't say it, but she could see the rest of the message in his eyes. *Our time is getting short.*

After a three-hour drive from Bayreuth to Passau, they dropped off their grandpas at the museum and drove to St. Stephen's Cathedral.

"Don't worry. The guys promised to give you plenty of video footage tonight to make up for the day trip," Dennis said as they got out.

"I don't doubt that. It'll be great. They seem to really pour out the stories when they know it'll mean my having more time to spend with you." She glanced around, trying to appreciate the sights of this medieval part of town. She didn't feel whole without her grandfather at her side. It was as if she were missing an arm. How was she going to handle it when they all went their separate ways? Her heart ached just thinking about it.

"I really appreciate your planning this day. This place is so beautiful." She paused and tucked her hands in her jeans pockets. Her fingers brushed her cell phone, and she thought about calling Jill to check to see if there was any news on Angeline. Then again, if Jill did have news, she would have called. She looked up at the baroque cathedral. There wasn't anything in Seattle that compared. It was white with a green roof—bronze, she guessed, that had tarnished over time. Intricate carvings graced the arched window frames. Angel statues rose from the roofline like messengers prepared to fly to the heavens at a moment's notice. If the exterior was this intricate, Ava couldn't even imagine what the interior looked like. Cathedrals like this were designed to give illiterate people glimpses of a glorious God, and it amazed her how common men had displayed that glory.

It made her think about her own life. Was she really living it in a way that displayed God? She wasn't sure. Especially lately. She had thought living a good life and doing the best with her talents was enough. Maybe it wasn't.

Her cell phone buzzed, startling her. Maybe it was Jill with news of Angeline.

"Hey." She held the phone up. "I need to get this."

"Sure." He turned his back, and she stepped several feet away. "Jill?"

"Guess again."

Jay.

Ava swallowed hard and then looked over her shoulder at Dennis. He eyed her curiously, and she quickly turned away. "Hi."

"I got your e-mail." His voice was tender and sweet, like it had always been. Hearing him, it was almost as if the breakup never happened.

He cleared his throat. "Is this a good time?"

Ava's knees weakened. She hurried toward a bench where an older couple sat. She sat on the end, turning her back to them. "No, it's actually not. I told you I'd call when I got back."

"I couldn't wait any longer to tell you I was stupid. I made the biggest mistake of my life. I'm half of the whole we used to be . . ."

She didn't answer. It had been everything she'd wanted to hear before the trip. Now she was a different person. This trip had changed her. She'd laughed, she'd cried, she'd feared, she'd doubted, and . . . she might even be falling in love with someone else.

Tourists milled around her, taking photos of the structure and lining up near the entrance.

She looked at the sky, seeing that the sun was coming out, hot and bright. She unzipped her sweater and took it off. Her whole body felt hot. Her heart ached.

"I can't talk about this now."

"I have to know one thing. Do you care about me at all?"

She balled her free hand into a fist and lowered her head. "You called me in Europe to ask me that?"

"No, I called to tell you that these months without you have been empty. But I did call to ask that too. I have to know."

"You hurt me." She lowered her voice to a whisper. "We should have been married by now."

"I just need to know that I still hold a place in your heart."

"Yes, of course."

There was silence on his end of the line.

"We'll talk more when you get back. Talk to you later, Av."

"Yes, okay." She hung up the phone, not quite sure what had happened. Her mind felt full of quicksand. A hand touched her shoulder and she jumped.

"Everything okay?"

She looked up at Dennis. "Of course. Just business matters in Seattle." She rose and brushed her hair off her shoulders. "I'm ready now. Are we going to take in some sights?"

Dennis chuckled and adjusted the rim of his baseball hat lower over his eyes. "Personally, I thought it would be nice to walk around, enjoy the sunshine, talk."

"You're right. A walk sounds nice."

They walked shoulder to shoulder toward a large river. The town around them was quaint, medieval. Small shops and cafés lined the streets.

"Are you hungry?" Dennis asked.

"Not really." She didn't tell him that her stomach was filled with a hundred butterflies. She'd wanted time to be with him and talk. Now that she had the chance, Jay had ruined everything. *Why did I tell him I still care? Stupid, stupid.*

Yet even as they walked, her mind took her back to the three years she and Jay had dated. They'd gotten along great. They enjoyed the same things. They'd seemed like the perfect couple. And then there was Dennis. She glanced up at him. How could this guy, who was both handsome and kind, care for her after all these years?

Somewhere inside, she still felt as if something would happen and reality would prove her doubts about him to be right. What if she was just someone he'd hang out with because she was his best option at the time? After all, she hadn't heard from him in fifteen years. Even back then, their relationship hadn't been grounded in reality. He'd been in a make-believe world, thinking that they could jump into marriage and a life together. She'd been the realistic one, telling him she wanted to finish college. That had always been in her timeline—followed by the husband, house, a dog, and 2.5 kids.

But now it was different. They were mature. They could support themselves. They could probably make it together. Then again maybe this was a fluke. They were in Europe. She took in the river, the medieval-looking buildings. She felt at peace with Dennis walking by her side. Real life never could be this good, could it?

"Let's walk along the trail by the Danube," he suggested, tucking his hands into his jeans pockets.

"That's the Danube?" She pointed to the wide, blue-green river ahead. "Like the song?"

"The one and only."

"I never thought I'd really see the Danube."

"What places do you *really* hope to travel to? Other than Paris, of course."

"I live in Seattle, so anywhere with sun. Hawaii maybe. Or Arizona."

"Is that the type of place you'd pick for your honeymoon?" He cocked an eyebrow at her.

"What do you mean?" She slowed her pace.

"You know, after a wedding. A honeymoon? Is that where you'd planned on going with your fiancé?"

Ava stopped and looked up at the large, arched walkway that led to an open-air market. The last thing she wanted to do was talk to

Dennis about her and Jay's plans.

"Look at those cute shops." She pointed to a narrow street and the small shops that looked like places Snow White's dwarfs would tend. "I want to get my mom a souvenir before I return. Do you want to look?"

Dennis didn't answer.

She looked at him, and his brow furrowed.

"Okay, since you don't want to answer that question . . . does Mr. Mystery Man have a name?"

She released an exasperated sigh. "Yes, it was Jay."

"*Was?* Is he dead?"

"No." She rubbed her arms. They couldn't stop their trembling.

"What happened?"

She ran her hands over her face. "I just got a note one day from Jay telling me that it wasn't going to work. That the wedding was off. It was sudden—and painful." A man and a woman walked toward them down the sidewalk, and Ava and Dennis stepped to the side. After the couple passed, she turned to him and rubbed her brow. "Do you want to know more?"

"Yes." Dennis waved to a little girl in a stroller. The toddler waved back. "How long did you date?"

They walked through some sort of park. The shrubs were manicured, flowers were planted in neat rows, and even the German children seemed to play in an orderly and quiet way.

"Three years." She shrugged. "Please let that be your last question."

"Do you want me to tell you about some of my girlfriends?"

"I don't think I want to hear."

"The list is short. It won't take long. There was Jane—a worship leader from my grandpa's church. And then there was Lisa, an intern from my grandpa's church. And finally Jennifer. She—"

"Let me guess, you met her at Grand-Paul's church?"

"He's quite the matchmaker. They were all pretty and nice and . . . they just didn't seem right. The longest relationship lasted six months, and she finally broke it off because she said—" He paused.

"What?"

"She said that every time I looked at her, I wasn't really looking at *her.* That it was as if I was seeing someone else, or at least wishing it was someone else. Those are her words, not mine."

Ava wanted to ask more, but at the same time she was afraid to.

"Look at that." Ava pointed to a hillside up ahead. A large castle looked like something from a fairy tale. Then again, she couldn't picture a fairy tale like this. "Could you imagine what it would have been like to have lived there?"

"Cold, drafty, and rat-infested would be my guess."

"Wow, so romantic."

"You want romantic?" He reached down and took her hand. His hand felt warm, and she let him lead her. They reached the river and followed a paved trail. As they walked, Ava looked over at the water that was more gray than blue. There were sailboats, and in the distance she saw a steamboat chugging downstream.

"So, how did Jay end it? You said he left a note, but there has to be more to it than that."

"It's not the most fun story to tell."

"I still want to hear it. I can't know you—really know you, Ava—if I don't know all of it—even that stuff that makes you cry."

Dennis stopped by a grassy hill, stepped off the trail, hunkered down, and patted the ground. Ava nodded and they sat side by side. She released a long breath and stared at the water.

"I doubt I'll cry, but what happened is that he— Jay was supposed to go to his tux fitting on Saturday. Friday night I got home from work to discover there was a large gift bag by my apartment door. I immediately knew who it was from. I'd given him the bag with his last birthday present inside and he'd saved it. There was a card on top of the bag—or what I thought was a card.

"I opened the envelope, and there were just five

sentences. 'Ava, I'm sorry. This isn't going to work out. I'm sorry. Have a good life. I'll be praying for you.' "

Her hands trembled, and she placed her fingers to her lips. "I haven't told that to anyone before. Even my friends. I told them he sent me an e-mail, which would have been easier. Maybe he would have gone longer than five sentences."

"What a jerk." Dennis spat the words. "He didn't even have the guts to tell you face to face and then to give you a gift—"

She shook her head. "It wasn't a gift."

"But you said—"

"I said it was a gift *bag*. Inside were just some of my things. My running shoes, which I'd forgotten at his house. Some CDs he'd borrowed. Some photographs of me that he'd taken and had framed. I—" She started and then lowered her head. Tears pooled in her eyes, which surprised her.

"You what?" His hand gently rubbed her back, and his touch made it even harder to hold the emotions in.

"Okay, you really want to know?" She lifted her face and wiped away a tear. "I couldn't have felt more worthless if he'd rented a billboard and posted it on the I-5 that he was dumping me. In fact, that probably would have been better." Her voice rose and others sitting near them turned, but she didn't care.

"It would have been much better if there was some big fight. We could have fought about work, or family, or anything. It would have been great if he would have yelled at me, and if I would have yelled even louder at him. And if I would have thrown something and hit him square in the forehead—that would have really helped. But I got a stupid note and all my stuff back. And when I tried to call a dozen times, he ignored the calls. And then he changed his number." A sob broke through, surprising her. She wiped her dripping nose with the back of her hand. "And so do you know where that left me?"

The motion of his hand stopped.

"It left me thinking and rethinking. Replaying our conversations and trying to figure out what the heck I did wrong. I did something, that's for sure." She swallowed hard and a hiccup escaped. "And I—I just have to make sure I don't do it again. It hurts too much." She turned and buried her face in his shoulder. "It just hurts."

"Oh, Ava." Dennis scooted closer to her and then wrapped both arms around her, pulling her tight. She felt warm, protected. She couldn't remember the last time she felt so cherished. She also couldn't help but think back to Jay's voice on the phone. Even after all he'd done to her, it still felt good to hear his voice. To know he cared. That he'd missed her.

They sat there for a while, her just resting in

Dennis's arms. He smelled like a spicy musk, and his T-shirt was soft on her cheek. A boat passed by, and passengers on the deck took photos of the town. She would be in their snapshots, forever captured in this embrace. She liked the thought of that.

"And you know what the saddest thing was?" she finally muttered, leaning back slightly.

"What?" Dennis paused and turned, looking into her eyes.

"When I got the note and looked into the bag, the first thing that came to mind was 'That's it? This is the man I was going to marry and that's all he had of mine?' "

"I can top that." Dennis's eyebrows peaked. "I have the beach towel that you used every time we went to the lake. The pink one with yellow flowers. I found it in my car after you left, and I still use it to dry my car after I wash it." He chuckled. "I also have the program from when we went to see *Grease* at the community theater." His tone grew more serious. "And the photos of us sitting on the roof of the cabin, trying to coax down the squirrels with raisins.

"I also have the three letters you wrote to me, including the one that said you met some guy at college." Then he took her hand. "After the big fight, I was going to go along with your suggestion that we just be friends, but even that didn't work so well—"

"The guy was Chris Anderson. He played football and was a total jerk. We dated for three weeks." She pulled her hand from his, mostly because she was afraid. She could feel the anxiety moving through her body like an electric current, a reminder of the pain of losing Jay and a realization she'd messed up this whole thing with Dennis all those years ago. Messed up big-time.

"I can't believe you kept all that stuff. It's crazy. Really crazy. And kind of creepy." She smirked. She rose and moved to the railing at the river's edge that overlooked the water.

"You meant a lot to me." He followed her, standing by her side. "I wish we could start over. Maybe this trip is a second chance."

Ava shook her head. "It's just like that summer. When this is done, I'll go back to my life and you'll go back to yours and we'll lose touch just like we did before."

"You don't really believe that. You're just saying that because you're afraid of getting hurt again. I can see it in your eyes. Besides, we're adults now. We have cell phones. Heck, e-mail has been invented. You really don't think I'll just return to my normal life and forget about you."

She turned and began walking.

"Ava, will you stop? Will you look at me?"

"I can't."

"Why?"

"Because you're right. I'm afraid." Ava slowed,

but she refused to look at him. She couldn't.

Dennis grabbed her arm. She paused, but she still refused to turn. "If I look at you, I'm going to fall in love with you. And if I love you, it's just going to mess everything up."

"What 'everything' is going to be messed up?"

"Nobody's perfect, Dennis. Even though I try my best, I'm far from perfect. And you're not perfect. And do you know what happens when two imperfect people get together?"

"What?"

"Disaster. Heartbreak. Pain. A big mess. Don't you see? I told you I was falling for Chris Anderson because he wasn't nearly as wonderful as you. If things didn't work out with Chris it wouldn't hurt so badly. It was the same thing with Jay. He was nice and handsome, but he talked too much. And he spent too much time at the gym, and his feet stank horribly."

Laughter burst from Dennis's lips.

Ava looked up at the sky, focusing on the white clouds being pushed across the sun. "I was grateful for those flaws because I figured then Jay could deal with all my flaws. I didn't have to be perfect, because he wasn't perfect. If things didn't work, I could remember all the things I didn't like about Jay and so much the better. I realized this after he broke it off. Realized it had been in the back of my head all along." She tucked her hands into her jeans pocket. Her fingers touched her cell phone, and she tried to push Jay's voice out of her mind.

"Is that what you thought about us too, that things wouldn't work out?"

"I didn't know how to deal with it. I felt too young to be making adult decisions. You wanted us to move near each other. You were talking about marriage in the near future. I had a list of things I needed to do first."

"I would've waited," he said quietly.

Even though he held her hands close, she refused to look at his face. She heard the pain in his voice.

Finally, she lifted her face and looked into his eyes.

"Don't you see, Dennis? I love your smile and your passion. I love the way you talk to me, and how you make me talk about things that no one else would care about. I love the way you think that the best day is one that you spend with your grandpa. And I love how beautiful and wonderful I feel when I'm with you."

"And the problem is?" he asked, scratching his head.

"The problem is that nothing that wonderful can last," she admitted. "It would end, and I'd be heartbroken big-time. I grew up with a single mom. That's all I've ever known. And while most moms dump on their exes, my mom did just the opposite. She told me how great and handsome and smart he was. No one came close to him. Every day I could tell she still thought about him. It was heartbreaking to grow up like that. She'd found someone she'd given her heart to and then had to live her life without him. I—" Tears interrupted her words. "I couldn't imagine that. I didn't want to live like that. I didn't want to hurt like that . . . so I found a way that I thought would hurt less."

"Oh, Ava."

Before she knew what was happening, his arms were around her again, pulling her into his chest. "I wouldn't have left." He kissed the top of her head. "It's no accident we're here, now, together. It's no accident at all."

He lifted his hand and brushed the hair from her cheek, tucking it behind her ear. "What I do want is to love you. And to be loved by you."

"Dennis . . . I don't—"

"You don't have to feel pressured to tell me how you feel yet. I just want to know if you think this is something worth pursuing—something that won't end when we fly two different directions. I have a feeling it could work, Ava. I have a feeling we could make it work."

Ava didn't answer. Instead, she stood on her toes, narrowing the gap between them, and brushed her lips against his.

Chapter Twenty-Six

After picking up their grandfathers, it took less than an hour and a half to get from Passau to Linz. When they got to the hotel, Ava couldn't help but smile as she saw the other veterans milling around, all wearing Eleventh Armored Division caps.

"You excited to talk to these guys?" Dennis reached over and squeezed her hand.

"If you are, don't let them know. You don't want them to tell you too many stories." Grand-Paul chuckled. "Theirs aren't nearly as interesting as ours." Then without hesitation, he and Grandpa Jack headed out to find their friends.

"I think I'll join them in a little bit." She yawned. Missed sleep last night was taking its toll. That and the fact she had too many things pressing on her heart.

"Why don't we meet downstairs in an hour?" she told Dennis.

"Sounds like a plan."

Dennis carried her luggage upstairs for her, and she opened the hotel door.

"Thanks," she whispered and then went inside. He looked down at her, as if wanting another kiss, but she quickly stepped back. "See you soon."

She carried her video equipment and small

satchel to the table and thought about checking her e-mail, but she was too tired. Just then, her eyes caught the address of the hotel on the stationery on the desk.

"Kaerntner Strasse," she mumbled. That sounded familiar. Ava went to her purse and pulled out the slip of paper on which she'd written down Angeline's address. It was the same street. What were the chances? Suddenly she was no longer tired. She grabbed her purse and camera and headed back downstairs. Outside the hotel, she checked the numbers. From the looks of it, Angeline's flat was only a few blocks from the downtown area.

Ava quickened her steps as she walked. How amazing it would be to end her trip by finding Angeline. Her grandfather had searched for her to no avail. Would God bring Ava to the woman just a couple blocks from the hotel?

The area changed from a business district to small apartment buildings as Ava approached the address she'd found online. A young woman was helping an elderly woman out of the car in front of it. Ava froze in place and her heart did a double beat. Would either of these women have the answer? She hurried to them.

"Excuse me. Do you speak English?"

The young woman lifted her head. "Little." She raised her hand and held up her fingers, showing just a small space between them.

"Do you know an Angeline Pirard? Does she live in this building?"

"*Ja*," the woman said. "She used to. She died few months ago."

Ava's heart sank. Had she missed Angeline by just a few months?

"But husband, he lives," the woman said. "Mr. Pirard should be home."

Mr. Pirard, yes of course. Pirard was her married name. Ava didn't know why she didn't think of it. Angeline would have most likely gotten married, which would make finding her even harder.

"No. No, thank you." Ava smiled and then took a step back. "I won't bother him at this time. But thank you for your help."

She turned and slowly walked back to the hotel, and the weight she'd been carrying returned. Finding the woman seemed even more impossible now. Doubt sent gray shadows across her heart.

Back at her hotel room, Ava glanced at the clock and was flustered to see she was already ten minutes late to meet Dennis, and she hadn't had a chance to check her e-mail to see if there was any news from Jill.

Forget the e-mail. She took in a deep breath, trying not to be too disappointed about Angeline. She still had an evening of interviews to look forward to.

She ran a comb through her hair, brushed her teeth, wiped smeared mascara from under her eyes, and was about to hurry downstairs when she noticed a note that her grandpa had written on the small desk. Her grandpa must have come by when she'd been out.

"Going with Paul to meet friends for dinner across the street. Meet us when you return."

Ava smiled and tucked the note in her pocket. The town wasn't very big, and she guessed it wouldn't be too hard to figure out where the restaurant "across the street" was.

She grabbed her camera and equipment and hurried downstairs. She scanned the small lobby, looking for Dennis. She didn't see him, and she was about to head outside when she noticed him standing on the small side deck just off the hotel's main patio.

From where he was standing, there was a good view of the main square and the large pillar statue. Gold-plated rays reflected light from the top. Heaviness weighed on her. She had to tell him about the phone call today. As much as she didn't like it, she still had feelings for Jay. Yet those feelings paled compared to how she felt for Dennis.

She approached him and placed a hand on his back. He turned to her, smiling. "Ava—"

She held up her hand, halting his words. "Before you say anything, there's something I need to tell you. That phone call today . . . it wasn't work. It was my former fiancé. It was from Jay."

Hurt flashed in his eyes and Ava thought she was going to be sick. She never wanted this. Never wanted to hurt Dennis.

"What did he want?" Dennis reached forward and took her hand as if holding on to a lifeline.

"He wanted to tell me he still cared. He wanted to know if I did too. I told him maybe, but now I know that's not true. After today I realized—"

"There you two are!" Grand-Paul's voice boomed across the patio, interrupting Ava's words.

"Yeah, we're here. Just enjoying the view. Beautiful place." Dennis stroked Ava's hair as he spoke, and Ava was certain she saw Grand-Paul's smile brighten at seeing their closeness. She'd wanted to tell Dennis more—how she felt about him—but now was not the time. She'd get another chance. She looked at him and smiled, hoping he believed that Jay wasn't the one she loved.

"Yes, well, it's pretty inside the restaurant too. Aren't you two hungry? Besides, there are some folks I want you to meet."

Ava poked Dennis's ribs with her finger. "I think it's time to go introduce ourselves. I have a feeling we're going to hear some stories."

"You think?" Dennis grabbed her hand and held it in his. Held it tight.

She squeezed it back. "Yes, I am looking forward to it. Looking forward to hearing the men's stories."

"But didn't you want to tell me something?"

278

Ava shrugged. "Later. Let's talk about that later."

Ava held her breath as she walked into the dining room of the small Austrian hotel across the street. As she scanned the room, she recognized many of the men. They were the same ones she had met her first night in Paris—a dozen in all. Yet there seemed to be something different about them. Or maybe the difference was in her.

Ava tried to remember names as her grandfather introduced his friends again. Bob, John, Arthur, Frank, Harold, Ray . . .

The restaurant was busy, and they found a round table in the corner. Dennis sat by Grand-Paul, and the look in his eye said that he never wanted to leave his grandfather's side. The realization that they'd soon be losing Grand-Paul hit her again, and she was thankful that they'd had this week together. Grandpa Jack sat by Dennis. He pointed to a small table near the back of the room.

"Ava, I've convinced a few of the guys to talk to you," Grandpa Jack said. "I asked the waitress to save that table for you."

"Really? That's, uh, great." Ava didn't have the heart to tell him that it would be hard to videotape with all the noise. She'd figure out a way. Ava scanned the guys' faces, and none of the men looked away or seemed intimidated. She had a feeling that if she had enough time, she could get each of them to tell her a story or two. "You told them I'm videotaping, right?"

"Yes." Grandpa Jack nodded. "Ray here said that was fine just as long as you taped his good side. But I told him that would be hard if he was sitting on it." Laughter burst from the guys, and Ava joined in, surprised. Her eyes widened as she looked at her grandfather, and she had a hard time catching her breath from her laughter. "Grandpa, did I hear what I just thought I heard?"

Grandpa Jack was as gentle as they came, but Ava had forgotten how puckish his humor could be when he was around his veteran friends. It was as if he could be freer with them—even freer than he was with his friends at home. Maybe because they'd seen him at his best and his worst, and they still respected him. Maybe because he felt young again when he was in their presence, and some of the spunk of his younger years dug its way out.

A man entered, and all heads turned his direction. Grandpa Jack tugged on her arm and then pointed. "That's Mitch Thompson—Major Thompson now. He has a great story about how he and his brother met up on the battlefield. You should talk to him about that."

"Jack! There you are," the man called from the doorway.

Mitch Thompson strode over to them, and Ava found herself sitting tall in his presence. He still looked tough, with his broad shoulders, square face, and crew cut. Even though he wore a simple blue blazer and jeans, he had an aura of command.

"We missed you on the bus, but I'm not sure you missed us," he teased Paul. "Heard you were gallivanting through Europe with a beautiful woman." Mitch looked at Ava and winked.

"Yes, well, Ava here didn't let us say no. She figured since we were here, we might as well see it all. How was your trip?" Grandpa Jack asked.

"Helluva trip, if I say so myself. Not what we thought, but we've seen a lot of the countryside. My only regret is not seeing Bastogne, but maybe that's for the best."

"Major Thompson," Ava dared to say, "my grandfather told me there's a story of you and your brother meeting up on the battlefield. I'd love to interview you sometime."

He cocked his head and looked at her, as if taking stock of her. Finally, he winked and he smiled. "Well, young lady. It's quite a story. If I do talk into that video camera you'll have to shoot my left side; it's the more handsome of the two."

More laughter rumbled around the table and Mitch looked puzzled.

"Yes, your left cheek is the best," one of the other guys said.

Ava tried to hold in her own laughter. She straightened her shoulders even more and lifted her chin. "Of course, Major. I'd be happy to shoot whatever side you'd like."

Her comment made him smile even wider. He squeezed her shoulder. "I knew I liked you."

Major Thompson asked the waitress for a quiet place in a side room. He then ordered the house special for Ava's dinner, and they exchanged small talk until it arrived.

"Feel free to eat while I talk, miss. I've lived around soldiers my whole life; nothing much distracts me from my mission. Enjoy."

"Thank you, Major." She set up her camera and then pressed RECORD. Then she dug into her food.

"There were six of us boys total. Two in the navy and four in the army. My oldest brother, Howard, was in Europe. He was an officer." Then he went on to tell her how their divisions met on the battlefield, how the two brothers found each other when their two units fought side by side. They were allowed one meal together before returning, not knowing if they'd ever see each other again. Thankfully, they survived and made it home.

"Well, thank you, Major. Thank you for your story."

"One more thing, miss; I think this is important. Look around and you'll see everyday heroes. Each time you perform an unselfish act in spite of your own desires or needs, it takes courage. I don't know about you, but the unselfish act does not come naturally to me. I am a self-centered person.

So it takes some effort and some courage to ask the God of grace to help me to be selfless."

Ava smiled, wondering how many men under the major's command had heard this speech through the years. She'd have to note where it was on the tape. It would work well for her video.

"You're right." She glanced at her grandfather, Dennis, and Grand-Paul, who had snuck in at the end of the interview.

The major rose and then left everyone with a firm handshake before walking over and finding a seat with another group of veterans.

Grandpa Jack smiled. "Mitch always was that intense."

"You're telling me. He was a twenty-four-year-old kid and acted like he was running the show," Grand-Paul said, chuckling. "At least it makes for an interesting Friday night."

Ava turned to Dennis. "Yes, and I'm thankful it's Friday. I don't have to turn in a video for tomorrow! I'm so excited I don't have to stay up late. I get to sleep."

"It also means tomorrow's the ceremony at Mauthausen. It's going to be a busy day and a hard one."

"We should head for bed, Jack. Let's give these young ones time to say good night without chaperones." Grand-Paul winked and stood. Then he started his slow journey to their hotel across the street. Grandpa Jack joined him.

"It really seemed you were enjoying those guys' stories," Dennis said.

"I did. They're great and I hope I get to talk to more of the guys tomorrow. They have so many tales. I want to hear them all, but . . ." Her voice trailed.

"But what?"

"The more I think about it, the more I see now that this is how God planned it—for us to travel separately from the group. If we'd been with all of them, I would have missed so much about my grandpa's story. Grandpa's not loud or bold. He steps out of the limelight. If there'd been all these strong personalities around, the videos I sent would be completely different, not to mention we never would have gone to the farmhouse, and I never would have heard the story about Angeline."

"That's true. Also, there's us. I don't think we would have had the chance to talk—not with all the old soldiers vying for your attention." He stretched his hand toward hers. She took it and allowed Dennis to fold her into his embrace.

"Are you ready for tomorrow?"

She nodded. "It'll be difficult but good. I'm excited."

"What about the day after and the day after that?"

Ava stepped back slightly and looked into his face, unsure. "What's the day after?"

Dennis smiled. "The beginning of the rest of our lives."

Dennis's words played through Ava's mind as she made it up the stairs to her room. She wished she could say that she was as optimistic about their future as he was. She still had to face talking to Jay. Ava had a feeling that only then—when she had closure with her ex-fiancé—could she commit herself to Dennis completely.

In her room, she checked her cell phone, but there were no messages. She turned on the computer and tried to connect to the Internet, but it wasn't working. She called the front desk and discovered the line was down.

She couldn't imagine how stressed she would have been if the Internet had been down on any of the other nights when she had to send a video.

Ava got ready for bed. She was amazed that it was not even midnight. As she lay there, she thought about everything. The trip. The old stories. The new stories. Jay. The day with Dennis. Sure, she hadn't found Angeline, but she'd work on that when she got back. She'd come to Europe thinking she'd visit a few sites, make her boss happy, save her job, and have a nice time with her grandfather. But what she'd found was so much more. Her chest felt full, or maybe it was her heart.

Yes, definitely her heart.

Chapter Twenty-Seven

There wasn't a cloud in the sky. Ava hung the camera bag on one shoulder and her satchel on the other, and walked away from the rental car. After leaving Linz, they made their way to the town of Mauthausen, near the concentration camp with the same name. Beyond the grass was a wide river, blue-gray. It flowed gently, peacefully. She set up and filmed the river for a few minutes and then scanned the hillsides. Lush, green meadows. Scatterings of trees. Just a few small farms dotted here and there.

Beautiful.

The countryside around the town of Mauthausen reminded her of the movie *The Sound of Music*. It had the same rolling hills and a large blue sky that seemed bigger than the one back home.

"It's the Danube." Her grandfather's voice interrupted her thoughts.

"Yes, and it's beautiful." She wanted to turn the camera on him but refrained. She continued to film the river and countryside and let the audio pick up his voice. She would film him later. Surely when he was part of the ceremony, he wouldn't mind having a camera in his face.

"It's beautiful here. I didn't expect this."

"It is." He cleared his throat. "That day started

out like this—the day that we got here the first time. But later it rained huge sheets of water. The Germans who surrendered at the concentration camp and were walking behind our jeeps back to headquarters were drenched. It seemed like God was crying with us."

Ava nodded and listened. She watched him and tried to memorize this moment—her grandfather, the beauty of the countryside. His words that tried to express all he felt but couldn't. His eyes that in a strange way explained more.

Ava smiled at his words, but she had something else she needed to talk to him about. "Grandpa, I've wanted to talk to you this whole trip, and I've failed. Before we go up there today, I need to apologize. That conversation we had at Thanksgiving—you were right. I was focusing all my attention on Jay and my job more than God. I'm sorry that I told you that my life wasn't any of your business. I can see now how brave it was for you to say something to me."

"Ava, dear, you were forgiven as soon as the words were out of your mouth. I knew you didn't like to hear my words, but I was hoping they would sink in."

He paused and looked to the high hill. In the distance, she could barely make out the tall, stone walls of the camp. Horror in the midst of beauty.

"I found God here, you know," he finally said. "As you probably saw from my letters, I struggled with my faith all through the war. How could God let all this happen? That's what I wanted to know.

"Then the day I opened those camp gates, He changed me. There were thousands and thousands of prisoners. They were no more than skin and bones. They told us about working in the quarry. They were beaten, starved. I saw what evil and sin does, and God reminded me that He was the way out. If we come to Him, continually, He opens the gates. If we follow Him, He leads."

He reached into his back pocket, and Ava could hear the rustling of paper. When he held them out to her, she noticed they were letters. "Here are three more letters I brought with me. There are more at home, but they're just news and boring reports. I'm not proud of my anger at God during this time. Looking back, I'm surprised I wrote home in my pained state. I suppose I had to get those feelings out somewhere, and deep down I knew my parents would love and accept me, no matter what. Two letters tell of my pain and the last one . . . well, a new freedom, but you'll see."

Ava tucked them in her purse. "Thank you, Grandpa, for trusting me with these. I'm eager to read them, the last one especially."

They stood there, watching the river for a while, and then she finally spoke again. "Has being here after all these years helped you find freedom in all of it?" She wondered about Chenogne, but she refused to ask. In his own time he would tell her.

"No. I can't say it has. Even at my age, I'm still a work in progress." He fiddled with the buttons on his dress shirt.

She finished filming and then packed her things. "Should we go see if the other guys are ready?" She didn't want to press and ask him to explain. He had enough on his mind today. Besides, it wasn't like they needed to find complete closure before they headed home. They still had weeks and months in front of them to talk, to understand.

"Sure. We don't want to be late," he said.

Ava glanced at her cell phone for the time. They didn't have to be at the camp to meet Martha, the head of the memorial committee, for an hour, but for her grandfather anything less than very early was late. She hadn't gotten cell service since they left Linz, and the Internet hadn't been back online that morning. She was glad she'd gotten off the last of her videos on Thursday. And if all went as planned, she'd send some footage of today's ceremonies when they traveled down to Vienna to catch the flight home tomorrow.

Has the time really gone this quickly? It didn't seem possible.

Dennis was waiting by the car when they approached. Grand-Paul was already seated in the front seat.

Grandpa Jack climbed into the backseat, slamming the door.

"I think they're eager to get there." She offered Dennis a hug.

Dennis kissed the top of her forehead. "I think so. Everyone should have a day when they're celebrated as a hero. Our grandfathers deserve this."

"Yes, they do."

The two-lane road up to the concentration camp from Mauthausen village was busier than she guessed it was any other time of the year. Cars snaked up the hill, as well as tour buses with advertisements in various languages displayed on their sides.

Men in yellow vests directed traffic—buses to a field on the right, cars to the left.

Dennis parked.

As they climbed from the car, her grandfather walked more slowly than he usually did, as if the heaviness of the memories made it difficult to move.

Ava had seen photos of Mauthausen concentration camp on the Internet. They'd been in black and white, but in color it looked the same. The only difference was the bright blue sky in the background.

The parking lot ended at a large flight of stone steps that led up to the next level. They took the steps slowly, Grand-Paul leaning heavily on his cane. At the top were a road, a wall, and a series of gates. Each gate was big enough for a car to drive through.

The road looked as if it had been recently paved. The closer they got to the top of the hill, the more crowded it became with people.

"Look." Ava pointed to an old man. He was short and stocky, and he wore a black-and-white striped cap and a black-and-white scarf.

"They wear those to show they were former prisoners." Grandpa Jack pointed.

"But why would they do that? You'd think they'd want to forget," Ava said.

"They've come back as an act of defiance," Grand-Paul explained. "To come here—especially after all these years—proves Hitler didn't win. Evil didn't win. They survived against the odds. They live."

"They also come to remember those they lost," Grandpa Jack continued. "They have no cemeteries to take flowers to. Many of them don't even know when their loved ones died, or under what circumstances. Yet, once a year they can come back and cry and mourn." His voice quivered as he spoke.

Another large group of gray-haired men clustered in groups. They stood at the base of a large monument. *There are so many of them.* A shiver ran up her arms, and she wished she could approach each one and ask to hear his story. Then again, she was having a hard enough time dealing with the stories she'd already heard.

Grandpa Jack patted her arm. "I'm going inside with Paul. He and I want to introduce ourselves to Martha and the memorial committee. They're saving us seats in front. You may have time to go take the tour before the memorial starts."

Ava nodded. "I'm going to walk around and get some footage. We'll see you inside."

Dennis took her hand and they continued on. They walked to the edge of the hill and looked down the steps leading into a large quarry. Vines had grown over much of the rock wall, but a set of long, steep steps was still visible. Ava set up her camera and videotaped a wide, sweeping shot. Then she turned and did the same with the camp, recording the tall, concrete fortress. When she finished, she turned back to the quarry.

Ava shook her head, trying to picture the slave labor under control of Nazi guards. "I wonder what they thought about as they climbed."

"I wonder if they believed they'd been put into a living hell," Dennis added. "Hardly any food, the hard labor. They didn't die as quickly as if they'd been put in the gas chamber, but they died all the same."

She turned away as the images in her imagination overwhelmed her. And she knew that those images, no doubt, paled compared to the truth of what had happened there. She turned her attention back to the crowds and the monuments and began filming. One of the metal monuments displayed a circle of men with their hands lifted. It was as if they were reaching to the heavens, begging for an answer.

The crowds pressed in, and after Ava packed up her camera again, she felt Dennis's hand on the small of her back.

"Ava, look."

He pointed to a curb where an old man and woman sat. The man wore a brown vest, white shirt, and dark-blue pants. His hair was neatly combed, but his worn shoes proved he was no man of means. The woman wore a faded flower dress and blue scarf. She looked like a Polish peasant. Like a grandmother in one of Grimm's fairy tales. The man pulled out a thermos and poured hot water into two small tin cups that the woman held.

She lifted the camera and recorded the couple making their tea. She swallowed hard, feeling both sad and proud. Sad they'd faced so much. Proud they lived to return.

Everything around Ava was a blur. She did her best to record all that was happening. She felt removed, looking through the small, square viewing screen.

They walked to the old barracks—the only ones left standing—and Ava thought about the stories of the skeletal men that both her grandpa and Grand-Paul had freed.

They walked through the gas chambers that looked like showers. Heaviness overwhelmed her, and it was as if death still hung in the air. Some of the white tiles were chipped, and she wondered if that was from prisoners trying to claw their way through the walls. Her stomach felt sick and her head hurt. She needed air.

"Dennis, I have to get out of here." She handed him the camera and turned and walked out the shower room door. The stairs that led down to the showers were packed with people, so she walked through the door to the right of the showers, which she thought would lead her outside, but instead she walked into an oven room. The room looked like any dim basement. Two double ovens—black, long, large enough for a body to be slid inside— were opened before her. The stench of burning flesh was still strong, and she covered her nose with her hand.

"Oh, dear Jesus." It was a prayer. A prayer of sadness for all those who had died this way. A prayer that she could make it back outside for fresh air. As she hurried forward, her mind replayed her grandfather's stories, and tears filled her eyes.

"Those poor, poor people," he'd said, and now she understood.

She stepped through the next set of doors. It was

a museum. Her grandpa and Grand-Paul were there. They were looking at a huge photograph of the liberation—the half-tracks, the people. Ava hurried up to them, and as she did, she realized what they were looking at. It was *them. They* were in the photo. They were young and crowds of skeletal survivors celebrated the freedom the Americans' arrival ensured.

She paused behind the two men, staring. Her heart pounded, celebrating. Celebrating the fact that they were able to come back and see this. See that they would not be forgotten. Grandpa Jack placed an arm around Grand-Paul's shoulders, and a lump grew in Ava's throat. Although the battlefield might never remember them, the people here would. The lives they saved had birthed new life, families that would live on.

"There you are." Dennis approached. "Martha's in a fluster that you're not in your reserved seats. The program starts in thirty minutes, and she's lining everyone up."

"We aren't going to have to give a speech or anything, right?" Grandpa Jack asked. "We just have to stand up there?"

"I don't think you have to say anything. They're just going to introduce you and the others to the crowd." Ava smiled. "You can do that, can't you?"

"Just as long as I don't have to give a speech." Grandpa Jack took Ava's arm, and they followed Dennis. "That's almost as bad as having a video camera in your face." He laughed, but it was a nervous laugh.

They found their places among the others.

Grand-Paul and Grandpa Jack had just gotten seated when Ava saw someone approaching out of the corner of her eye. It was an older man, but he walked with quickened steps. Tears streamed down his face and he walked with arms extended.

"*Danke.*" The word emerged in a sigh as he stood before Grandpa Jack and took his hands. He rattled off something else in German that Ava couldn't understand. Then the man lifted his sleeve and pointed to the burgundy number tattooed into his arm. "*Danke!*" he cried and then turned to Paul. "*Danke.*"

The survivor moved down the line, walking in front of the seated veterans, pointing to his prisoner tattoo and thanking the Americans one by one.

Tears streamed down Ava's cheeks, and she quickly wiped them away. Her heart flipped through emotions—sadness at what those prisoners had gone through. Pride about her grandfather's part. Joy over being able to bring her grandfather back here again. Grief at knowing that Grand-Paul wouldn't be with them much longer.

Five minutes before the ceremony was to begin, the crowd took their seats. Looking behind her at row after row of people, Ava gasped when she saw someone she recognized across the crowd. It was Rick . . . the camera guy from Seattle. Next to him was Clark the co-host from the morning show.

"Oh my goodness."

"What is it?" Dennis asked.

Ava opened her mouth to explain, but the ceremony started and the crowd quieted. She leaned over to whisper in his ear. "Two guys are here from *my work*."

Dennis's brow furrowed, and then he followed her gaze. It was then, as Ava looked harder, that she saw that someone else was with them. A woman who looked to be in her sixties. Clark had his arm around the woman's shoulders, and he pointed to the stage. The woman nodded and excitement filled her face.

It was the rapid beating of her heart that gave Ava the first hint of who the woman was. Why else would Clark and Rick have come so far?

Chapter Twenty-Eight

Martha greeted the crowd first in German and then in English. Ava had less than a minute to wonder if the memorial committee knew about Angeline before Martha approached the podium to introduce the veterans who were there for the ceremony. Other parts of the ceremony would follow, but this would come first.

Fourteen veterans were in attendance. The first was called to the stage, and the roar of the crowd was comparable to the cheers at a play-off game. The first man approached the stage, and the crowd jumped to their feet. The next name was called, and the ovation rose in volume.

One by one, the veterans were called to the front. Each one had a family member accompany him. Each one was presented with a plaque and then led off the stage to the standing ovations of the tens of thousands of cheering men and women—Holocaust survivors, their family members, and others who'd come to celebrate liberation.

Paul's name was called, and Ava squeezed Dennis's hand. He rose and guided his grandfather to the stage. A lump grew in her throat. How frail and pale Grand-Paul was. They should have picked up on his illness sooner. They should have known.

More names were called, and Ava waited for Grandpa Jack's name. Finally she heard it. He was the last one, and Ava guided him up. But just as he accepted his plaque, she noticed movement toward the stage. Her mouth dropped open as Clark approached. Martha's face beamed as she stepped back and offered Clark the microphone.

"Mr. Andrews. I'm sorry. I don't mean to interrupt, but there's something else we'd like to present to you, sir. Or rather, someone else."

The cheering of the crowd started off strong, as with the others, but when they saw someone different onstage, they quieted. Ava looked to Clark, wishing he'd tell her exactly what was going on. Martha translated Clark's words.

Clark had a handheld microphone, and Ava turned to see her grandfather's reaction. His hand tightened on her arm. Ava wrapped an arm around his waist.

"Mr. Andrews." Clark turned so that Rick could get him on film, and he flashed his million-dollar smile. *"Mornings with Clark and Laurie* recently heard from your granddaughter—our very own producer, Ava Ellington—that you did a very heroic thing during the war. Do you want to tell us about it?"

Martha translated and then Clark pushed the microphone in front of her grandfather's mouth.

His eyes widened, and he scanned the crowd. Then he looked at Ava. "Ava, I don't know what he's talking about."

Ava stepped forward and took the microphone from Clark's hand. Her fingers tightened around it, and her chest seemed to double in size. Grandpa Jack would soon find the answer to the question that had haunted him for so long.

"As his granddaughter, and the one who joined in this search, I can answer that, Clark. My grandfather helped a little girl in nineteen forty-five. Her name is Angeline, and he's wondered about her ever since. We don't know if she's alive or . . ." She let her voice trail off.

Clark nodded and grinned, and then he leaned forward and spoke into the microphone, still in her hand. "If you think you're speechless now, sir, I don't know how you'll feel after this. We have that girl you saved with us. Of course, she's not a little girl anymore. She's a mother, grandmother, and nurse living in California. And, Mr. Andrews, just as you thought of her, she also thought of you. She always wondered about the American GI who saved her. Angeline, would you please come up here?"

Tears filled Ava's eyes as she noted the awe on her grandfather's face. Gasps filled the crowd, followed by cheers. The cheers grew louder as a middle-aged woman climbed the steps to the stage, opening her arms to Grandpa Jack.

"Thank you, thank you. I've always wanted to meet you."

Her grandfather looked at Ava and then at the woman. His eyes narrowed and he studied her face as if trying to see the resemblance. "You— you're Angeline?"

The woman nodded. "I am."

Her grandfather lifted his hand and touched her shoulder, as if checking to see if she was real. Only then did he step into Angeline's embrace.

His hands trembled, and Ava wrapped her arms around him, making sure he would stay up. She swallowed down the emotion, and as her mind cleared, she realized that the audience was on their feet, cheering.

Clark continued talking about how the show tracked Angeline down, but Ava wasn't interested in that. All she could focus on was the look on her grandfather's face. The woman wasn't what Ava had expected. She was American, and only the slightest accent could be heard in her words. She was thin, with blond hair streaked with gray and swept into a bun at the base of her neck.

"It's really you?" he said. "My little girl."

He swayed slightly, and she held on to him. Clark again attempted to put the microphone in her grandfather's face, but Ava pushed it away.

"He needs to sit down," she urged. "This is too much."

"Come with me. I'll take you to a quiet place so you can reconnect," Martha said, leading them off the stage. The cheers rose in volume, and Ava could feel their vibration, as much as she could hear them. Ava followed Martha, and as she passed the first row, she wondered if she could ask if Dennis and Grand-Paul could come too. But as she looked down the row to meet Dennis's gaze, anger flashed from his eyes.

She smiled at him, but Dennis shook his head and turned away.

With one look from Dennis's face, the excitement over finding Angeline deflated like a balloon that had lost its air. *How can he be upset? Doesn't he see how amazing this is that they're able to reconnect?*

Martha led them to the bookstore near the front gates. They walked through the store through a doorway in the back. Inside was a small office, and as they entered, Grandpa Jack turned to Angeline.

"Do you have it?" he asked.

Angeline nodded, understanding. Then she opened up her purse and pulled out a small box. "It's too small for me to wear now, but I've always kept it." She opened the box, and there was the necklace Grandpa Jack had told Ava about. It was just as Ava remembered he'd said—a small pearl and a little silver bird.

"My aunt Sabine told me the story. She was the one who raised me in the States after the war."

"And the couple at the house?" Grandpa Jack sat in the office chair.

"Strangers. We were from a village near Bastogne. Before we left, our whole block was destroyed and my father was killed. I remember walking around in the dark and cold with my mother and hearing all the loud noises and the flashes of lights. I know now that they were big weapons and that there was a huge battle, but at the time I didn't know what to think. My mother told me I was going to be okay, that God was watching over me."

"She said that?" Ava smiled.

"Yes, my mother had a strong faith in God. That was her—the woman in that room who had died."

"Your mother?" A sob erupted from Grandpa Jack's lips. Trembling hands covered his face. "I am so sorry. I didn't mean to kill her. I shot into the room thinking there were Germans inside."

"You? No." Angeline kneeled before Grandpa Jack. "It was not you." She pulled his hands from his face and took them between hers. "Before you got there, the Germans came in. They were angry. One of them wanted to take me. My mother refused, and he shot us both."

The color drained from Grandpa Jack's face, and his eyes were wide. "It wasn't my bullets?"

"No." Angeline shook her head. "I know this for a fact."

"Grandpa!" Ava hurried to him. "After all this time, you are innocent. You didn't do it."

He lowered his gaze. "Of this, Ava. But I'm far from innocent."

Ava didn't know what to say. The woman again embraced her grandfather. "Thank you. I'm here now because of you." But even with the woman's words, his shoulders did not soften.

The woman fingered the necklace in her hands, and they listened as the cheers outside died down and a man's voice could be heard over the sound system, giving a speech in German.

Grandpa Jack lowered his head. "I'm so sorry. Maybe if we had gotten there sooner." His lower lip trembled.

Angeline took his hand between hers. "I have faith. I know I will see her again. It was a miracle I was saved. God sent you to save me. We shouldn't question His ways." The woman stroked Grandpa Jack's hands as he no doubt had stroked hers those many, many years ago.

Ava leaned forward in her seat. "And then what happened? After the ambulance took you away?"

The woman covered her mouth with her hand, as if trying to control her emotions. She lowered it and continued. "I—I remember waking up in some type of tent hospital. I wanted my mother and father, but they were gone. I cried for them even though I knew this. A kind doctor cared for me. Then they sent me to another hospital with more wounded soldiers, or at least I think that's what happened. I was so young; it's hard for me to remember." She looked into Grandpa Jack's eyes. "I do remember you, though. I remember your face as you carried me."

"You speak really good English. I can tell you weren't raised in Europe," Ava said.

"Oh no. Our first stop was France. I remember being taken to a hospital with other children, and the administration there contacted my aunt."

The woman placed a hand over her heart and

closed her eyes. She took in a deep breath, and her forehead bunched, as if her mind was replaying a painful memory.

The woman's eyes opened, but instead of looking into Grandpa Jack's face, she studied his hands. "There were so many changes. I lost my home, my family, my country, and my language. My aunt, you see, lived in San Diego, California. Unbeknownst to me, my mother had sewn my aunt's address in my coat." The woman sighed. "I wonder how Mother knew to do that. We traveled by ship when I was well enough. I was raised with cousins and knew the love of a family." A smile brightened her face. "But even though so much was lost . . . my life was saved. Thank you."

Grandpa Jack nodded and then wiped his tear-filled eyes with the back of his hand.

"I've had a good life, Mr. Andrews. I love my husband and our three sons. My husband, David, would have been here, but he's been ill. It was a quick trip. I found out about you—about this memorial service—and five hours later I was on a plane. I'm honored to meet you."

Grandpa Jack opened his arms for another embrace. "I won't forget this," he managed to say. "As long as I live, I won't forget this."

Even though Ava wasn't happy with the way Clark had handled things, she was awed that this had happened. She also wondered why Jill hadn't called her. Jill was good at many things, but keeping a secret wasn't one of them. Ava wished she had known; then she could have schooled Clark on how to handle things. She could have written a better script for how this played out.

Angeline and Grandpa Jack talked for nearly an hour, sharing about their families and reliving the events that had led up to that day when God brought them into each other's lives. Then Martha returned and informed them that the ceremony was over and that there was media waiting outside to talk to them.

Ava hadn't expected there to be more media, and she looked to Grandpa Jack to see his reaction. He nodded and seemed calmer than he had been when he'd been on the stage. He rose and stretched his arms out to Angeline.

"I live in Northern California," he told her. "It would be wonderful if Ava and I could travel down to see you some time." He pulled her into a hug and held on.

"I'd like that, Mr. Andrews." She pulled back and then placed a kiss on his cheek.

"You can call me Jack."

"Okay." She nodded. "All these years I called you my guardian angel. I'm thankful to finally know your name, Jack."

"Are the other guys out there already?" Grandpa turned to Martha and straightened, like the old soldier he was, ready to report to duty.

"Actually . . ." Martha paused. "The media is

just interested in talking to you, sir—and Angeline, of course."

The words didn't sink in until they walked out to a sea of cameras and reporters. Ava scanned the crowd, and although she saw some of the other veterans and their families, she didn't see Grand-Paul or Dennis.

"Mr. Andrews, Mr. Andrews, can you please tell us what it was like to finally meet Angeline after all these years?" one reporter called with a thick German accent.

Ava took her grandfather's hand. She looked at him and was surprised when he jutted out his chin and answered.

"It's nothing that I ever imagined possible. I'm thankful for my granddaughter's curious nature. I'm thankful to have a new friend in Angeline." He turned to the woman. "I think I'll be able to sleep well tonight. Better than I have in sixty years, now that I know the little girl I've thought about for so many years—" His voice caught in his throat. "Now that I know Angeline is safe."

He acted so bold, so confident. Ava's chest swelled with pride.

The media continued asking questions, and her grandpa and Angeline answered them the best they could—about the war, their lives after the war, and their new friendship.

After a while, her grandpa's speech slowed. He was growing weary. "I'm sorry. No more questions," she said to the sea of reporters.

"Just one more?" It was Clark's voice.

Ava turned to him, and he winked at her. Next to him stood Rick, with a big smile on his face. He'd always wanted to do on-site videography and reporting—and here he was.

"Okay, just one more," she conceded.

"Mr. Andrews," Clark said, "you've said a few times to these reporters that you're no hero. You said that you only did what anyone else would have done in that situation. Personally, I do feel that you're a hero, sir, but I do have to wonder if you question your own heroism because of other reasons. Mr. Andrews, can you tell me about Chenogne? Can you tell us about your part in the lives lost there?"

A gasp escaped Ava's lips, and her grandfather slumped beside her. She reached for him and grabbed him, holding him up. Angeline grabbed him from the other side.

"Who told you that? Did Jill?" Ava's mind felt like mush. Surely Jill wouldn't do that. It made no sense. Nothing made sense. All she knew is that she needed to get her grandfather out of this chaos.

They needed quiet. They needed space. Dark clouds descended on every bright spot the day had offered.

Ava gripped her grandfather's arm tighter.

"Hold on to me, Grandpa."

He obediently slipped his hand around her arm. More voices and more questions sounded around her, but Ava ignored them. She stretched out her hand, motioning for the people crowding them to step to either side.

The air seemed heavier than normal, and thick, as if she was still breathing in the dusty air from the oven room. Her grandfather's steps were small, and the gravel on the ground in the parade area beyond the bookstore made it hard for him to get his balance.

Thankfully, the reporters parted, allowing them to make their way out of the gates.

Even as they walked away from Angeline, away from the camp and toward the car, Ava wondered what she should do. She needed to find Dennis. She needed to get her grandfather back to the hotel. She needed to apologize.

She wrapped her arm around him, holding her grandfather up, and they walked down the sloped hillside to the parking lot.

"Grandpa, I'm so sorry. I never meant for this to happen. I had no idea—"

"Ava, it's not your fault. Anyone who took the time to look up our unit would know about Chenogne."

Ava nodded, but she knew that wasn't the truth. Clark knew about Chenogne because she'd mentioned it to Jill. Ava wondered if Rick had pursued Jill in order to get the story he wanted. She wouldn't put it past him.

Ava bit her lip, and then her shoulders relaxed just slightly when she saw Dennis and Grand-Paul waiting ahead.

"Are you ready to head back?" Dennis unlocked the door with a hard edge to his voice. "I think we've seen enough." He looked at her, shooting darts into her eyes. His jaw was tight, his hand balled into a fist on the top of the car.

"Yes." Ava knew they'd just seen what had happened. She wished she could rewind and stop that last question. If she could change anything about this trip, that would be it.

"That's pretty amazing, Jackson, meeting up with Angeline like that," Grand-Paul commented, feigning cheerfulness.

"Not something I'd imagine in a thousand years," Grandpa Jack said again, his voice shaking.

Dennis said nothing. He just drove in stony silence.

At the hotel in Linz, Grandpa Jack and Grand-Paul stood at the doorway to the hotel, but they didn't go in.

"We're heading across the street," Grand-Paul explained. "We're meeting the other guys for dinner."

"Can I meet you later, Grandpa?" Ava asked. "I'm really not hungry."

"Of course." Grandpa Jack patted her hand. "You should get some rest. It was hard work taking care of me today." Grandpa Jack gave her a tired smile, and the smile just made her feel worse.

"I'm with Ava," Dennis said. "I don't really think I could eat right now, but I might be over later."

She could tell he was trying to keep his tone even, but his words jerked as if only thin threads held the angry ones inside. Dennis placed his hand on the door to the hotel and pushed, striding inside without saying a word to her.

The old guys headed across the street, and as soon as Ava noticed they'd made it to the front door of the restaurant, she walked into the hotel and to the stairs that would take her to her room.

At the stairs, which swept like a wide arch into the lobby, Dennis waited. He was looking at a photograph of a young boy with his dog on the wall. Ava hurried to move past him—before she had to explain.

"Ava?"

She paused on the first step.

She didn't turn around, didn't look at him. She could tell from the tone of his voice that he wasn't happy. Other people moved around the lobby, but she ignored them all.

"I can't believe you did that," Dennis said, speaking to the back of her head.

She slowly turned. "You can't believe I enlisted my team back home to find this girl—this woman—so that my grandfather could see her before he dies? Not a day went by that he didn't think about her."

"You didn't have to do it like that. You exploited your grandfather by bringing the national media into this. He would have been content enough just seeing her."

Anger bubbled inside Ava.

Dennis pinched the bridge of his nose, looking weary, confused. "You turned the ceremony into a circus. When did this day stop being about our grandfathers? When did this become about *you?*" He lowered his hand and released a heavy sigh. "I suppose nothing has changed. I should have known. It's always been this way."

His blue eyes appeared darker as he looked at her, void of the light that had been there the last few days, and she could see he was no longer talking about the cameras. The events today had apparently aroused the bitterness nestled deep inside him, as if the media's advances were a stick poking a wasp's nest, stirring up what was already there.

"Excuse me?" Ava gripped the railing to the stairs leading to the second story. The black iron felt cold under her grip.

"You heard me. It's always been this way."

"I heard you, but I don't understand. What do

you mean *always?*" She jutted out her chin.

"You know what I'm talking about. That summer—it was the best of my life. I had everything figured out. I was going to spend my life with you. I—" Dennis paused. "I already had the ring."

Ava's hand grasped her throat. "You bought a ring?"

"It was my grandmother's ring."

"But you never proposed. How did you know I wouldn't have said yes?"

"Because when we talked, and I asked about your plans, you said you wanted to go to college. You said you wanted to be the first one in your family to graduate, and that you wanted to be on television and make something of yourself. Marriage wasn't on your mind."

"Of course I said that. I was eighteen years old. I did have those dreams; I wasn't going to lie."

"I would have understood if you wanted to go to school, but how could I have shared my heart when you didn't see me in your future? If you'd asked me, my answer would have been different. What I wanted more than anything was *you.*"

Ava took another step up the red carpeted stairs so she was as tall as he was. His face was just six inches from hers. The resurrected pain in his face ripped at her heart. His anger cut her to the core like a knife to the gut.

She pointed a finger at his face. "Did you ever

consider that I would have given it all up if—" Her throat tightened. "If you had just followed me?" She heard footsteps behind her. Ava pressed her lips together and waited for the person coming down the stairs to pass. A woman walked by and gave them a curious look. Others in the lobby were also watching.

When the woman was out of earshot, Ava continued—her voice lower and more controlled. "You can't do this, Dennis. You can't blame it all on me." She shook her head, and then she focused on his eyes. His gaze was hard, his eyes narrow. "You're the one who started returning my letters. And today . . . you assumed the worst about me." Ava moved to go, and suddenly her body felt weary, and she questioned whether she could carry herself up the stairs.

"Where are you going?"

"To my room. To work. I have a video to work on, remember?"

"I bet you do." Dennis lowered his voice. "You have those ratings to keep track of."

Ava paused her retreat, and her throat grew tight. She tried to swallow, but it wouldn't go down.

She balled her fists, turned, and strode back down the stairs toward him. "Wow, Dennis. If you believe my job is most important, you don't know me. I'm driven but not heartless. And since you were the one to bring our past into this conversation, just because I didn't think the timing wasn't right didn't mean *we* weren't right. We could have taken the time to get to know each other. To fall more deeply in love. To build our dreams together. It would have taken time for me to figure out that life doesn't always have to go by my agenda—I'm still figuring that out—but I'm confident that with you around, I would have gotten there. You would have become my dreams, Dennis."

She took the steps two at a time to the second story. She had video clips to edit and a plane to catch tomorrow. If she was lucky, she'd finish picking out the best clips before she and Grandpa Jack joined the other veterans on the bus that would take them to the airport in Vienna.

Though her work was challenging, she hoped it would help get her mind off of so many other things, especially the realization that her motives weren't always as noble as she'd like to think. Somewhere between her high opinion of herself and Dennis's cutting observation was the truth. A truth she didn't always like.

Yet even thinking about a video made her head hurt. She didn't have to finish it tonight, but she would have to wrap it up over the next couple of days to have it ready to air by next week. The thing was, she needed the perfect story to tie up all the segments, and that would be hard. There was nothing perfect about what had happened today.

Her video would have to be different than the reunion, because from what she had seen today, Clark and Rick were already using that.

Back in her room, she set up her computer and the camera. Tears pooled in her eyes, and she wiped them away with the back of her hand. Her throat hurt, and her stomach lurched. Even though she worked to get her mind off everything that had happened, her emotions weren't swayed so easily. She felt miserable. Ava couldn't believe this was her last night in Europe, and this was how she was going to spend it.

Tomorrow she'd be back in Seattle, and the day after that at work. She'd get cheers from her team for all her video work and for making the reunion story possible. And she'd have to have a serious talk with Jill. Ava didn't know if she could be friends with someone who'd given away the information on Chenogne.

Not that she knew the truth of her grandfather's involvement in Chenogne—not that she'd ever know.

When she got home, she'd clean her apartment, go through her mail, attend church, and try to ignore the wedding dress still hanging in her closet. She'd meet her friends for coffee, but she'd still be thinking about her grandfather and about the people whose paths she'd crossed, if even for just a moment.

And now she'd think about—no, obsess about—

the fact that Dennis had been ready to propose but never did. She'd imagine what their life would have been like and she'd be miserable.

Ten minutes later she connected the cable from the video camera to her computer and then lay on her bed, stomach down, hair in her face, waiting for all the video footage she'd taken at the Mauthausen camp to transfer.

"Stupid, stupid, stupid," she mumbled, unsure if she was talking about Dennis, or herself, or this day, or her life in general.

"I don't understand," she said, turning her head and peering out the window at the steeple of the cathedral. "I liked my life. I was happy with my job. I was perfectly fine scheduling cooking segments and bad author interviews." Ava punched her pillow, and even though she said that, she knew it wasn't the truth. Still, the discontent she'd felt then was much easier to deal with than the renewed heartache.

A knock sounded at the door, interrupting her words. She glanced at the clock. It couldn't be Grandpa Jack. He had a key. And she sure hoped it wasn't Clark or Rick. The last thing she wanted was to see them. And the last thing they'd appreciate was finding her like this.

Dennis.

What if it was him? Apologizing not only for today but for letting her go so long ago? What if he finally realized that her intentions had been good after all, no matter how things had turned out?

The knock sounded again. Ava jumped from the bed and hurried to the mirror on the wall. She straightened her blouse, wiped the makeup from under her eyes, and then ran her fingers through her hair. She stood with shoulders back and then opened the door.

A frail man stood there—Paul.

Her shoulders deflated. Then she scanned the hall.

"Sorry, I'm the only one here. Didn't mean to disappoint you."

"No, I'm sorry, Grand-Paul. It's always good to see you. I thought you were going to dinner." She offered him a quick hug. "You're feeling okay, aren't you?"

He accepted the hug and then nodded sadly. "Yes, I'm doing well. I wish the same could be said of you."

She brushed her hair back from her shoulder. "I'm fine, really. It was a long day, that's all." Ava nodded as if agreeing with her own words. "Whew, and I still have this video to work on. Actually, I'm not sure that it'll even be needed now that my studio sent its own crew and all. Still"—she patted his hands—"I'm going to do it, and I'm going to do my best, just like someone really special told me once."

Grand-Paul nodded. "I'm sure it will all work

out. I think we can ask God to help us with that. What your grandpa Jack said in Bastogne is true. Maybe we do need to pray more—even about the small things. I'm willing to try if you are."

Ava nodded, noting a softness in Grand-Paul's gaze that she hadn't seen before. Peace, even after all the craziness of the day.

"Being around my grandpa has had an effect on you. I can tell. It's had an effect on me too."

"And being around Dennis has impacted me too. Waking up to find him reading his Bible and praying encourages me." Grand-Paul winked. "Your grandfather and my grandson are not perfect, but they seem to know who to turn to when they need help. It's what I found on this trip. I remembered how much peace God could give me. I remembered Him."

Ava swung the hotel room door open wider. "Would you like to come in? I'm sorry I didn't think to invite you in sooner."

"No, I am heading over to dinner. I just wanted to see that you're okay. I know we'll see each other tomorrow on the bus, but I just wanted to make sure you didn't head out anywhere. You never know what a night like this could bring." His eyes brightened with a twinkle.

Ava crossed her arms over her chest. "Yes, I'm here, and I'm fine. I'll look forward to catching up tomorrow. Will you tell Dennis good night for me since I won't have a chance?" Hearing about his doing morning devotions had taken away the edge of the anger that had been there before.

"Of course I will. And promise me you'll come by and see me in Florida. If there get to be too many clouds in your life, sunshine is only a flight away."

"I know, Paul. I promise I will." She gave him another hug, remembering how she wanted to ask him to be a guest on the show someday soon. But she wouldn't ask now. She'd talk to him later about that, if at all. The last thing she wanted was to be accused of taking advantage of someone for ratings.

"Don't give up on this day yet, Ava," Grand-Paul said in her ear as he gave her a quick hug. "Never give up. Sometimes the future isn't what we expect, but when we get there, it often isn't as scary or as overwhelming as we first thought."

"Thank you. I'll remember that. I'll never forget this trip . . ." Her voice trailed off. "And I'll never forget you."

"How could you?" He kissed her cheek. "I'm unforgettable." Then he held her arms and looked into her eyes.

"And don't give up on my grandson. He can be difficult at times, but so can each of us. That was my other prayer, you know. I've been praying it since Bastogne. I thought it would be a great place to start."

"For us, Dennis and me?"

Grand-Paul nodded. "Yes, for you. Both of you to find the love you're looking for—in each other."

Chapter Twenty-Nine

Ava punched in Jill's number. She didn't bother figuring out what the time zone was. She needed to talk to Jill. The idea that her friend would sacrifice her grandfather's respect for a "surprise" story was eating Ava up inside.

The phone rang.

"Hello?"

"Jill."

"Oh my gosh, Ava, how did it go? Was it the most exciting thing ever? Was your grandpa completely surprised?"

"Yes, he was. So was I. And not in a good way."

"What? Are you serious? Ava, that was the best reunion ever. I can't wait until we air it!"

Ava took in a deep breath and then breathed it out slowly. "Finding Angeline was great, although it could have been done differently."

Ava placed her pillow against the headboard and leaned against it. She felt fidgety inside, restless. Not just because of this phone call, but everything. "But that's not what I'm mad about. Why in the world did you talk to Clark about

Chenogne? How could you do that? That was between me and you—friend to friend. It was horrible, Jill. Everyone was so excited, talking about the reunion with Angeline, and then Clark had to bring that up—the deaths. How could he? I've never seen my grandfather's face so white. I thought he was going to pass out." A sob burst forth. "My grandpa doesn't know I had anything to do with it. He assumed that the reporter just researched it and found out for himself."

"I didn't tell anyone. I swear, Ava. Clark must have read my notes, and then he must have done some research on his own. Maybe he just assumed the village was connected to Angeline." Jill heaved a sad sigh. "I'm so sorry that hurt your grandpa. Will he be okay?"

"I think it will be fine. I'm going to find him and explain."

Returning to her desk, Ava logged out of her computer. She wasn't going to worry about the video. She wasn't going to worry about anything but working things out with her grandfather.

Ava got up from the bed and walked to the window. She stared down at the Austrian street, looking up and down the sidewalks for Dennis's familiar walk, but she didn't see him.

"I'll see you in a few days," Jill said. "Again, I'm so sorry."

"See you soon."

Ava ran a brush through her hair and then just as

she was slipping on her shoes, Grandpa Jack returned. He entered the room, and when Ava glanced up, she saw that the major was with him. Ava smiled to see that after all these years, he was still taking care of his men.

"Sorry, sweetheart, but it's a madhouse out there," Mitch said. "The reporters won't leave Jack alone. I think your grandfather's a little shaken up."

"They followed us from Mauthausen to Linz?" Ava moved to her grandfather's side, leading him to his bed, where he sat.

"Couldn't eat a bite of my meal. They just kept asking questions." Grandpa Jack shook his head.

Mitch nodded and then ran his fingers through his gray hair. "It's a big story. The idea of a World War II vet being reunited with someone he saved has caught the attention of the world. My daughter called me from the States. A video clip of their first embrace in over sixty years is already on YouTube."

Ava could only imagine Todd's excitement about something like this going viral. It would take their show to a new level. It would gain viewers, advertisers. A week ago she also would have been excited, but when she looked at her grandfather and saw his weariness, she wanted nothing more than to protect him.

"I don't know what to do. I imagine if the media followed us here, they'll follow us to Vienna, too, and then be waiting when we get home," she said. "We can't let that happen."

Ava turned to her grandfather. "We have to leave now, tonight. We have to get out of this madhouse."

Ava drove Major Mitch's rental car to Vienna. He'd insisted she take it, saying he'd find a ride with one of the other guys. Ava's only regret was not finding Dennis or Grand-Paul to say good-bye. She'd left a note, hoping they'd understand and promising to touch base with them once they got back to the States.

"Ava." Her grandpa's voice trembled as he said her name.

"Yes?" She paused, glancing over at him.

"I need to clear something up. I feel like I have a Sherman tank parked on my chest, and I'd like to tell you something. It's . . . about Chenogne." He clasped his hands on his lap. "I want to tell you what happened. What really happened." His voice shook, and he placed a hand on hers. His skin looked tissue paper–thin.

"Are you sure?"

He nodded.

"Thank you. I do want to hear, but you need to know something first. It's my fault. Their asking you about that today was because of something I did," she confessed. "I asked a friend to look up information for me, and somehow it spread from there. It's not what I planned. I was trying to figure out what was bothering you so much. I should have waited until you were ready to tell me." As she said those words, she thought of Dennis. He had told her to wait, to give it time. She was sorry now that she hadn't listened.

"Oh, Ava." He sighed. "If I hadn't been so secretive, then you wouldn't have had to ask for help. It's just hard." His voice caught in his throat, and then he cleared it. "The only other people I told were your grandmother and Paul. I knew Grandma had loved me, and Paul has stuck with me. I just have to trust that you'll continue to love me too. I trust that you'll understand I was a kid who didn't know what to do other than to do as I was ordered."

"Of course. I know that." She eased her foot off the gas pedal as she maneuvered a turn.

He let out a soft groan. "We had only been on the outskirts of Chenogne, which is not far from Bastogne, for twenty-four hours. Our commanders knew what they were doing. They put the right troops and weapons in the right places at the right time, and we started gaining ground. We scared the Germans; they didn't know what hit them." He paused and then shook his head as if trying to shake out a memory. "Many of the Germans surrendered."

Ava bit her lip. She'd made the wrong conclusion after hearing Jill's story. She also realized she never did receive that e-mail from the librarian as Jill had promised. *It was the Germans who were the prisoners-of-war—the POWs.*

"I saw a white flag waving from a stone house," her grandfather continued. "I shouted to the German soldiers and called them out. I expected a dozen maybe. They were walking like they were half-dead, beaten down. I think in the end there were sixty of them. I don't know why they were surrendering to me. I was just one guy. Later, I realized they probably felt safe—" Emotion caught in his throat.

Tears filled Ava's eyes, and she quickly wiped them away, focusing on the road. She wanted to tell him to stop. She didn't want to hear him say the words. Still, she couldn't stop him. She had to know for herself.

"A sergeant showed up. He said to take them over the hill. I knew what was going to happen. We had orders, you know. After the Malmédy Massacre—when the Germans had killed many of our American soldiers who'd surrendered—we were told to take no prisoners. We were to do to them what they had done to our guys."

"So what did you do?" The words escaped her as a heavy breath.

"I turned them over to some other guys from my unit. Not long afterward I heard the gunfire."

"Oh, Grandpa." Ava took his hand in hers and squeezed. "I'm so sorry you had to go through that. I'm so sorry that you had to live with that memory all these years."

His shoulders shook.

"I can still remember their faces. I can still see them, Ava. Those German soldiers trusted me," he whispered.

"I still love you," she said. "I know now . . . and I love you." She viewed the dark countryside passing by outside the car window, realizing the war had changed everything. The countries she'd driven through, the men who still remembered. Their children and grandchildren—at least the ones who chose to listen.

"A few hours after that, we headed to the Bastogne-Marche highway. I couldn't feel bad any longer. I had a job to do. But as we moved down the road, I saw them—dark forms lying in the snow. It's the image that I wake to nearly every morning. It only goes away with prayer. Some things only change with prayer."

"Does God help you to forget?" Ava asked.

"No." Grandpa Jack shook his head. "He reminds me I'm forgiven—for big things and small things. He tells me to look ahead, not back. He reminds me of heaven, where there will be no more tears." He sighed.

"Have you read the letter yet, Ava? The last one?"

"No, not yet, but I want to."

"When you do, it will help you to understand.

God showed me many things through the war, and He's still showing me. Like today." He looked over at her. "Today I learned we don't need to be afraid of sharing our whole selves with those we love."

Ava glanced at the sparse boarding area, wishing there was a place to lie down. Airports would make a killing if they offered reclining chairs for rent by the hour. She'd give fifty dollars for the chance to lie down and shut her eyes.

Next to her, Grandpa Jack slept. He sat up straight except for his chin, which rested on his chest. His eyes were closed, and if she listened closely, Ava could hear the smallest snore. He no doubt was weary from all that had happened at the camp this morning, and from their drive down to Vienna.

She thought about pulling out her computer, but she didn't have enough brainpower for that. Instead, she pulled out her phone. She considered calling Dennis, but she didn't want to hear the anger in his voice. No, she wanted to forget about today and just hold on to the memories of yesterday. Yesterday—their day at Passau.

Before they'd left, she'd gone to Dennis and Grand-Paul's room. No one had answered the door, so she'd written a note instead and slid it under the door.

A part of her hoped that Dennis would call her

when he found the note, but another part of her wondered if another fifteen years would pass before she heard from Dennis again. She hoped not. Despite their last fight, she missed him already. She smiled, thinking of how he'd kissed her.

She thought about Jay too, but only heaviness filled her chest. Warm heat rose up her neck. She should never have responded to his text. It was dumb to get flustered by his phone call. Why had she been so stupid? Even if Jay tried to make up for the broken engagement, she knew now he wasn't the type of man she wanted to spend her life with. What she loved about Dennis was his relationship with God, his care for the less fortunate, and his dedication to Grand-Paul and Grandpa Jack. It saddened her to know that her work had hurt the older men. That Dennis's fears had played out. It hurt even more to consider what he thought of her.

She let out a heavy sigh and sent up a silent prayer. If she couldn't have Dennis, she prayed God would continue to change her, to teach her to be more patient, to care for others more than herself, to believe God could make wonderful things happen when we allowed Him to and didn't force our own way.

Ava pulled out the letters from her grandfather. She read the first two and couldn't help but feel sorry for him. They were angry letters, telling his parents about his friends who had been killed. They were statements declaring there could be no loving God if He allowed such violence to happen. They were dated in February—not long after Chenogne, and during his battles through Germany.

She folded them and put them into their envelopes and then pulled out the last one.

May 15, 1945
Dear Mom and Dad,

Today I was delivering bread to the camp, and an old man—one of the prisoners—approached to talk to me. He knew English well and told me he used to be a professor at the Germany university, but since he was Jewish, this is where he ended up. The whole time we talked, he told me he would be returning to find his family. He and his wife had sent their children to live with family in Canada, and he knew they were safe. He hoped his wife was safe too. The thing that amazed me about this man—who was thin and covered with sores—was that he didn't talk about the past. Many of the prisoners tell us all the horrible things the Nazis did, but not this man.

Mom, I asked him about this, and his answer made me think. He told me he was free. He'd been liberated from the darkness. He told me the gates had been opened. He also prayed for me. He said I was chosen by God to be one of the liberators.

I have thought about those words over and over. Chosen? I'd volunteered to fight. I was placed in my division, but I didn't feel chosen for anything. Also, if I was chosen for this, did that mean I was chosen for the battlefield too?

I'm not sure if I wanted to be chosen, but being able to open those gates has made all the battles worth it. I think my friends who died would think so too. Their deaths made freedom possible.

"Miss, we're ready to leave now." The airport attendant's words interrupted her reading. "If you and your grandfather would follow me—"

"Yes, just one moment please."

Ava gathered her things, but not before she read the last paragraph in her grandfather's letter.

Like the man I spoke to, we all have a chance to focus on the future over the pain of the past. It's a lesson that might take me a lifetime to learn, but one that's worth knowing. Also, most of the time, being chosen means accepting the pain with the joy and knowing the joy is greater because the pain was there.

Love,
Jack

Ava swallowed her emotion as she rose. She put the letters away and then helped her grandfather to the plane, finding it hard to believe the trip was over. Finding it hard to believe they were leaving Europe. They were leaving this place, but they carried so much home with them. So much.

Ava just wished that she and Dennis had worked things out, but after reading that last letter, she knew she couldn't give up on love so quickly. She had to hope. If she didn't, what would she have?

It would take adjusting her focus. Looking to God, trusting Him, and then looking to those He wanted her to love for life, imperfections included.

Chapter Thirty

"Ava, aren't you off the plane yet? Todd wants to know your response to the video he e-mailed you. He's thinking of having—what was his name? Yeah, *that* guy here. Seriously, it's so sweet. Call me."

What in the world is she talking about? Ava sighed as she listened to the message from Jill, getting into a rental car.

Grandpa Jack sat in the passenger seat and his eyes stared out the window as if confused to be seeing Seattle instead of Germany or Austria outside the window. She wondered if he was already missing Paul like she was. Dennis too.

Ava hadn't been able to bear the thought of her grandfather going back to California and her to Seattle, so she'd talked him into coming up and staying with her a few weeks while the media fanfare faded. She knew it was only a matter of time before the media tracked him down, and she didn't want him to have to deal with all the hoopla by himself. At least when the hounds finally tracked him to Seattle, she'd be there to fend them off. Though he had worried about the state of his lawn when he returned to the trailer park, he'd reluctantly agreed.

When she called her mom from the Amsterdam airport, where they had a connecting flight, she also told her mom that Grandpa Jack should have someone around to make sure he was doing well physically. What Ava hadn't told her mom was that she wasn't ready for them to go their separate ways just yet.

Outside it was dark, and the bright lights of Seattle filled the horizon. It was beautiful, but it didn't seem right. Something was missing. Even with her grandfather here, there was still a big hole that she knew only Dennis and Grand-Paul could fill.

There was one more message, and Ava clicked to listen.

"Ava, you're not ignoring my calls, are you?" It was Jill's voice again. "I heard that you were getting home early. I know you won't have time to rest, but do you think you can make it to the studio by ten o'clock? Todd needs you here, and he says that whatever you do, don't watch the video that's in your e-mail in-box. He says if you do, you'll be fired, and he'll get the word out to every studio in the world not to hire you."

She shook her head, still not understanding, and then she turned to her grandfather.

"You tired?"

"A little."

She glanced at her watch. "I have to go to the studio in the morning. Do you want to come?"

"Maybe not. I think I might have to take after my granddaughter and sleep in."

Less than six hours after she'd made it home, Ava strode down the long hall of Studio 28. Then she turned and opened the studio door.

"There you are." Jill rushed to her and opened wide her arms. "Are you ready?"

"Ready for what? I'm not even sure what this is about."

"Well, there's a video, you see, and it gave us an idea for a, uh, future segment. We don't want everything set up at first. We just want you to react."

"React to what?"

Jill placed a hand on her hip. "You'll see. You just have to trust me. And don't worry; this is taped. It's not live. If you don't like it, we won't use it."

The door opened and Todd approached with a smile. "Ava, the video segments from Europe were fantastic. I don't know why you're producing. You're a star in the making. Now get up there onstage and sit. Laurie has something she needs to talk to you about."

Ava did as she was told. Then the wardrobe coordinator came up and touched up her makeup for the camera. A smile filled the woman's face.

"Ready?" Laurie brushed her dark curly hair over her shoulder.

Ava shrugged. "I'm not really certain what this is about."

Laurie nodded and smiled toward the camera and the new cameraman Ava had yet to meet.

"Today we have a special guest with us on *Mornings with Laurie*. You all know Ava Ellington from her trip across Europe with her grandfather. And many of you may be tuning in because you caught the reunion of Ava's grandfather with a woman he saved in the war as a small child. But what you don't know—what I recently found out—is that there was much more to this reunion story than meets the eye. You see, while Grandpa Jack was being reunited with the old battle-sights, Ava was spending time with someone from her past. Watch this."

The studio lights dimmed and an image flashed

on the large video screen behind them. It was a picture of her and Dennis when they were eighteen. Ava's heart pounded, and she wrung her hands on her lap. *What in the world?*

The photo disappeared, and then Dennis's face filled the screen as a video played.

"Hey, Ava, this is Dennis. Hanging around with you over the past week has inspired me. And when I happened to meet up with Rick and Clark here—" The camera turned around to Clark and Rick's faces. Then it turned back to Dennis. "Well, I asked them to help me make a video of my own."

Dennis looked up into the sky, as if he was trying to find the right words, and then he looked back into the camera.

"First, I need to apologize for my outburst today. I was wrong. I didn't give you the chance to explain. I'm thankful that Clark here explained what had happened. He had wrongly assumed Chenogne was the name of the town where your grandfather found Angeline. Can you forgive me? I acted pretty lousy today."

Tears pooled on her lower lids, and even though she knew he couldn't see her or hear her, she nodded.

"Now, my grandpa packed this ring when he heard you were coming, just in case. I'd hate to disappoint him. I'd hate to have my heart broken, and I'd hate to be standing in this hall all night.

I'm going to head to your room, sweep you off your feet, and ask you the question I've waited fifteen years to ask. You see, Ava, I have to tell you that I'm completely in love. For the last fifteen years I've carried a secret love around for the girl I knew. Now I'm even more deeply in love with the woman you've become."

The camera scanned back, and Ava could see that Dennis was standing at the bottom of the stairs in the foyer of the hotel in Linz. In the background she could make out the media forming outside the hotel, but Dennis didn't seem to notice.

Dennis smiled at the camera one last time, and then the video ended. The screen behind Laurie went black, the lights came back on, and Ava glanced around the set. It seemed foreign, and she had a feeling this wasn't where she wanted to spend the rest of her days. She also felt alone.

Ava placed a hand over her heart. Tension built inside as she wondered what happened when Dennis realized that she wasn't in her room—wasn't there to watch the video. That she was already heading back to the States.

She focused on Laurie.

"Ava, do you want to tell us what happened?" Laurie asked.

"I left. I wasn't in my room. I was already headed back to Seattle."

Laurie smiled and then nodded. Then she looked at someone over Ava's shoulder.

"You may have left, Ava Ellington, but this time I knew what to do. I knew to follow." It was Dennis's voice, and it wasn't coming from the video.

Ava stood and turned. In the dimness off the stage, she could make out his handsome features. She could see the love in his blue eyes. "Dennis."

Dennis strode up to the studio stage, and she rose and folded into his arms. He held her close. Held her tightly.

"You weren't easy to catch, you know. Good thing my grandpa has good connections and we found a plane just as fast as yours."

She snuggled her face into his neck. "I don't want to let go. I don't ever want to let go."

"Are you sure?" Dennis chuckled in her ear. "If you don't let go, you won't get to see what I have in this box."

She watched as he pulled a small box from his pocket.

Ava released him and stepped back. At the same moment, Dennis sank onto one knee. He opened the box and held up the ring. It had an antique setting that held a small diamond.

"Ava Ellington, I want to trek through life with you. I want our journey to last to the end of our days. Will you marry me?"

Ava covered her mouth with her hands. She nodded.

"Is that a yes?"

She lowered her hands.

"Yes, Dennis, over a million miles and through ten thousand days, yes."

Cheers arose from the studio room around them, and Dennis placed the ring on her finger. Then he stood and gave her the most gentle of kisses.

"Looks like my prayers were answered!" It was Grand-Paul's voice. Ava turned, and her heart leapt to see him. And by his side Grandpa Jack stood.

"You two were in on this? Grandpa, how did you pull that off? I just left you back at home not an hour ago." Ava laughed.

"Of course we're here. We were trained to be wherever we're needed most." Grand-Paul winked. "I have to say, after the long journey, this victory at the end of the trip makes it worthwhile."

Ava looked down at the ring on her finger and then back to Dennis. "I love you. And I forgive you." She smiled.

"Can you forgive me a thousand times more?" His eyes were focused on hers. "Because I'm sure I'm going to mess up many times, Ava."

She winked. "I think I can schedule that in."

He chuckled. "Good, but don't get too caught up in those plans. Right now all I want to think about is you and me. Together for life."

"Sounds perfect," Ava whispered. "Like a journey to look forward to. To remember."

Author's Note

Dear Reader,

In 2000 I was on vacation with friends when I heard a heart-breaking story. Fifty-five years prior, in a small northern Austrian village called Mauthausen, white flakes fell from the sky. The month was May. It wasn't snow that tumbled down, but ash. I first heard the story of the tens of thousands of people killed, of the ash that poured from the crematorium, from a historian who gave us a tour of the concentration camp. My heart broke as I tried to imagine the horror.

Among those familiar with World War II history, Auschwitz and Bergen-Belsen are commonly discussed. But there are many lesser-known concentration camps. One of them is Mauthausen, named after the nearby village.

Mauthausen

As early as 1939, prisoners began arriving at the small train station at Mauthausen. A full two years before the bombing of Pearl Harbor, this once peaceful community was already experiencing the horrors of war. And by January 1941, the Mauthausen-Gusen camp was the only "category three" camp in Third Reich history, meaning it was a camp of no return. To be sent there was to be given a death sentence. Men, women, and children were either killed soon after their arrival or else worked to death in quarries and munitions factories.

Historians estimate that between 120,000 and 300,000 people perished in the Mauthausen camp system. Most who entered the large gates never exited, but in May 1945 everything changed. American troops had fought through France, Belgium, and Germany and finally crossed the Austrian border. The first American GIs to arrive at the camp were from the 41st Cavalry Recon Squadron, Eleventh Armored Division, Patton's Third US Army. The men opened the gates and brought the prisoners what they never expected—freedom—followed by food, clothes, and the care of medics.

When the camp's historian, Martha, told me about these men, I knew I wanted to meet them and to hear their stories. What was it like to grant these prisoners their freedom? How had it affected them? When I arrived home, I researched their

Men of the Forty-first Cavalry
on an M8 tank

experiences and contacted their division's veteran organization to ask if it would be possible to interview any of the men. I was overwhelmed by the response. The men invited me to their annual reunion in Kalamazoo, Michigan.

A friend traveled to the reunion with me, and as we entered through the hotel doors, I saw gray-haired men with their Eleventh Armored Division caps sitting in small groups and sharing old war stories. We'd just finished checking in to the hotel when a younger man approached. "Are you the author?" he asked. "I've had men lined up all day waiting to meet you."

Sure enough, those I'd connected with through letters were waiting with their photos, their stories, and their tears. After all these years they had not forgotten. I talked to Arthur and Charlie first. They'd been best friends during the war, and

Eleventh Armored
Division patch

fifty-five years later they still finished each other's sentences. Thomas, LeRoy, and Tarmo were next . . . each one telling me his story. Many more men, each with his own personal experiences, poured out their hearts to me. During the week they held a special ceremony to honor their friends who'd died and to remember the people they'd liberated. After all these years they knew that what they'd done mattered.

I attended two more reunions over the years, one in Buffalo and the other in St. Louis, and interviewed hundreds of veterans. I wrote two historical novels about their experiences, *From Dust and Ashes* and *Night Song*, but it was the relationship with the men that forever changed my life.

You see, my grandfather was also a World War II veteran, but I'd never taken time to sit down with him and hear his stories. I was afraid the stories would upset him. I didn't want him to have to think about those times any more. It was hard for me to connect my sweet grandfather with

Veteran of the
Eleventh Armored Division

someone who fought in war so long ago. What I forgot was that he had been young once, and his fight helped secure my freedom. What I didn't remember is that the memories were always with him, daily, even if he never talked about them. After Grandpa Fred passed away in 1999, I wished I'd taken the time to listen.

Meeting the men of the Eleventh Armored Division gave me a second chance to listen. I saw their tears and quivering chins as they told me the stories of battles in Bastogne and the Siegfried Line. I saw their drooped shoulders and heavy hearts as they explained what they lived through when they liberated Mauthausen and its subcamps. I'd lost my grandfather, but God gave me a hundred more grandpas. What a gift.

One of my most amazing experiences was to receive an e-mail from a woman named Hana.

She'd heard of my book and knew I'd interviewed some of the veterans. She asked if I'd interviewed any medics. Then she told me an amazing story. Hana was born on a cart just outside of Mauthausen. Her mother had survived a prison term at another camp and was transported to Mauthausen at the end of the war.

Hana was just three weeks old when the Americans arrived, and she was very ill. The filthy conditions had given her a skin infection, and sores covered her tiny body. No one expected her to live. Yet one of the medics saw the small baby and knew he had to do something. Even though it took most of the day, he lanced and cleaned all of Hana's sores, saving her life. Over the years she'd wanted to find the medic but didn't know where to start.

I was amazed by Hana's story and told her I knew one medic. Maybe he remembered who that man was. I gave Hana his contact information and soon heard the good news. My friend LeRoy "Pete" Petersohn was the medic who'd saved her life! The two were soon reunited. After all these years Hana was able to look into the eyes of the man who saved her and to thank him. After all these years Pete was able to meet the woman he saved. "Baby!" he called out when he met her.

In the ten years since I began interviewing these veterans, most have passed away. Some of them— realizing their days on earth were coming to an

Eighty-first Medical Battalion vehicle on
the snowy road to Houffalize

end—returned to Europe one last time with their family members to walk along paths they'd never forgotten. Those trips inspired this novel.

Remembering You is a work of fiction, but the experiences of the men are true. The experiences of Ava are also true-to-life. I was busy with life when God pointed me to an amazing story and to even more amazing men. I'm so thankful I took time to listen and care. I'm so thankful I allowed these men to share what—and whom—they remembered most.

Thankful for those who've come before us,
Tricia Goyer

Questions for Discussion

1. What are some of the major themes of this book?

2. Do you have a family member who served in World War II? Does this novel change your thoughts about his or her experiences? In what way?

3. What is one thing you learned about World War II that surprised you?

4. How did the war affect Grandpa Jack and Grand-Paul? Do you think those effects are typical among World War II veterans?

5. Throughout the book Ava wants to help Grandpa Jack reconnect with someone he met during the war. Would you have done the same thing as Ava? Why or why not?

6. How do you think the story would have been different if it had been written from Grandpa Jack's point of view?

7. If you were to meet a World War II veteran, what questions would you ask?

8. Have you ever been to Europe? How does your view of Europe change when seeing it through the eyes of veterans who fought there?

9. What is unique about the relationships in this novel? Which relationship touched your heart the most?

10. How does the relationship between Ava and Grandpa Jack change or evolve through the course of this story?

11. Do you think Ava made the right choice in opening her heart to Dennis?

12. How was Ava and Dennis's relationship different the second time around?

13. How do the characters change spiritually? Do you find those changes to be realistic?

14. What is the one thing that's lingered with you after you put down this book?

15. Have you read some of the author's other books? How is this story similar? How is it different?

About the Author

TRICIA GOYER is an award-winning author of fourteen novels, many of them set during the World War II era. She has interviewed more than one hundred war veterans to make her stories come alive for her readers. Among her published historical novels are *Night Song*, which won ACFW's 2005 Carol Award for Long Historical Romance, and *Dawn of a Thousand Nights*, which won the same award in 2006. She has also authored nine nonfiction books and more than three hundred articles for national publications. In 2003, Tricia was one of two authors named "Writer of the Year" at the Mount Hermon Christian Writer's Conference, and she has been interviewed by *Focus on the Family*, *Moody Mid-Day Connection*, *The Harvest Show*, *NBC's Monday Today*, *Aspiring Women*, and hundreds of other radio and television stations. Tricia and her husband, John, have four children and live in Arkansas.

Guideposts magazine and the
Daily Guideposts devotional book are
available in large print editions
by contacting:

Guideposts
Attn: Customer Service
P.O. Box 5815
Harlan, IA 51593
(800) 431-2344
www.guideposts.com

Center Point Publishing
600 Brooks Road ● PO Box 1
Thorndike ME 04986-0001 USA

(207) 568-3717

US & Canada:
1 800 929-9108
www.centerpointlargeprint.com